MUTANT
CHRONICLES

MUTANT CHRONICLES

MATT FORBECK

Based on the screenplay by Philip Eisner

BALLANTINE BOOKS • NEW YORK

A Del Rey Mass Market Original

Copyright © 2008 by Campfame Limited and Mutant Chronicles International Inc. MUTANT CHRONICLES and related logos, characters, names and distinctive likenesses are trademarks and registered trademarks of Mutant Chronicles International Inc. and/or Campfame Limited. All rights reserved. Published by arrangement with Mutant Chronicles International Inc.

Published in the United States by Del Rey Books, an imprint of The Random House Publishing Group, a division of Random House, Inc., New York.

DEL REY is a registered trademark and the Del Rey colophon is a trademark of Random House, Inc.

ISBN 978-0-345-49905-9

Printed in the United States of America

www.delreybooks.com
www.mutantchroniclesthemovie.com

OPM   9   8   7   6   5   4   3   2   1

Dedicated to William King for working so hard on the original roleplaying game line with me and for many years of treasured friendship

Special thanks to everyone at Paradox Entertainment, especially Fred Malmberg, Joakim Zetterberg, and Thommy Wojciechowski

Thanks also to everyone at Del Rey, especially Keith Clayton and Susan Moe

Finally, thanks to Simon Hunter and the *Mutant Chronicles* cast and crew for bringing this story to life

1

The skies had been pissing rain for so long that Captain Nathan Rooker was sure God—if there was such a thing—meant the place to be used as His personal toilet. Nathan knew that he'd been warm and dry at one point in his life but couldn't remember when that had been or what it had felt like. All he knew now was the slick cold of the never-ending rain and the horrors of the everlasting war.

Nathan glanced both ways along the sodden trench. Every one of his soldiers stared up at him, their eyes devoid of anger or hope. Curiosity showed only in the fact that they'd raised their heads at all.

"Heads up, lads," he said as he trudged through the mud. "Put a smile on it."

The soldiers went back to huddling under their gear, trying to preserve the tiny bits of warmth that would stave off a trip to the infirmary or the grave. The rain sluiced off their helmets and coats as if they were little more than statues, frozen in place until the call went up for them to defend this sodden stretch of earth once more or, worse, to charge across it.

Finding a thin ladder of wet iron propped up against one wall, Nathan climbed it and peeked out over the edge. "Bloody bastards," he said. "Let's see what's on today's menu of shit."

Tracer fire zipped over his head as he peered out over the

no-man's-land that separated his Capitol forces from their Bauhaus foes. Gray smoke crawling with tendrils of a foul yellow drifted across the battlefield, curling around the miles of barbed wire and into the countless trenches that crisscrossed the muddy landscape like the distant canals of ruddy Mars. For a moment, Nathan considered donning his gas mask, but he couldn't stomach the stench of the filter again—at least not until the gas came too close to ignore.

Artillery fire flashed in the distance, silhouetting the battered edges of the horizon with a flash bright enough to burn through the rain and haze. A dull report crumped from the same direction just before the shell whistled overhead.

Something would happen soon, Nathan knew. He could smell it in the air. The Bauhausers would tire of trying to shell them out of their holes and would come storming across that battered patch of land to give it a shot by hand. The only question was when.

Nathan slogged off to his left, through a ditch that seemed more sewer than trench. The sky flashed above him, then stayed lit. He looked up to watch a flare scudding beneath the clouds like a trapped sun hunting for a way out. Then a blast from one of Capitol's own big guns snuffed it out like a match in a hurricane.

Nathan heard the big Bauhaus 880 let loose another of its nearly yard-wide shells. He knew it took four men just to lift one of those loads, much less slam it into the breech of one of those building-size guns. The fact that Bauhaus's Ducal Militia could manage it so quickly spoke loudly of their dedication and training.

Nathan worked his way through the maze of trenches, glancing up at the well-worn handmade signs that marked each intersection: Marilyn, Betty, Alison.

The irony of naming wartime trenches after women didn't escape Nathan. Did the names come from girlfriends or mothers? he wondered. Perhaps both. He didn't have the energy to explore the metaphors.

He turned up Alison to find a squad of soldiers scraping a meal of cold meat out of dented tins. They stood at his approach. One soldier kicked a resting buddy with his soggy boot, but the sleeping soldier didn't move.

Nathan waved the kicker off. "Let him sleep." Soon enough the order might come for them to go over the top of the trenches, and the soldier's rest would become permanent.

Nathan looked the kicker in the eyes. When the trooper had been fresh out of boot camp, he might have shivered at the sight of Nathan's bars. He'd been here too long now, seen too much. His eyes showed nothing at all.

Nathan fished out a tin of food and handed it to the soldier, who accepted it without a word. Then he pulled out a pack of cigarettes, lit one, and handed it to a soldier who looked like he might freeze to death without it. "Enjoy."

He gazed at the others: soaked, miserable, and ready to die. At least they were still alive for now, a better fate than that which had befallen many of their friends. "All the fun at the fair, eh?"

There was little Nathan could do to improve his soldiers' lot, but he was determined to do it. Some of them would die under his command, maybe even today, and offering them a cold bit of kindness was the least he could do.

"Hunter back?" Nathan said.

The men shook their heads. There had been no news.

Nathan wondered what was taking the sergeant so long. He'd expected Mitch to report in an hour ago. He wondered if the patrol had wandered too close to the enemy lines, but he knew—hoped, at least—Mitch was too smart for that.

Nathan slogged past the men. He patted one on the shoulder and gave the kicker an understanding nod.

He couldn't say much to raise their spirits. They'd heard

all the hollow platitudes before and long since learned to despise them or treat them with the blackest humor.

Nathan headed for the nearest medical tent. He hoped he wouldn't find the patrol there, but there weren't many good reasons for Mitch to be this late. Most of those causes would have sent the survivors to seek a doctor's help.

One of the soldiers farther down the trench scratched his scalp with both hands as if he meant to scrape it off. As Nathan neared, he spotted the captain's bars and forced himself to stop.

"Sorry, sir," the kid said. He wrapped his fingers around the rim of his helmet to keep them from reaching for his hair again. "Bugs in the rug, sir."

Nathan gave the young man a mirthless smile. "Scratching makes it worse."

A soldier standing guard over a triage alcove behind the scratcher snorted softly at that. From his gray face, Nathan knew he'd seen enough of this war to crush his soul. There was nothing Nathan could do for him that wouldn't be met with derision, whether displayed or not.

"Is Hunter's patrol back?"

The sentry nodded. "What's left of it." He jerked his head toward the alcove behind him.

Nathan grimaced as he ducked around the corner and parted the grimy curtain that separated the alcove from the main trench. Inside, bare incandescent lights burned from a canvas ceiling that kept out the worst of the rain. Wounded and dying soldiers—impossible to tell which was which—lay racked along the walls in gore-caked cots that lifted them above the filth.

Many of the men groaned in pain. Some tried to scream, but they'd long since blown out their voices on the battle-field, shouting for help that always took too long to come. Now they could only rasp about their agony instead.

The brightest lights in the place hung from a cord over a stainless-steel operating table set up in the middle of the widest part of the trench. Someone had slapped it up there years ago as a temporary measure, and there it had stayed. Nathan couldn't imagine how much blood had run off the table's edges since then. Rivers, for sure.

"Put pressure on the exit wound!" a medic named Winter said. His desperate tone told Nathan the soldier was a lost cause.

Despite that, the second medic—Talamini—kept working at the soldier's wounds, packing them with gauze while Winter pulled out a bone saw and started an impromptu amputation.

It was like trying to keep a riptide from taking a sand castle down. There was no hope for the soldier, Nathan knew. Even if the man lived, chances were that infection would take him within days. But the medics didn't stop trying, not until it was over.

Finally, the blood stopped running. The soldier's hacking breaths halted. The medics stepped away from the table, leaving the soldier lying there, still.

In a proper hospital, even one just behind the battle lines, one of the medics might have called out a time of death. Here, such details didn't matter. The man was dead, and that was the only fact that counted. One less soul to be fed into the Capitol war machine.

Nathan stared at the fallen soldier's face: Slade. He'd been one of Mitch's men. The captain sucked air through his teeth.

The medic in charge of the operation reached for Slade's dog tags. He had no time for niceties, and they needed the table for the other damaged souls lining the trench around them.

A hand snaked in from behind Talamini and snatched Winter's blood-spattered wrist. The medic let go of the tags as if they'd burned his fingers.

The man who'd grabbed Winter's arm reached out and

held Slade's dog tags, then gave them a sharp yank. The chain around the dead man's neck snapped.

Nathan stepped up and closed Slade's unblinking eyes. He looked across the man's body at Sergeant Mitch Hunter as the man threaded Slade's dog tags onto a chain heavy with a dozen other sets.

Mitch looked like shit. Mud and blood caked his skin and clothes. The only things clean on him were his eyes, and they were bloodshot and dead, focused on something a thousand yards away.

"What happened?" Nathan had to ask, even if the answer was clear. The patrol had had its collective ass handed to it.

Nathan hadn't wanted to send those soldiers out into that meat grinder, but he'd had no choice. Better to send a single patrol out to trigger a trap than the entire platoon.

He hadn't asked Mitch to go. The man hadn't even bothered to volunteer. When Nathan had asked for someone to take on the suicide mission, Mitch had just stood up, and his men had fallen in line behind him, then marched off to their doom.

"Ran into Cog armor five klicks out." The Bauhaus military's emblem looked like an eagle with its wings stretched wide. Instead of feathers, though, its wings showed the teeth of Bauhaus's corporate cog.

"How strong?"

Mitch stuffed the chain of dog tags back into a pouch on his belt before answering. The tags inspired loyalty in some of the men, Nathan knew, who took heart in knowing that their sergeant would carry on in memory of them. For others, though, the sheer number of tags Hunter carried spooked them. No one wanted his to be the next on that chain.

"Five ATCs."

Nathan blinked. Five armored troop carriers. "A full platoon."

This must be the offensive he'd heard rumors about for weeks. He'd almost started to think that it would never come, that it had all been part of a Bauhaus strategy to psych the Capitol infantry up for a nonexistent foe, a feint before the true attack. Or maybe it had been a ploy of Capitol's own morale department. Nothing bound soldiers together like impending doom.

Now here it was.

The medics started to stuff Slade's body in a bag. They'd long ago taken to putting one of the black sacks down on the table before laying a soldier on it. Then, when they had to use it, they could get the corpse packed up and lugged off in seconds.

"We left them bogged down in the wire, but they called in our position and walked eight-eighties up our ass."

Mitch's voice betrayed no hint of emotion. He showed neither fear of the oncoming attack nor grief for his fallen men. Such things were luxuries he denied himself, as Nathan knew he must too.

"Once they clear the wire, they'll be right fucking on top of us." Nathan grimaced. Bauhaus was finally coming at them, and there wasn't a damn thing they could do to stop it. Even with Capitol's big guns slamming away at the line of invaders, the Cogs' armored troop carriers could just roll right in.

"Just another day," Mitch said.

As if to punctuate Mitch's words, the lead medic zipped Slade's body bag closed.

2

It had been so much easier back in the Academy on Mars, Nathan thought: "Fight for freedom!" "Defend Capitol!" and dozens of other slogans. Back on Mars, under the bright red sky, the husk of Earth—which some called Dark Eden—had seemed like a nightmare used to scare children.

Now Nathan not only lived in that nightmare, he fought and killed in it.

Most of humanity had long since fled the planet of its birth. In fact, most people had never seen Earth through anything other than a telescope. Born on Mercury, Venus, Mars, or the Imperial archipelago in the asteroid belt, they eked out their lives blissfully distant from Earth's dark skies.

The Third Corporate Wars had touched every part of the solar system, but they'd smashed what was left of Earth to pieces. Most of the planet had long since been abandoned and returned to the wild. A few outposts still held treasured bits of civilization. Although the four megacorporations had once abandoned the place, the Brotherhood had stayed, keeping the place under its protection for decades.

But now war had come to Dark Eden again.

It made sense. In this neglected land, each of the corporations could set up its own protected enclaves from which it could wage its side of their extended proxy war, battling over bits of turf that no one outside the Brotherhood gave a damn about.

Like right here, right now.

Nathan picked up a periscope out of the mud and wiped off its lenses. Then he slapped it up against the trench's upper edge and peered through it. Through the viewfinder, he spied a number of Bauhaus ATCs—more than the five Hunter's team had spotted—rolling in their direction.

"Here they come!" Nathan put down the periscope and glanced along the length of the trench. None of the soldiers sat huddled on the ground any longer. The time for hunkering down to wait was over. They stood ready, lined up before the rickety ladders that would take them over the top of the trench and into no-man's-land. They bore their rifles before them, each of them having stopped to give his weapon a final cleaning before the battle began.

They'd waited so long for this moment, killed so much time, and now that it was here, every second seemed precious.

Mitch knelt down and grabbed a dead soldier who'd been left to lie where he'd fallen, most of his head taken off when he'd peered a few inches too far over the top of the trench. He patted the corpse down, then slipped his hand into its shirt pocket and pulled out a still-dry pack of cigarettes.

"I guess dead men don't smoke, huh?" said one of the privates. Mitch paid him no heed.

To Nathan's left, a chaplain by the name of Parente— seconded to Capitol by the Brotherhood—prayed loudly for them all in Gaelic. The man's holy symbol glittered from where it hung around his neck: a cross over a downward-pointing triangle. Nathan always thought it looked like a short spear with an unwieldy handle, and he sometimes felt the same way about the Brotherhood. It could be useful, even dangerous, but was never entirely under anyone's control but its own.

Nathan gazed up at the sky, hoping to find some sign of God. He saw only tracer bullets zipping over the trench, their glowing trails lighting the sky like falling stars raining down from the black heavens.

He remembered what real stars looked like, although he hadn't seen them since he'd been ordered to move himself and his family to this forsaken chunk of dirt. He wondered now, as he often did, what Adelaide and Grace were doing at that moment. He silently joined in the chaplain's prayer for a moment, petitioning for his life, not for his own sake but for that of his wife and daughter, safe in their home many miles behind the front.

"Amen," Parente said solemnly as he used a long, silver aspergillum to splash holy water on the men near him.

"Thanks, Padre," said a large soldier as he slung his M516D—a double-barreled pump-action shotgun—over his shoulder. He wiped off the water along with the rain that sluiced down his face. "I feel all cleansed and shit."

Nathan rolled his eyes, but Parente just splashed El Jesus with holy water once again, as if it would rinse off the soldier's latest sin. He clearly wasn't offended. Here on the battlefield, he'd heard too much profanity for it to faze him any longer, and the others had given up trying to shield him from it.

"It's a good sign, actually," Parente had said to Nathan once. "It means they've accepted me as a soldier, as one of them rather than a representative of the Brotherhood. That's the first step."

"What's the next?" Nathan had asked.

"Getting them out of this damned war alive. But that's your job, not mine."

"Sergeant?" Parente said to Mitch. "Would you receive grace?"

Even in the middle of war, at the moment before they were most likely to die, the chaplain kept reaching out.

Nathan had to respect that even if he knew the man's efforts were as doomed as those of his platoon.

"You'll never reach men like Hunter," Nathan had said to Parente. "He's too far gone."

"The Brotherhood is patient. In the long run, faith outlasts all."

Mitch had heard that and snorted. "In the long run, Padre, we're all dead." Then he'd stared out over no-man's-land. "For us, maybe in the short run too."

Mitch ignored the priest and lit his cigarette. El Jesus grinned at Parente, pride and pity warring on his face. "Top's going straight to hell."

Parente gave a resigned sigh and trod off down the trench to offer solace to whatever other men he might find. El Jesus winked at Nathan, and the captain found it hard not to smile at the man's infectious mood. Despite having orders to march into the maw of the Cog war machine, the man shone like the blazing sun in Mars's red sky. Nathan wondered if he'd learned this while living in the Danger Zones of San Dorado or if he'd just been born that way. He wished he could summon a fraction of the man's heart.

Instead, Nathan pulled another periscope from next to the ladder in front of him and cleaned the lens on this one too. The dead soldier behind him had given up on being able to see out of the thing and had paid for his impatience with his life. Nathan took his time, making sure the optics were clean, then raised the top of the scope over the trench's lip.

The ATCs were closer now, and the Cogs' 880 was hammering their lines harder, softening them up. Soon the shells would stop, but only when the ATCs drew close enough to disgorge their lethal cargo: a full squad of Bauhaus soldiers each.

"They're nearly with us," he said to his men.

The Capitol guns would kick in soon, Nathan knew. The commander on the hill behind them, on which the nearest gun was mounted, was careful with his ammunition. He had only so many shells and didn't care to blow them on long-range shots that probably would only shower their already-filthy foes with mud. He liked to wait until each shot would do the most harm.

Nathan hoped he wouldn't wait too long.

"You know your top kick used to be an officer," Nathan said to El Jesus. He took one last look through the periscope, then brought it down.

El Jesus raised a large eyebrow at Nathan's words.

"That's right. We went through the Academy. Was gonna be one hell of an officer and a fine human being. One morning he woke up with a screaming case of I don't give a fuck."

Nathan reached down and pulled on a tarp bundled up over something tucked under his ladder. It gave way, revealing a waterlogged case of whiskey beneath it. The rain had long since soaked away the print on the box, but the contents inside were still safe.

"Give a fuck about what?" said Mitch. "Every yard we take, every Cog we kill, all we do is make some fat fuck's stock go up two points."

"Yeah, but it's all about the money, isn't it, Sergeant?"

Mitch snorted. "Ends up that way when they give out cash bonuses to officers based on body count."

Nathan opened the case and pulled out a bottle. He looked down at the label and the Martian brand emblazoned across it, the triple moons riding high above the stylized red planet.

"You know," Nathan said to Mitch, "sometimes I get the impression you don't believe in the rightness of our mighty corporation."

It was a weak joke. Nathan had lost any idealism about his job too. He found it hard to remember what it had been like to feel that way about Capitol. The last time he knew he'd had it had been during his training with Mitch at the Academy.

That had been several worlds ago.

He wondered if the Bauhausers on the other side of the battlefield cared for their corporate masters back on Venus. Or were they like the soldiers dug into the trench with him here, worn souls, tired of war—of life too—but ready to do their job at any cost? But did any of them truly know the price?

Nathan didn't expect Mitch to reply, but his old friend surprised him.

"They don't pay me to believe, sir."

Nathan handed the bottle to Mitch. The rain washed the dust from it as it passed between them.

"No, they don't," Nathan said. "They pay you to fuck shit up."

Mitch almost smiled at that. Instead, he took a long pull from the bottle, then handed it back to Nathan.

The captain tipped a bit of the warm whiskey into his mouth. It tasted rotten, but it burned all the way down into his stomach. The warmth spread from there throughout his body, from the top of his head to his toes.

He wiped his mouth with the back of his hand, then passed the bottle to El Jesus. He knew the corporal would take a belt and then pass the bottle down the line. It was a ritual, perhaps a hollow one, but one the soldiers would respect. At this point, it was all they had left.

3

Something in the back of Nathan's head told him that the time for action had come. Perhaps he could unconsciously feel the vibrations in the earth from the treads of the Bauhaus ATCs. Or it might have been a sixth sense he'd formed about such things after having been in countless battles.

Maybe he was just sick of waiting.

"Get up!" He had to bellow to make himself heard over the nearly constant roar from the big guns spitting death over their heads. "On your feet! Get on your feet!"

Mitch and El Jesus stood straight up and began a last-second weapons check. As they did, those nearest them followed suit, and then those nearest them, and on down the line.

The bottle passed faster now. A soldier stood up to receive it, took a swig, then passed it on to the soldier next to him. He then checked his weapons and slapped a fresh, fully loaded clip into his assault rifle.

Nathan watched the procession for a moment, then reached out and nudged the man nearest him, who'd gotten tired of watching and sat down. The captain had just gotten the others to their feet, and he couldn't have them all following this man's lead.

"On your feet, ladies!" Nathan hollered. "Show those Cogs your war face!" Word passed on down the line.

El Jesus flashed all his teeth in a boyish grin, then pumped his shotgun.

Holy Cardinal, Nathan thought. *He is young. He's actually enjoying this.*

Finally, a soldier took the last pull from the bottle. After nearly gagging on the backwash, he smashed the bottle on the ground and raised his rifle to the ready. That seemed to be a signal to the others that the time to hit it had come.

As a unit, the drab-clothed soldiers hauled themselves up their ladders, pushing the ends of their guns up over the lip of the trench before them. In an instant, the trench bristled with them, sticking up like the quills on a porcupine's back.

Standing alongside his soldiers, each of them perched on top of a flimsy ladder or another makeshift stool, Nathan stared out into the hellish fields of no-man's-land. The never-ending rain had made a swamp of the once-green fields. Puddles of water glistened in the sharp glow of tracer bullets, flares, and exploding mortar shells. Some of them joined together into bodies of water large enough to qualify as lakes if they'd been more than a foot deep.

Despite the chaos happening overhead, though, Nathan saw nothing stirring on the ground before him. A part of him, he realized, had wished that the ATCs would be waiting for him and his men when they topped the edge of the trench. To see the enemy would be a welcome change from the usual routine of duck and cover.

The big Capitol gun thundered then, signaling the start of the fight in earnest. Nathan missed the flash, but the crump got his attention. The shell exploded in a violent mess of mud and the bodies of whichever poor soldiers had been in its way.

Tracer fire zinged overhead again, closer this time.

"Let's step to it! Lock and load!" Nathan readied his rifle. Although wet, it was clean and ready, and he knew its cool barrel would soon run hot.

On Nathan's signal, the men stepped up on the wooden,

mud-caked rail running the eastern side of the trench, then slapped their rifles down over it.

They knew not to fire yet, but Nathan feared one of them would lose his nerve and start shooting before he ordered it. "Easy, lads," he said, trying to soothe their jangling nerves. "Wait for it. Easy."

Nathan peered through the rain-soaked night again, straining to see the Bauhaus soldiers as a Bauhaus ATC roared up to the thickest part of the snarls of barbed wire to disgorge its cargo. The golden Bauhaus cogs emblazoned on its front and sides glinted in the glare of the overhead flares that had turned this rain-soaked night into a bright, black-mantled day. The massive machine—all flat, armored sides and sharp, angry angles—trained its main machine gun on the trench and laid down a sweeping sheet of covering fire as the main hatch burst open on the side closest to the trench.

A mob of Bauhaus troops stormed down the ramp made from the ATC's open hatch. In the absolute madness of the moment, it struck Nathan how much they looked like his own soldiers. Maybe the months stuck here on this horrible ball of mud had worn off all the bits that made them different.

In the end, they were all soldiers sent off to fight a war for people who'd never held a gun in their lives. They had more in common with one another than they did with their superiors. At the moment, though, none of that mattered more to Nathan and his soldiers than killing these bastards before they killed them instead.

The Cogs came fast and low, charging straight for them. For a moment, they didn't seem human, but that had to have been a trick of the light. Or maybe it was Nathan's training as a soldier kicking in, dehumanizing his foes so they'd be easier to kill.

He decided it was time to give in to that training.

"Let 'em have it, lads!" he shouted.

The Capitol line erupted in a fusillade, and the Bauhaus troops responded in kind. This was war, all right, the keen moment of battle they'd dreaded for so long. Nathan couldn't help feeling relieved that it was finally here.

Men fell on both sides of the line, most without a word. Those who weren't killed instantly by the bullets that struck them were often knocked out or went into shock. A few, though, maintained consciousness and bellowed in horror and pain.

Those were the worst. The dead Nathan could ignore. The dying distracted everyone around them, and in the middle of a battle he couldn't afford any distractions. That sort of thing would just end up with more of his men killed.

Nathan blocked out the screams as best he could and kept firing, firing, firing, letting the bullets blast out of his gun as fast as they would go.

Then El Jesus spotted something.

"Incoming!" the big corporal yelled.

Nathan peered into the darkness in front of them to see if he could pick out what had alarmed El Jesus so much. He couldn't make out a damn thing but bullets, mud, and blood.

Then he noticed that the mist toward the horizon had turned thick and yellow and was billowing their way.

"Gas!" Nathan yelled. "Get your masks on!"

Nathan dropped to the ground and struggled with his mask for a moment before pulling it into place. This was the sort of thing he'd been trained for back in boot camp so many years ago, but this was no drill. If he failed to get the mask on in time—or put it on incorrectly—he would be dead. He had no room for error.

Satisfied that his mask was snug and functional, Nathan glanced about to see most of his soldiers managing to get their gear on as well. One man farther down the line still lagged behind the others, though. He'd just gotten his mask out of his bag when the yellow smoke washed up to the edge of the trench and then spilled into it, filling it in an instant.

The soldier, a man named Bisley, took in a lungful of the pale yellow stuff and dropped to the mucky excuse for ground. He began to cough in short, violent hacks. A moment later he vomited, then fell over on his back, blood frothing from his mouth in dark pink bubbles.

The soldiers who had managed to get their masks on in time looked to Nathan for guidance. His voice useless under his mask, he signaled for them to stay put. Even with the enemy this close, their best defense was the mud in which they'd dug their trench. If they could leave as little of themselves exposed to the impending assault as possible, they might survive long enough to take out the attackers as they closed.

Nathan's troops vaulted themselves back up their ladders and leveled their rifles over the field of battle like the combat-tested veterans they were. And then everything broke down.

Unable to communicate with his soldiers by voice or by hand signals, Nathan lost all control over them. They had to rely on their training or instinct, or both. In some cases, it seemed they fell back on neither.

One soldier began firing blind into the thinning mist, shooting at the invisible Bauhausers who had to be out there somewhere. Most of the others, hoping their compatriot had seen something, joined in, chattering away at the smoke in short bursts from their assault rifles.

Whether the Capitol soldiers hit anything, Nathan couldn't tell. He held his gun still but ready, conserving his ammunition and waiting for a target to present itself. He saw Mitch doing the same, slapping the soldiers nearest to him to their senses. El Jesus kept near his sergeant, his shotgun still silent, although the end of it jerked back and forth at every sound.

Then gunfire blasted back at the troops from the thickest

parts of the mist. Capitol troops dropped into the mud, parts of them blown off by bullets. Some screamed for a few moments before death took them. Others fell into horrible moans that seemed they might never end.

The remaining Capitol troops returned fire at their unseen assailants. Bullets spattered Nathan with mud as he blasted away into the retreating swirls of smoke. Somewhere in the middle of it all, he heard the deep growl of a massive engine amid the staccato crack-crack-cracks of rifles and chain guns.

The piss-yellow smoke fading now—the Bauhaus troops wore no protection against it—Nathan ripped off his gas mask. The damned masks got in the way more than they helped when it came to fighting like this. The poison burned his eyes and nostrils and tickled the bottom of his lungs, but he could see clearly again, unhampered by the mask's narrowed vision.

The ATC's machine gun fell silent as its troops closed on the trench, the gunner unwilling to cut down his own troops to get at the ones hunkered down in the mud.

4

The Bauhaus troops came at the trench hard and fast. As much as Nathan hated the Cogs, he had to admire their training. They didn't flinch in the face of the Capitol defensive fire, never turning back for even an instant if a fellow next to them dropped to the ground, dead before his face hit the mud. A moment later, they were at the lip of the trench and then were leaping in.

Nathan took down two of the Cogs before they reached him, but another came racing in right behind his fallen friends. Nathan jumped back into the trench and waited for the Bauhauser to reach the muddy lip before dropping him with a shot to the chest.

On either side, Bauhaus troops descended into the trench to do battle with the Capitol soldiers. There were just too many of them coming in too fast to stop them all. Gunfire burst out all around the captain now, and he hugged the trench's muddy wall to avoid the worst of it.

To the south end of the trench, a Bauhauser tore apart a Capitol private with a knife. Behind him, another Capitol soldier stabbed him in the back with a trenching tool. Blood erupted from the Bauhauser's mouth, and the soldier who'd killed him thrust up the small shovel in triumph. A moment later, a burst from an assault rifle brought him down too.

Nathan glanced behind him and saw that the way was

clear. He opted to do the only responsible thing when faced with such odds.

"Fall back right!" he shouted at the top of his lungs. "Fall back right!"

Facing out into no-man's-land, right would be to the north along the trench, away from the bulk of the Bauhaus invaders. If he could get his soldiers together and find better ground on which to make a stand, they might have a chance to survive the day. Otherwise, with the visibility as poor as it was, the Cogs would pick them apart.

As he broke north, calling out the new orders, Nathan ran into a private named Robertson. He slapped the man on the shoulder and pointed for him to move, but the soldier refused to move his weapon from where he had it trained back down the trench.

Nathan slapped the man again.

"I'm not retreating!"

Nathan recognized the defiance in the soldier's eyes. He'd spent most of the last few years of his life trying to beat it out of his men, although he knew he'd never succeed. The ideals of freedom were too deeply ingrained in the minds of Capitol's citizens for even its best soldiers to ever surrender them.

Many times, Nathan had realized that this dedication to freedom set Capitol apart from Bauhaus, Mishima, and Imperial. The other megacorporations—even the Brotherhood—treasured obedience and the hierarchy of their societies. Not so with Capitol. It was their worst weakness and their greatest strength.

"Retreat, hell!" Nathan said to the man. "We're advancing in the opposite direction!"

The other soldier smiled at that and lowered his weapon. As he did, a barrage of bullets tore into him and drove him to the ground.

One of the shots ricocheted off Nathan's helmet, knocking it away into the mud and sending him sprawling along the trench.

Stunned, Nathan reached up to wipe the water and muck from his face. His hands came away covered in his own blood, the red liquid blending with the black dirt. His ears rang so loudly that he wondered if the bullet had turned his helmet into a bell, with his skull as the clapper stuck inside.

Nathan shook his head to try to clear it but failed. He stared down at Robertson's body and wished the man had listened to him instead of bickering about orders. If he had, both of them might have lived.

Nathan flopped over onto his back and saw the Bauhaus soldier standing over him, the tip of his Panzerknacker assault rifle still smoking. The Cog pointed his weapon down at Nathan, his finger already tightening on the trigger. Nathan had lost his assault rifle when he'd fallen, but he still had a Bolter pistol in his belt holster. He commanded his hands to draw it, even though he knew he'd be dead long before the barrel cleared its leather casing.

A burst of gunfire sounded, and despite himself Nathan closed his eyes. A moment later, he opened them and saw the Bauhaus trooper no longer standing over him but lying in a rapidly cooling pile at his feet.

Nathan stared up at the man in disbelief, then at the unfired gun in his hand. He turned around and saw Mitch standing there, his M50 lowered back to the ground as his eyes searched the mists behind Nathan for a new target.

Still woozy, Nathan raised his pistol at Mitch. The sergeant dived forward, out of Nathan's line of fire, exposing the well-armed Cog charging up behind him. Nathan squeezed his pistol's trigger and pumped three sharp shots into the man. The last one caught him in the face and obliterated his head.

"Fuck," Mitch said as he got back to his feet. "For a second there I thought you were going to shoot me."

"For a second I was." Nathan looked Mitch in the eyes.

That had been too close. He felt fear clawing inside his stomach, trying to gouge its way out. "I don't make it out of here, you look after the girls."

Mitch flinched at that. Nathan knew his old friend would take care of his wife and daughter whether he asked him to or not. At that moment, though, he needed to ask, no matter how uncomfortable it might make Mitch.

Mitch reached down and hauled Nathan to his feet. "Can't I just buy you a drink?"

As they stalked through the trench, looking for other men, Nathan heard the too-familiar muffled *whump* of Bauhaus grenades exploding in another trench. Those damned potato mashers could blast a whole squad apart if they landed in the right place. He hoped they had sailed wide.

Then Nathan heard the shell from the big Capitol gun overhead roar. He snapped back his head and stared through the rain into the inky sky.

The flash from the gun froze the shell in the air, leaving it hanging there for an instant like the sword of Damocles. A heartbeat later, it smacked down in no-man's-land. Nathan hoped it tore another one of those Bauhaus ATCs apart.

The explosion's roar deafened Nathan for a moment, making his ears ring with pain. The blast threw up a tidal wave of rocks and dirt that splashed all the way back to Nathan's trench hundreds of yards away.

Nathan struggled to breathe for a moment and wondered if his ears had started to bleed. Even the rain seemed to stop, the droplets being blasted away by the tremendous explosion.

Then the rain fell once more, as if it had never stopped, and time started rolling again.

Most of the Capitol soldiers had followed their captain's orders and fallen back. That left Nathan and Mitch with El Jesus and two mud-caked grunts, Bonner and Naismith.

Nathan opened his mouth to chew out the men for ignoring his orders, but El Jesus cut him off before he could get started.

"Can't get through to Betty, and Marilyn's fucked."

Nathan frowned. That meant the Bauhaus forces had overwhelmed the two nearest trenches. The Cogs must have sent an ATC full of soldiers against each of the trenches. The battle had gone poorly here, and it sounded like the neighbors to the north and south hadn't fared much better.

Nathan stopped and glanced around. The tracer fire and shells had stopped, but the sound of small-arms fire seemed to come from every direction but down. They had to figure out some way to hook up with the central command and reevaluate the situation. But which way could they turn?

Nathan rubbed his chin as he made his decision. "Take Mary Jane and link up with Slick Nancy."

The soldiers around him nodded. The circuitous path would take them out through the back trenches and, they hoped, to the rear echelons of the Capitol forces. With luck, they'd get there in one piece.

Nathan wiped the mud from his face again and realized, maybe for the first time, that he'd lost his helmet. He wondered how bad the wound in his head was. Had the bullet just lacerated his scalp, or was he losing gray matter with every step? He figured if Mitch hadn't told him to sit down yet he had to be fine.

Bonner noticed Nathan rubbing his bare head, and the soldier took off his helmet and tossed it to the captain.

"Sir!" Bonner said. "Heads up!"

Caught off guard, Nathan still managed to snatch the helmet out of midair. He stared at it for a moment, then realized he needed to give it back. He'd lost his own equipment, and there was no reason for Bonner to suffer for that.

As Nathan held the helmet out to Bonner, Mitch started to chew the man out. Nathan had heard the diatribe before. "Never give your gear to another man, especially your helmet. It's fitted to your fat head, not his!"

Although Mitch didn't seem like he gave a fuck about anything, Nathan knew that his sergeant cared about the men who served with him. Moments like this only drove that home. Nathan had commanded dozens of sergeants over the years, but none of them had been as loyal to his men as Mitch.

"You keep that fucking bonnet on!" Mitch said to Bonner.

The young man nodded silently. He opened his mouth, maybe to explain that he'd only been trying to help a superior officer, but the bullet that blasted through his skull, bursting it like a blood-filled balloon, cut him off.

Even as Bonner's body fell, Mitch, El Jesus, Naismith, and Nathan returned fire. Whether or not they hit anything, they would never know. They ran off in the other direction rather than take the time to check.

5

Mitch Hunter had seen enough of war in his life. He'd joined the Capitol forces as a way to serve his corporation, the one he'd been born into. His parents had been Capitol citizens, and his ancestors before them, as far back as anyone could remember. They'd all served in the forces. That's what they did.

Now, for the life of him, Mitch couldn't understand why.

Maybe the worlds had changed. Maybe it had been him. He'd killed people on four different planets, several asteroids, and three moons, including Luna, which he hadn't seen once on his entire tour of duty here.

Sure, in most cases those people had been trying to kill him too. He'd been defending not only himself but Capitol's interests around the system. But he'd had his fill of blood, no matter how noble the reasons for which it had been spilled.

He didn't know what he was fighting for anymore. He just knew he wanted to survive it.

Mitch moved up to take point as the four soldiers made their way north up the trench. He would have hoped that Nathan had guessed right and that his plan would steer them clear of the fighting until they could rendezvous with the rest of the Capitol forces.

But Mitch had given up on hope. Take each moment as it comes, and react with your gut. That's all he had left.

El Jesus came stumping up behind him, as subtle as an elephant and just as solid, his shotgun at the ready. Nathan and Naismith brought up the rear, with the captain sometimes reaching out to lean on the private's shoulder to steady himself.

Mitch crouched low and moved fast, his rifle out in front of him, his finger on the trigger. The trick with chasing through the trenches like this wasn't in shooting anything that crossed his path. It was in making sure he didn't shoot somebody on his side.

No trace of the yellow gas curled through the trenches here. The rain seemed to have finally stopped too. Now that he thought about it, it had been waning since the Cogs had launched their attack. They'd probably waited until the weather cleared a bit so that the rain wouldn't wash their damned gas out of the air. Then they'd hit, and hit hard.

Mitch came to a corner and slowed as he reached it. As he curled around it, he froze.

"Top?"

El Jesus's voice sounded like that of a little boy. Mitch shook his head without looking back, signaling for the man to be quiet.

Every instinct he had screamed at him that something was wrong, but he couldn't say why. Then he knew.

It was quiet.

He could hear gunshots and cannon fire, but off in the distance, far away. Here in the trenches, there wasn't a sound louder than the squelching of the boots of the three troopers coming up behind him.

He considered calling out, but he knew that was the wrong thing to do. Someone might be hiding out there—someone from Bauhaus—and shouting would give away his position.

Mitch crept forward a bit, and as he did, the mists began to peel back like layers of curtains. The trench widened out here. They drove supply trucks this far into the place and dumped off goods that sometimes even made it to the troops stationed farther in.

Usually this intersection stood clogged with troops coming and going. Guards were stationed there at all times. Right now, though, no one was there at all.

No, Mitch corrected himself as the mists thinned more: no one alive.

Corpses littered the ground from one side of the trench to the other. Mitch's guts tensed from the fear that the rest of the Capitol forces had been slaughtered, leaving only the four of them to stand alone against the Cogs.

As he moved forward like a strong and silent tiger, he got a better look at the fallen. They'd been torn to pieces. It seemed like a helicopter had crashed here, rotors first, and chewed through everyone in the place. But no charred hulk of a vehicle lay resting in a crater in the center of the trench, just arms, legs, heads, torsos, and parts impossible—or plain painful—to identify.

"Jesus Christ God almighty," he said to no one.

Mitch heard someone behind him—it had to be Naismith—puke into the bloodstained muck.

"Motherfuckers," El Jesus said in a voice weighty with horror and rage.

Mitch pointed to a shoulder lying off to the left. It bore the insignia of a Bauhaus Blitzer, one of their special forces. Remnants of other Bauhausers lay scattered about the place, mixed in with the Capitol corpses in equal measure.

Mitch heard El Jesus stifle a gasp. Whatever had happened here, it had killed everyone around, regardless of which side he'd been on.

A voice in the back of Mitch's head screamed at him to turn back, to go racing down the trenches in the other direction or leap up the nearest ladder and charge off into no-man's-land or straight into the open fields behind the front.

Instead he picked his way forward, trying to avoid stepping on anything that had once been part of a living man.

Several times he failed.

At one point, Mitch stopped to look at something that seemed like a bloody mask half-buried in the mud. In an instant, he realized he was staring at the back of a severed face.

As he bit back the bile that threatened to rise in his throat, Mitch heard movement from above the trench. He swiveled to the left, training his weapon above the trench's lip, right about where a soldier's chest would be if he charged at them out of the darkness.

Nothing stood there. Nothing moved at all but the mists, which swirled about in a pattern that reminded Mitch of a speedboat's wake.

After a long moment staring up at the settling mists, Mitch turned back to the open part of the trench and came face to face with a dark-haired, sharp-chinned man in a Bauhaus officer's uniform.

The man seemed as shocked as Mitch. He must have just emerged from one of the other trenches that emptied into this central area and then stumbled into Mitch and his friends. Right now, though, how he'd gotten there wasn't important.

Mitch swung the butt of his rifle about and smashed the oberleutnant in the face. The Cog staggered back, bleeding but unfazed.

Mitch resolved to hit the man harder this time and brought the rifle around in a sharp, twisting jab. Once he knocked the man down, he would have enough room to train his gun on him and blow him away. Better yet, he'd keep the man silent and question him about any compatriots hiding nearby. He didn't want any gunshots to bring them running.

Instead, though, the oberleutnant blocked the incoming

blow with his arm. He then grabbed Mitch with his free hand and pulled him into a savage headbutt.

Mitch reeled back, the rifle tumbling from his hands and disappearing in the mud. He knew he'd never find it in time. Opting for a silent kill, he drew his combat knife instead. The Cog did the same.

Mitch held his ground and waited for the oberleutnant to come to him. He knew that the others would come to his aid in mere seconds. He only needed to keep himself alive until then.

The Cog seemed to sense this and launched himself at Mitch. He feinted to his left, then stabbed right, his well-oiled blade gleaming in the dim light. Mitch blocked the man's arm with his left hand and then drove in hard with the knife in his right.

The Cog leaned in under Mitch's strike and tried to head-butt him again. This time Mitch was ready. He snapped his neck back and took the blow on the tip of his chin.

The oberleutnant kept at him, this time bringing up his knife toward Mitch's guts in an attempt to disembowel him. Mitch knocked the man's hand away, but the Cog kept hold of the knife. In a smooth move that Mitch had to admire, the man switched to an overhand grip on the knife and then put all his strength and weight into stabbing it down at the sergeant.

Mitch reached out with his left hand and caught the ober-leutnant's wrist. The point of the knife came jabbing straight toward his face, stopping only inches from his eye.

As the Cog grunted in frustration, Mitch brought his own knife around toward the man's exposed neck. A single, sharp blow, and the man would be dead, his blood gushing out of his throat.

This time, Mitch ended up the frustrated one. The Cog spotted the incoming blade and managed to get his free hand up in time to grab Mitch's wrist in a grip like a vise.

The two of them stood there, holding each other's knives at bay with one hand while trying to stab their foe to death with the other. The deadly dance paused when both men froze at the sound of a half dozen weapons being cocked at them.

6

Mitch recognized the sounds of his compatriots' weapons being chambered with bullets and shells. The pump action on El Jesus's shotgun was unmistakable. Still, he couldn't bring himself to feel too good about it. The three Bauhaus troops who'd appeared behind the oberleutnant dampened his relief.

Standing in the middle of a vicious knife fight surrounded by a gunfight, Mitch remained calm. "Panic never helps," he'd often told his soldiers, even in the face of certain death.

He hoped the oberleutnant had trained his men as well. It would take only one nervous trigger finger for this standoff to devolve into a bloodbath, and there had been enough death that day. The stench of the already rotting corpses and the freshly scattered bowels would have been enough to make Mitch's head swim if the last remains of the Bauhaus gas attack had not already taken care of that. He breathed through his mouth and strove to stay cool.

The oberleutnant took advantage of Mitch's apparent hesitation in the middle of their fight to renew his efforts with his knife. Mitch's grip on the man's wrist tightened in time. He pushed the Bauhaus knife away and at the same time pulled back on his own blade.

The oberleutnant—Mitch could read the name Steiner on his chest now—held Mitch's arm just as tightly, suspecting the sergeant of some kind of trick.

"Murderer," the Bauhauser said in his German-accented English, his voice shaking as he spoke. "Has war driven you mad?"

Mitch said nothing, just stared at the man with cold eyes. He didn't struggle with Steiner any longer but held him right where he was. He didn't want to kill the man, but he would not hesitate to drop him if necessary.

Nathan spoke up from behind. Mitch never took his eyes off Steiner, never gave the man another chance to make a move.

"My men didn't do this."

Steiner gaped at Nathan's words, grasping their enormity. If the Capitol troops hadn't done this, then who could have? As Mitch watched, he saw the answer dawn on the oberleutnant's face. Disgust and rage followed close behind.

"You accuse me?"

Mitch barely parted his lips to spit out his soft-spoken accusation. "Yeah."

Steiner's lip curled in hatred.

Mitch understood. They were both professionals, veterans of countless wars. But the carnage here had gone beyond all that.

Mitch didn't care too much for humanity as a group. He'd seen too much of the worst of people over the years. But whatever humanity might be, this was a crime against it.

Mitch stared into Steiner's eyes. As far as he could tell, the man's horror and disgust were real. He and the other Cogs hadn't committed this atrocity either. But if they hadn't, who had?

Mitch heard someone behind him starting to get sick. The tension—or maybe the awful smell—had gotten to Naismith again. Mitch hoped that one of the Bauhaus troops wouldn't see this as his chance to drill the private into his grave. His grip on Steiner's wrist tightened, and he felt the hand on his arm do the same.

Mitch risked a glance back toward Naismith to see how the man was faring. The soldier leaned forward and opened his mouth to puke. As he did, a blade the length of a sword emerged from between his teeth like a horrible bone-colored tongue.

Naismith tried to scream but gagged on the boneblade instead. Then the blade jerked backward just as fast as it had appeared, pulling Naismith's corpse back into the obscuring mists with it.

Everyone but Mitch and Steiner spun about to face the encroaching mists. Mitch was ready to go for his sidearm too, but he didn't trust the oberleutnant not to stab him as soon as he dropped his knife.

One of the Bauhaus troopers fell over then, his body slapping into the gore-crusted muck without a word, much less a scream. Something in the mists, which seemed as close and cloying as ever, dragged the body away, blood still gurgling from the dying man's mouth.

Mitch and Steiner looked each other in the eye, then dropped their arms at the same time. A silent agreement had passed between them. They might be enemies, but they were professionals too. They could put their animosity aside for the moment to deal with this new threat.

Afterward, of course, all bets were off, but for the moment they would work as a team.

Mitch stuffed his knife back in its sheath with one hand as he reached for his pistol with the other. He had it clear and pointed out toward the mists in a split second.

It heartened Mitch to see that Nathan, El Jesus, and the two other Bauhaus troopers had all come to the same conclusion as Steiner and he. That proved the barest comfort, though, against the unknown threat coming at them from the all-consuming mists.

Something moved in the shadows next to Nathan, and Mitch opened fire. The others did the same. Some fired at the elusive figure near Nathan, and others blasted away at ghosts of their own.

Mitch couldn't make out what he'd been shooting at, but he knew there was more than one. Dark, twisted shadows loped along the edges of the mist, barely out of sight. He felt like a sailor dumped into a dark and shark-infested sea, struggling to fend off the unseen predators, never knowing from which direction they might strike next.

He fired at each shadow he saw, either single shots or controlled bursts, but nothing out there complained about the results. A few of the bullets ricocheted off something, and others blew back splatters of mud from where they smacked into the trench's floor or walls.

The sound of six guns blasting away at the mists rang in Mitch's ears, and he cursed the noise. They might have had to deal with only a few of their foes at the moment, but if there were any others out there on the battlefield, the racket would be sure to bring them running.

Somewhere in the mists, he heard a radio operator calling for evacuation. The man's voice ended in a wet gurgle before he could finish.

El Jesus's shotgun blasted away holes in the mist, actually blowing the smoke back for precious moments, opening small windows into it. They closed nearly as fast as they formed, but they proved at least that the world didn't end at the limits of the mists.

Mitch wondered if this was what hell was like.

He spied something moving fast past one of the gaps El Jesus had blasted open. Its skin was the color of a fresh corpse: pale, slick with rain, and bereft of the warmth of blood.

Another blast sounded, and Mitch spotted a pair of burning red eyes staring back at him. He swung his pistol about and fired two quick shots at it, but the thing—whatever it was—had already disappeared.

The mists closed in harder until Mitch could barely see

a dozen feet away. Something long and sharp—another boneblade perhaps—sliced out of the glowing white mists and opened up El Jesus's thigh. Mitch shot at where a man's body should have been behind the blade, but the blade disappeared into the mists again.

The big man grunted against the pain, shoving it away, and kept firing. Blood ran down his leg but did not spurt. He would live, Mitch knew, if that was the worst that happened to him this day.

The odds on that, though, didn't look good.

A trooper standing near Mitch—not Steiner, who'd disappeared, it seemed—fell apart in a bloody burst as a blade reached out and sliced him lengthwise in two. Lifeblood geysered from the man's remains as the pieces of him slid into the muck.

Mitch opened up with his pistol, emptying it into the area from which the man had been slaughtered.

"I'm out!" He dropped the useless weapon. He then spied a trench sword lying in the mud, still grasped in a severed hand, and snatched it up, prying the dead fingers from its grip.

"Ah!" El Jesus was trying to move, and the pain nearly stopped him dead. "My fucking leg! My ankle!"

As Mitch brought up the long, vicious blade, he spied a shadow rushing straight for him. Desperate not to end up like the last man who'd held the sword, he put all his weight into his swing and sliced straight at his attacker.

The blade connected with something solid, and Mitch felt the impact jar his arms to his shoulders. The shadow moved away silently, even as something solid slapped to the ground before him.

Mitch looked down and saw the end of a once-human arm lying at his feet. He picked it up and looked at it. Where the fingers should have been, a long, serrated blade of bone jutted out of the wrist, as if the forearm had somehow mutated into a new, savage form. Instead of blood, a viscous black fluid oozed from the open stump.

Mitch bit back the vomit that rose in his throat and glanced around. The shadows had stopped circling them for the moment, perhaps because the soldiers had finally hurt one of them. Or maybe they were readying a final assault.

Assessing the situation, Mitch glanced about and saw only Nathan, El Jesus, and himself. Steiner and his men had disappeared, either dead or fled. He had no inclination to go looking for them.

We're fucked.

El Jesus nudged him and pointed with his shotgun toward the south again. At least it seemed like that direction. In the mist, still in the middle of a fight, it was impossible to tell how badly they might have been turned around.

A pair of burning eyes stared at them from the edge of the smoke. Shadows massed behind the hidden creature, joining and leaving it at random.

This was it, Mitch knew. Within the next few moments, the creatures—whatever they were—would attack, and it would be all over.

El Jesus raised his shotgun. He couldn't have had much ammo left in it, Mitch knew. Nor could Nathan, who still bore a smoking pistol in his fist.

Mitch held the stolen sword before him like a talisman to ward off evil spirits. No matter when the attack came, or how, he vowed to take as many of the monstrous bastards with him as he could.

Then a blazing light washed down on the three soldiers from above. With the gunfire still ringing in his ears, Mitch hadn't heard the transport moving in. It scudded toward them, then hovered for a moment as the light played on the three soldiers.

The shadows retreated before the light, scurrying back

into the sheltering mists before Mitch could get a better look at them. He wasn't sure he wanted to.

Now that he could hear the airship's engine, Mitch recognized it as belonging to a Capitol troop transport. It had probably come in from the rear echelon to see what had gone so terribly wrong and maybe to pick up any survivors.

The airship moved off then, the light trailing back toward them for as long as it could. Soon, though, it was gone.

Nathan slapped Mitch and El Jesus on their backs, shouting at them as the chopper moved off. They needed to get to the landing zone fast. "LZ!" he said in their ears. "Get to the LZ!"

Mitch glanced over at El Jesus's leg. The big man grimaced at him through gritted teeth and nodded that he'd be all right. Mitch grabbed him by the shoulder, and with Nathan on their heels, they sprinted for the landing zone.

7

Mitch got several steps ahead of El Jesus before he realized the big man was lagging behind. Without a word, he reached back and pulled the corporal's arm over his shoulders, doing what he could to help support the man's weight on the side of his wounded leg.

Nathan stumbled up to try to help, but Mitch waved him off. The captain was already weak from the bullet that had creased his skull earlier, and Mitch knew he couldn't carry both him and El Jesus at once. If Nathan managed to keep his own legs moving, that would be enough.

Mitch remembered the last time something like this had happened to him. Then it had been Nathan carrying him through the jungles of Venus. They'd been part of an operation to free up a Capitol mining facility that Bauhaus claimed had been built on their soil.

Of course, Bauhaus had unilaterally declared itself in sole control of the entire planet, so any facilities owned by someone else constituted trespassing in its view. The Capitol President wasn't about to put up with that, so he'd sent in a brigade of the Capitol Ground Forces to make his point.

Mitch and Nathan had been unfortunate enough to be called on to serve in that action. It had been one of the first times they'd been on a real battlefield, and Mitch remembered how nervous they'd both been.

"You're just eager to flex those captain's bars," Mitch had said, ribbing his friend.

Nathan had ignored him. The two of them had been involved in a terrible argument when they'd gotten the orders to ship out. Despite the vows the two friends had made to each other, it had been over a girl. A woman, really, but not just any woman.

Adelaide.

Mitch had loved her from the moment he'd seen her, and Nathan had too. Both of them claimed to have seen her first, but that hadn't mattered. She'd seen Mitch first and fallen just as hard.

For a long time, the three of them had been inseparable, a trio of pals united by their mutual adoration. In the end, though, Addy had chosen Mitch as the one to take to her bed.

The orders to go to Venus had pulled Mitch from that precious place, a fact for which he knew he would never forgive his corporation. Weeks later, he and Nathan had found themselves part of the brigade that formed a protective circle around that damned hole in the ground the President treasured so much.

It wasn't as if the mine had all that much to offer. It was just a mine, a thousand miles from the Bauhaus metropolis of Heimburg. There were plenty of other places to put a damned mine, even on Mars, where Capitol's people belonged.

But the Board of Directors had decided to take a stand against Bauhaus's hostile takeover, and they'd chosen to plant their proxies here.

"What the fuck are we doing here?" Nate had asked as he hauled Mitch out of the jungle. "We're a couple of smart, handsome guys. We could have made something of ourselves in the business corps."

"You can't add," Mitch had said through gritted teeth,

trying to shove aside the pain that stabbed through his side where the bullet had passed through. Later, he'd find that it had missed any essential organs and that he'd heal fine, but at that moment he'd wondered if he'd seen his last Martian sunset with Addy at his side.

"And you have authority issues."

"Says who?" The blood seeping out of Mitch's side had started to run into his boot.

"It's in your record."

"You've seen my record?"

"It's not?"

Mitch smirked through the pain. "What's your point?"

Nathan grunted as he shouldered Mitch over a rotten log that had fallen across their path. "We'd never survive in the business world."

Mitch thought of the three other soldiers they'd lost while out on patrol, not to mention the injury done to his side. "We're not doing so well in the military, pal."

He heard a Hussar reconnaissance plane chug along overhead, trying to spot them through the dense canopy. For an instant, Mitch thought of trying to bring it down with his assault rifle, but the moment of madness passed. He laughed at himself, and pain lanced through his side, almost causing him to tumble to the ground.

"You should go on without me," Mitch said to Nathan. "I'm only slowing you down."

"And what would Addy say to that?" Nathan said. "I could never go back to Mars again."

"We'll both get killed."

Nathan smiled at his friend. "Leaving together or not at all, so quit your whining and move your ass."

"Yes, sir."

Mitch knew that Nathan had every reason to leave him there in the jungle to die. Just before they'd left Mars, the man had confessed his love to Addy. She'd told Mitch, of course, and he and Nate had fought about it on the entire long trip to Venus. By the time they had touched down outside the mine, their CO, Colonel Santino, had ordered them to shut the hell up and get along.

Mitch hadn't been able to believe that Nathan could betray him like that, to go after his best friend's woman. Addy was something special, sure, but not worth destroying a friendship over. Apparently Nathan didn't agree with that exactly.

Now, all Nathan had to do was let Mitch go and save himself. No one would have blamed him. Hell, Mitch had practically begged him to do it. Then he would have had Addy all to himself.

But Nathan would have none of it. As far as Mitch could tell, the thought of abandoning his friend had never crossed the man's mind. It was one thing, it seemed, to steal a man's reason for living and another entirely to let him die.

After a harrowing hour ducking the Bauhaus net of air and ground patrols, the two finally made it to the mine's gate. Once they got there, though, they found the tall, steel doors locked to them.

"You can't come in," Santino said, hollering down at them from the top of the gates. "We can't risk letting the Cogs drive a tank in through the door while it's open."

"So throw down a rope!" Mitch said.

The CO just shook his head.

"You set us up, you cheap fuck!"

Santino smiled. "Just following orders, boys. The Board of Directors needs an intercorporate incident here to strengthen its claims before the Cartel arbitrators. You are that incident."

While Santino was still chuckling, Mitch pulled out his pistol and, in one clean move, blew off the man's head. The corpse came tumbling over the top of the gate and crashed to the ground in a bloody tangle of broken limbs.

The guards atop the gate trained their weapons on Mitch

and Nate. "Thanks, pal," Nathan said. "You just got us killed."

Mitch tossed his pistol to Nathan and let himself slump to the ground.

"I'm not going to shoot you, Mitch," Nathan said.

"Arrest me," Mitch said.

Nathan froze at the suggestion. "What?"

"Arrest me. Press charges. I just killed a superior officer."

"That's the death penalty."

Mitch just stared up at Nathan from where he'd fallen. "In the long run, we're all dead."

Nathan signaled the guards to come down and take Mitch prisoner. Most of them had been good men, uncomfortable with implementing Santino's scheme. Now that the man was dead, they saw no reason to keep his plans any more alive than he—especially since Nathan had provided them with a convenient excuse to let someone else decide whether one of their fellow soldiers had to die.

"Fuck me, Top!" El Jesus said now as Mitch hauled his heavy carcass up the last hill. The transport sat there on the crest, the entire place lit up like a parking lot, waiting for them to come. It was a monstrous beast of a craft, almost impossible to put into the air, but as Nathan often liked to say, with enough diesel fuel you could move anything.

As if to prove itself, the airship hovered there, just inches off the ground. This would have to be a lightning-fast recovery, and if the pilot caught a glimpse of what was following the troops he was waiting for, he'd climb his ship into the sky in an instant.

"Come on!" Mitch said, shoving up under El Jesus as he pistoned his legs beneath him. "Just a bit further."

They passed an M89 heavy machine gun on a pivot mount as they made their way up the hill. The unit had set it up as a last line of defense for the landing zone, but now it stood empty, its gunner missing or dead.

For a moment, Mitch considered taking over the gun to blast the beasts in the shadows, but he knew that would condemn all three of them to death. Nate was too weak to help El Jesus to the transport, and he would have refused to go on without at least one of them.

He charged on past.

As he reached the lip of the hill's flattened top, he glanced back to see the shadows getting closer. With the transport on the other side of the clearing, he knew they'd never make it.

Nathan came to the same conclusion. Mitch saw him hesitate there next to the rotary machine gun and then head for it.

"Nate!"

Mitch tried to stop, but El Jesus kept going. The big man could barely see straight. He could only keep his head down and focused on the transport straight ahead of them. If he stopped, Mitch knew that El Jesus would fall over and never get up again.

"I'm right behind you!" Nathan said. "Go!"

Mitch cursed his friend, El Jesus, and every officer Capitol had ever had, but he kept the big man on his shoulder moving. As they lurched forward, he heard the M89 whir to life and then open up on the creatures chasing them.

"Come on, then!" Nathan roared at the things coming at him through the mist. The gun's long *brrraaappp* sounded like a never-ending crack of thunder rolling down the mud-slick hill.

As Mitch reached the transport, he shoved El Jesus up onto the boarding platform. The copilot stared down at them, looking as white as a ghost, and Mitch feared to ask him what he'd seen.

He didn't have the time now anyhow. He had to go back for Nathan.

As he turned to leap down from the boarding platform,

Mitch heard the M89 fall silent. It couldn't have run out of ammunition so soon.

"Fucking mutants!" Nathan stepped away from the gun and pulled out his knife. "Come on. Let's have it!"

Mitch's heart sank, but he couldn't give up. Just as his feet were about to leave the transport's platform, he felt El Jesus's meaty hand wrap around his arm. He tugged at it, but the corporal refused to let go.

"Lose the hand!" Mitch said, snarling at the pale shot-gunner.

"Fuck you!" said El Jesus. "You're not going back!" The man was so wiped, he could barely move, but his grip stayed on like a steel strap.

Mitch punched El Jesus in his wounded leg, and the man let go. He turned to stare out at the open stretch of land between the transport and where the machine gun sat shrouded in the mists.

"Nate!"

Mitch knew he should leap off the transport and rush to Nathan's aid. That's what his friend would have done for him. At least that's what he told himself.

"Go!" Nate's bellow echoed through the mists.

In his heart, Mitch knew better. Nathan was already dead, and he'd given his life for his friend. He couldn't let that sacrifice be in vain. Right?

As if in answer, the mists gathered tighter around the transport, and the shadows came stumping over the crest of the hill. There had to be dozens of them, maybe hundreds.

There was no chance Nathan had survived.

The pilot shouted back from the airship's cockpit, "Where's everybody else?"

El Jesus leaned back and slammed his fist against the bulkhead that separated the cockpit from the transport's main platform.

"There's nobody else!" the big man said. "Let's go, moth-erfucker!"

Mitch felt inertia try to pull him back to the earth as the transport lurched into the sky and left the landing zone. He watched the pool of light grow smaller below and then behind them. The lights began going out from the edges, one at a time at first, and then they snuffed out all at once.

8

Young Michael Stenmark had never seen his grandfather so agitated in all his years. The old man's hands shook as he sat at the desk, his eyes closed as he listened to the mysterious series of long and short beeps that fought through the crackling static that filled his headphones. Grandfather Patric had the volume turned up so loud that Michael could hear the beeps the moment he walked through the door.

The trip up the mountain from his bare stone acolyte's cell in the simple home just down the ridge had nearly frozen the boy solid. The blizzard raging outside had blocked the path to the radio tower, and Michael had wondered if the old rusted radio dish—which stood bigger than the radio shack itself—would still work if covered with so much snow. He thanked the Cardinal that another boy had been assigned the duty of keeping the thing clear.

Grandfather Patric scrawled the last letters of the message on the parchment as Michael approached the table. His lips moved as he read the words over one last time. His hand shook as if palsied as he shoved the paper into the boy's hands.

Michael took the paper without a word and stuffed it into a pocket on the inside of his acolyte's robes for safekeeping. He steeled himself with one last warm breath before charging back out into the snow.

As dawn broke over the mountains, Michael trudged

back down through the snow, past his humble home, and down into the gorge below. The snow grew thicker the lower he went, until it was as high as his chest. He pushed on.

At first he tromped through the snow. Then he had to crawl through it. At one point it was so deep that he felt like he was swimming through it.

Many times Michael thought of giving up, of turning back, but he knew that his grandfather would not understand. Better for him to die here in the snow, trying with all his might to push forward, than to return to his grandfather's shame.

The message was important. Despite not having read the scribbling on the paper, he knew that. He'd never seen his grandfather shake so.

If he turned back, if he went home, he would have to face his grandfather. The old man had never beaten him, but this could be the first time. Even worse, he knew that his grandfather would then try to get the message through himself, and Michael was sure that attempting such a journey would kill him.

Finally, Michael came to the drop-off, the part of the gorge that fell away hundreds of feet down to a trickle of a frozen river below. He worked his way down the treacherous path, knowing that one slip could send him sliding out over the edge and to his doom. He wondered if he would be scared the entire way down or if he would have enough time to regain his senses and even proclaim a quick prayer of penitence to the Cardinal before he hit the ground.

As Michael turned a corner in the path, the monastery loomed on the other side of the gorge before him. It seemed more like a fortress than a church, tucked away in the side of the mountain.

Michael made his way toward the massive stone bridge that stretched all the way across the ravine, and he looked up to see the rising sun caught in the stained-glass rosette hanging in the center of the place's Gothic facade. The sight always stole his breath, and he often felt as if this was the closest he would ever feel to the Cardinal, right in this moment of awe.

The snows had been cleared from the bridge, and when Michael reached it, he broke into a sprint. After fighting through the deep snows for so long, it felt good to finally stretch his legs, and he widened his stride as far as he could.

When he reached the entrance to the place, he stopped and stared up at the carvings over the tall, ironbound doors. There were no guards there, no one to greet him, but he did not find that strange. The monks would be in morning prayers at the moment, and they had not had an unannounced visitor since long before Michael had been born.

Michael let himself in through the small door set in the center of the two huge doors. He felt like a thief sneaking into the dragon's lair, although he'd been here nearly every day of his life. Inside, he could hear the soft echoes of the monks chanting their prayers in their solemn, steady tones.

Michael ran toward the chanting, and it grew louder with every step. He could hear the words now, not just the music, and he began to chant along with them under his breath.

9

When Brother Samuel had awakened that morning, he'd known something horrible had happened. He could feel it in the depths of his soul, and it disturbed him to his core.

Despite his growing sense of dread, Samuel had gone about his regular morning routine without a word. Up before the first hint of dawn had shown above the edges of the surrounding mountains, he had bathed in the icy waters that ran in a stream from the mountaintop all the way down to the monastery. Then he had dressed in his coarse red robes and hung the symbol of the Brotherhood around his neck.

Although it was heavy, he no longer felt its weight. When he removed it, he noticed that he felt lighter in its absence, so much so that he feared he might float away. The metal icon grounded him spiritually and physically, and without it he was rootless.

Last of all, he put his hands together, folding his thumbs and index fingers over each other, and prayed. He had done this every day since he'd pledged his soul to the Cardinal's eternal cause: protecting humanity from the evils that could destroy them all.

The bickering between the megacorps, inevitable as it was, only did the Dark Symmetry's evil work, driving wedge after wedge between the peoples of man so that they could not form a united front against the darkness. Nowhere was this more apparent than in the Cartel, the intercorporate organization founded to further the few aims on which all the megacorporations could agree.

The corporations sometimes seemed to forget that they had the Brotherhood for that. The Cardinal had long ago taken charge of the safety of their souls, and what could be more vital than that?

After a meager breakfast, Samuel made his way to the monastery's chapel. There he met the other monks at the appointed time, and together they prayed. At first he led them in a series of chants, and then he opened his copy of the Book of Law.

The monks spent almost every hour of daylight scribing new copies of the Book of Law by hand. That was the charge of the Directorate known as the Mission. It would have been simpler to use technology to copy the books, but that would have allowed the foul influence of the Dark Symmetry to alter the copied text in ways both subtle and horrible.

Some said humanity had taken a turn for the worse when it had been forced to give up the ways of technology to survive. The Dark Symmetry had made such amazing devices not only unreliable but deadly. The First Corporate Wars had broken out over such issues, and it had taken the Cardinal's leadership to bring humanity back from the brink of destruction to which it had driven itself.

No book made in the monastery was ever more than two copies away from the Book of Law kept in the monastery's vault. The first thing every monk did upon becoming a scribe was to make his own copy of the book from that sacred text. He then used that edition as the basis of the copies he made for other people.

As the chanting fell silent, Brother Samuel opened his copy of the Book of Law, set it on the lectern in front of him, and began to read aloud to the robed monks assembled before him:

Ár nathair atá ar neamh, naofar d'ainm
Go dtaga do ríocht
Go ndéantar do thoil ar an talamh mar a dhéantar ar
   neamh.
Ár n-arán laethúil tabhair dúinn inniu . . .

As he led the others through the catechism, the door at the back of the chapel creaked open on its rusty hinges. Samuel made a mental note to have Brother Bergtig oil them at the next opportunity. Then the boy named Michael came into view, and Samuel's heart sank. There would be time for taking care of creaky doors later.

Samuel frowned not in displeasure at the boy but at the message he knew he must bear. Although the monk did not know the contents of the boy's note, such vessels never carried good news. The Brotherhood was happy to let good tidings crawl, but it fired bad news from a cannon.

The boy drew a piece of parchment from inside his snow-crusted robes as he strode into the chamber. The child's hands were almost blue from the cold, and his fingers felt like icicles.

Samuel took the note and opened it. The news was worse than he could have imagined. His fingers tightened on the boy's shoulder, and his face drained of color.

Samuel placed the note into the Book of Law and closed it. He picked it up carefully from the lectern, then nodded for the monks to begin their workday. "In nomine Cardinalis," he said to them softly. The chamber's perfect acoustics carried his words to every set of ears.

As Samuel turned to leave the chamber, he heard the boy padding along behind him, ready for a new assignment, a response, anything. Samuel turned to the boy and shook his head. He gestured for Brother Stefan and Brother Conner to take care of the boy. If he had a hot bath soon, he might keep all his fingers.

Satisfied that the boy was in good hands, Samuel ducked into a nearby stairwell and began to climb. The stairs wound upward forever, spiraling higher and higher into the mountain's living rock. Windows shaped like natural formations let in sunlight every so many yards, allowing a weak light to stream into the shadows and show Samuel the way.

When he reached the top, Samuel found himself standing before an iron door sealed by many large locks. A monk stood by the door, waiting for him. She carried a naked blade in her hands.

Severian's Book of Law would be kept in her cell, he knew, there for her whenever she needed it. With her assignment, straight from the Cardinal, she would need her sword far more often than the book's words.

Despite her stolid composure, Samuel suspected that Severian was surprised to see him. Few people ever came up this way, and only if they had the most vital business. Still, no emotion showed in her wide, dark eyes.

Samuel reached out, and the monk bowed her head as he took a key from a chain around her neck. He inserted it into the lock and turned it in a specific way. Then he nodded to Severian.

The door swung wide. It creaked even more loudly than the chapel door had.

Samuel entered the tiny chamber beyond the iron door first, with Severian close behind. Sunlight streamed in from the skylight, illuminating the room. Lichen encrusted the rough-hewn stone walls. Ancient swords bearing Celtic patterns stood in the center of the room, covered with dust and cobwebs as if they had not been moved for the last thousand years. They hung in a circular rank around a lectern, and on the lectern sat a single leather-bound book, simple and unassuming. Samuel walked to it and picked it up gingerly, hefting it in his hands as if it were as precious as a newborn child.

This, Samuel knew—as few others did—was the original Book of Law, the first set of the Chronicles ever scribed. That alone would have been enough to make it a sacred tome of the highest order, but there was more to it than that.

This particular book contained certain chronicles that had never been copied into any other book. The knowledge held in it was too dangerous to be disseminated widely, even to other members of the Brotherhood. But the time had come for it to be revealed and put to use.

10

Samuel did not feel comfortable in the boardroom. He came from a world devoted to prayer and wisdom, not stock prices and balance sheets that could value a life in something as crass as crowns. If he had had a choice, he never would have set foot in such a place—the Earth headquarters of the intercorporate council known as the Cartel—but the Cardinal had personally requested he do so, and so he did without question.

The boardroom stood at the top of the Cartel's towering skyscraper. Weak sunlight filtered down through the gray clouds outside and across the wide stone balcony that fronted the panoramic windows, and fought through the smoke-filled air inside the room to provide what little illumination the ambassadors there would permit. They preferred to have shadows in which to skulk, away from the eyes of their underlings.

Not that any of the masses they supposedly represented would ever be permitted inside the first floor of this tower, much less allowed to enter the opulent sanctum—at least none of those who had not somehow curried the favor of these most powerful people. Some of them clustered here around their masters: needless translators jabbering away in their native tongues, secretaries recording verbatim every word said in the chamber, concubines brought to put their employers' virility on display.

It made Samuel sick. He longed for his simple, unclut-
tered cell and the monastery's clean mountain air. All he had
with him, though, was the silent Severian, who had not spoken a word since coming to the monastery, and this ancient
Book of Law, but that would be enough.

Standing at a lectern placed at the foot of the obscenely
large table around which the four groups were gathered,
with Severian standing behind him, he read from the sacred
Chronicles.

*"Before the first dawn, there was a battle in Heaven. The
Enemy was cast out and fell to Earth, an evil star."*

He looked to the chairman of this council, a regal man
named Constantine. He, at least, listened. Samuel could not
say as much for the ambassadors sitting beneath the banners of the Capitol star, the Mishima sun, the Bauhaus cog,
and the Imperial lion. He could read the disbelief in their
faces, in the way they had held themselves when he had entered the room, in the falsity of their smiles as they had
greeted him. They had no place for the Cardinal's wisdom
in their hearts, but that did not mean that Samuel could give
up, not with the fate of the planet on the line.

*"Broken in body but not in Pride, consumed by Envy and
Hate, it conspired to remake Man in its own Image. And
thus the Enemy created a Machine. A Machine that stripped
the souls from the dead and dying and replaced them with
its own Dark Essence."*

Samuel saw the Bauhaus representative roll his eyes at
this, and one of the man's retinue of sycophants had to stifle
a snicker. The monk knew how this sort of thing sounded to
worldly men. He'd been one once himself, a lifetime ago.
Would he have believed what was written here in this ancient book, in the steady hand that had used ink and quill to
speak through the centuries to the future of humanity for
the time when its prescience would be needed most?

Probably not, he had to admit. But Samuel had seen
many things since he had been a part of the corporate

world. He'd long ago renounced the so-called conventional intelligence and given over his life into the Cardinal's hands.

Men did not believe in what they could not see, and even then they refused to fully engage with the mysteries of the universe. They denied the very idea of the Dark Symmetry as superstition and lies, and they laughed at the notion that people of goodwill could use the light to fight against the darkness.

In these black days, though, their laughter rang hollow.

"When the great star fell to Earth, Neachdainn, Founder of our Order, united the ancient tribes of Man. Together they defeated the Enemy and sealed his Machine beneath the Earth."

Neachdainn had been one of the first Druids, the people who had lived in this land over two thousand years ago. Cardinal Nathaniel Durand I had built the Brotherhood on the rock of their beliefs and on the actions they had performed to save all of humanity so long ago.

Samuel could tell by the blank looks from the ambassadors that none of them had heard of the man. He knew that they each attended services in the Brotherhood cathedrals every week. They paid their respects to the Cardinal, but only with their lips and their gold. They kept their hearts to themselves, sheltered in the darkness of their souls.

The monk closed the book. What he had to say next came not from its words but from the Cardinal himself. Samuel was but a mouthpiece for this pronouncement, although he agreed with every word as if it had originated from his own tongue.

He knew that he had to speak truly here to gain their attention, much less their support. He was a mere monk, used to speaking only to other brothers, but he had to connect with these people somehow.

How long had it been since he'd left the monastery? He had lost track of the years in that timeless place. From what he had seen of civilization since he'd returned to it for this mission, it hadn't changed much. Perhaps only for the worse.

Samuel spoke clearly and slowly. He looked into the eyes of each of the ambassadors as he formed the words. They met him with strength—even defiance. Only Constantine seemed to hear what he had to say, but he kept speaking.

"But now war has broken the Great Seal, and its wheels turn once again. Every soldier that falls in battle, every woman and child taken in the night becomes an Enemy of Man, another demon bent upon our extinction."

He knew they had seen these things. He could not have avoided the reports himself if he had tried. News of the mutants rampaging throughout the world had taken up every last second of radio and television, every inch of newsprint. They knew what was happening, of course, but they had no idea why, no inkling of the truth.

"Ten beget a hundred, a hundred beget a thousand, a thousand beget a million. But even now there is hope. The Chronicles prophesy that one will rise to follow the path of Neachdainn into hell itself and deliver mankind from oblivion."

Samuel ended there and let silence fall over the room. He gave the ambassadors time to contemplate his words, to consider them and the course of action they demanded.

For a long while, no one spoke. This unnerved the monk, for he knew that most times these men jockeyed for the chance to make themselves heard, to trump their fellows in timing if not substance.

The silence stretched on longer. Then the man from Bauhaus spoke in his lilting accent.

"Asinine. You begged an audience with this council. You claimed to have knowledge of these mutants. And you tell us fairy tales."

The man glanced around at the others as he spoke, and

their righteous nods gave him their tacit assent. Embold-
ened, the Cog put his fist down on the table and made a final
pronouncement.

"There is only one way to fight an enemy: with blood and
iron."

11

Although Corporal Paul Lamb had never left the planet of his birth, he had fought battles on nearly every part of Earth. He'd never been in one like this.

The transport that had brought him here, from the home to which he'd supposedly retired from conflicts like this, had passed over the region where all of this had reportedly started. He'd peered out through the tiny window in the side of the plane and spied thousands of the so-called mutants streaming like ants out of the ancient plain that had now become a crater.

A fighter had nearly collided with the plane as it strafed the mutants, and then it came back for another pass. The bullets had almost no effect. They mowed down a line of the creatures as the fighter passed over them, but an instant later the open space disappeared as the survivors filled the gap.

Just thinking about it as he stood here in these trenches, which smelled of newly moved dirt, made him sick.

"You all right, mate?" a man next to him said in an Imperial accent much like Paul's own. The tag embroidered on his uniform's shirt said OLSSON.

Paul looked up past the man at the brilliant skyline of the city they'd been ordered to defend. He couldn't understand what hope they might have. If the enemy had made it this far from that damned hill, how could they be stopped here?

Paul just shook his head. He didn't feel like talking much.

"None of us are," the man on the other side of him said. His voice carried a strong Mishiman accent. His tag said ISHIMORI. "Last month, I was in a war along the coast of Africa. We fought against the Imperials there. Over farming rights."

Ishimori stared at Olsson. "I might have been shooting at you."

"Or vice versa," Olsson said.

Paul nodded. Glancing down the trench, he could see patches on the shoulders of every soldier, declaring from which corporation he'd been seconded. Imperial, Mishima, Bauhaus, Capitol—they were all here.

"It's not natural," Ishimori said, looking up at the dark, storm-tossed sky. "We should be fighting *against* each other, not *with* each other."

"It's the way of things," a dark-skinned Capitol soldier named Watts said. He stood tall and broad-shouldered, his head shaved entirely clean. He toted his M606 machine gun over his shoulder like it was made of plastic rather than cold steel. He had the way of a veteran about him, and Paul instantly felt a kinship with him.

"How do you mean?" This came from a Bauhaus soldier by the name of Emmert.

"Think about it," Watts said. "We're like one big family here. Humanity, I mean. We fight like hell with each other every chance we get. Sometimes over the stupidest fucking things."

The large man paused to unlimber his weapon and place it butt-first on the fresh earth.

"But if someone from outside the family tries to fuck with us?"

Paul nodded, as did the others.

"We are all right there for each other," Emmert said.

"We bond," Ishimori said. "Become a team."

Olsson chuckled at that. Paul started to ask him what

was so damn funny, but a flight of bombers roaring over-head cut him off. Once the planes had passed, he tried again.

"It's not funny at all," Olsson said, a wry grin on his face. "It's just—think about it. If we weren't here as a team, what would we be doing instead? Killing each other straight off."

"Once this is over, don't you think we'll go right back to that?" Emmert said. He stared at the others with his bright blue eyes and then at the twisted series of open tunnels around them. "I wonder if we'll get orders to turn on each other before we leave these trenches or after."

"You're making one hell of an assumption there," Watts said.

The Bauhauser snorted. "You don't think we'll be at each other throats as soon as this is over? How typically naïve."

Watts grunted and shook his head. "You're assuming this'll ever end."

Ishimori grinned, and the others joined in with nervous laughs. Soon even Paul found that he had to echo them. He couldn't say why, though, as he didn't find a damn thing funny about it.

Ishimori fished into his shirt and pulled out a battered pack of cigarettes. He took one and handed the pack to Watts.

"Those things will fucking kill you," the big man said. As the others cackled, he tugged a cigarette out for himself and then passed the pack on to the next man.

Ishimori pulled out a lighter emblazoned with the Mishi-man sun. With a flick of his thumb, it produced a steady flame. He lit his own cigarette with practiced ease, shelter-ing the lighter from the wind whistling down through the trench.

It smelled of raw ozone, bringing news of a coming storm. The scent of burning tobacco shoved that odor away.

Watts leaned forward, and Ishimori lit the man's cigarette

too. One by one, they bent forward and shared in the communal fire, then took their individual pieces of it back to enjoy.

They sat there for a moment, each of them savoring every last drag of his smoke. Paul choked a bit on his but held it down. He'd given up smoking a decade ago when he'd retired from the Capitol Navy, and his lungs wanted to argue with his decision to renege on his unspoken promise to keep them clean.

Then the sirens started to howl. Paul wondered if he'd ever see his wife and son again.

12

Samuel struggled with the urge to curse as he led Severian back into the Cartel's boardroom. Over the past two days, the battle against the mutant threat had gone just as he had predicted: badly. The undead legionnaires and their obscene kin had streamed out of the pit in an endless river of death that had flooded the streets of the city and all but washed the people who lived there away.

The Cardinal had offered Samuel the chance to leave on one of the Brotherhood's rockets, but the monk had refused. As long as there was a breath of hope on the planet, he knew his duties laid here. At his request, the Cardinal had arranged for another meeting with the Cartel's local council.

Oddly, the Brotherhood had not had to pressure the council for the meeting. "Constantine has been asking for you," the brothers in the communications station at the Sacred Dome on Luna had told him.

That, Samuel hoped, would make this easy.

"Welcome, Brother," Constantine said as his underlings escorted the two monks into the boardroom. "I've been hoping you could make it."

Samuel glanced around the room. The sycophants, secretaries, and concubines had vanished, leaving only the four ambassadors behind. Constantine sat at the table's head, framed in the dim light that streamed in through the wide, grimy windows.

Workers had stripped most of the opulent decor from the walls, and a few stragglers still struggled with the last bits. A pair of the workers dropped a giant, brassy cog on the floor, and it cracked nearly in two. They cursed, then scurried away in fear, but the Bauhaus ambassador dismissed them with a wave.

"Leave it," he said. "It is only a symbol."

The room stank of unbathed bodies, and each of the ambassadors bore stubble on his chin. The wrappings from countless meals sat crumpled in a corner where someone had swept them away.

Constantine gestured for Samuel to sit, but the monk declined. He did not care to be seen as an equal to these men. He was not there to talk endlessly about the fate of the world. He had come to ask for their aid and then act.

Constantine nodded his understanding to the monk, then turned back to the ambassadors.

"How much time do we have?" he asked.

It was a question to which Samuel was sure the man knew the answer. It had been asked for the monk's benefit.

"Twenty days," said the Mishiman ambassador. "Less, maybe."

The woman's English was flawless. She'd dispensed with both her translator and the ruse that she couldn't understand what the others said in front of her.

Constantine weighed her words carefully, then spoke. "Begin the evacuation."

"Evacuation?" Samuel could not believe his ears. The Cartel was giving up?

Constantine ignored the comment and addressed the other ambassadors. "We will move all key personnel to the offworld colonies and reassess our situation."

Samuel knew then why Constantine had asked for him to be present. This was no discussion, no meeting of the minds, but a passion play acted out for his benefit. This way, the cowards would not have to report their decision directly to the Cardinal. Instead, they would make him their messenger boy.

He was not about to let them slide away so easily. As the Cardinal's representative here, he had a duty to lift the scales from their eyes and make them see the light.

Samuel spoke in a soft voice. "Am I to understand that you would abandon the Earth?"

The ambassadors averted their eyes from Samuel and glanced at one another. Only Constantine could meet the monk's icy gaze.

"Yes, Brother. You understand well." The man's sadness weighed down his voice, and Samuel noted the sag in his once-proud shoulders. "We are finished here."

The monk forced himself not to snarl. The ambassadors seemed to understand that the meeting was over, and they stood up to leave.

"Even with every ship you have, how many millions will you leave behind?" Samuel asked.

No one answered him. The ambassadors were too busy packing their briefcases, each of which had been stuffed to overflowing with reports, notes, and sheaves of other documents. Only Constantine remained in his chair, in no hurry to leave.

The monk felt his temper rising, and he began to shout.

"And do you think the Enemy will stop with this world?"

He'd hoped it would not be a rhetorical question, but the councilors all took it as such.

"He will not. He will follow you. He will follow you no matter where you run!"

The bureaucrats ignored his words. It was as if he wasn't even in the room. The Imperial ambassador started for the door, with the others close on his heels.

Samuel picked up the sacred Book of Law that was chained to his wrist and slammed its bulk down onto the polished table with all his might. It sounded like a gunshot echoing in the large chamber.

Every head in the room turned to stare at the monk. The workers had all left at the word that the planet would be abandoned. Only the councilors, Severian, and Samuel remained.

"THERE IS STILL HOPE!"

The ambassadors looked to the monk now, hesitation in their eyes. Although they had made up their minds to leave, Samuel knew that he still had time—just not very much of it.

Constantine stared at the monk as if he were little more than a child in a room full of adults. Samuel knew that the councilors had debated this course of action for days. Even profit-driven souls such as these would not so easily give up an entire planet to the Enemy.

People like these obeyed the cold logic of the balance sheet, not the warm mysteries of life. Still, for them to agree to abandon their corporations' investments in an entire planet—and not just any planet but the very cradle of human life—meant the issue had to have become dire beyond words.

"What hope?" Constantine asked. The tone of his voice said that he knew there was none, but Samuel thought he detected a hint of desperation under the world-weary cynicism.

Samuel had his answer ready. He had known it since he'd first stepped into this boardroom days ago. He just had to convince these men he was right.

"Fulfill the Chronicles! Give me twenty soldiers and a ship!"

How much simpler could it be? So it had been written, and so it should play out. Samuel cursed the fact that he did not have these resources himself. The Brotherhood had long ago left behind Earth for Luna, and its holdings on the mother planet were limited.

Till now, the Cardinal had been able to rely on the good-will of the megacorporations to provide his followers with what they needed in any situation. None of them wished to incur the Cardinal's wrath. Had the situation here become so desperate, though, that they would be willing to deny Samuel such a comparatively minor request?

"What could twenty do that our armies could not?" Constantine asked.

The ambassadors nodded at this, and Samuel swallowed hard. It was a fair question, but he had the answer. These men knew nothing of the strength of individuals, the power of a small team to do what entire brigades could not. They lacked the imagination necessary to even conceive of such answers to their problems.

As the Cardinal had once said, "When you have a large enough army, the solution to every issue is war."

Samuel spread out his fingers and put his hands on the table before him, framing the Book of Law in his arms. "They can go where an army cannot. They can go down into the earth."

He paused for a moment, letting the import of his words sink in. "They can destroy the Machine."

Samuel gazed into the ambassadors' eyes one by one, searching for any sign of hope. Instead, they wore their disbelief like armor that turned away his words as if they were mere rain. Their armor, though, had become so rigid that it no longer allowed them to move. It might as well have been a coffin, for they would soon be buried in it.

Samuel opened his mouth to speak one more time.

"I know how this must sound to men of science, men of commerce. But I am a man of faith. And I am asking you—I am begging you—to have faith.

"Not in me. Not even in this."

Samuel rested his hands on the Book of Law before him. He knew that all the answers they required were written there, ready for all who were willing to read them. But he could not rely on that now, for these people would not open their eyes to its wisdom. He had to urge them not to have faith in the Chronicles.

"But faith in man. Faith that the ones you will leave behind deserve a chance.

"Please."

13

Dorothy Lamb scrambled around her family's apartment, packing like mad while her son sat on the floor of their parlor, listening to the radio. Outside, the sirens howled like banshees, signaling that the end was near.

She tossed some of Peter's clothes into the suitcase, alongside hers, then raced into the kitchen to find some food and water. *Take things that will last,* she told herself. *There's no telling how long we'll be gone.*

She pulled the packs of wartime rations off the shelves of the pantry. She tried to grab too many at once, and several fell to the floor, where they broke open, spilling across the tiles. She cursed to herself, knowing there was nothing to be done about that now.

She rushed into the parlor, where she found Peter trembling on the floor, his face in his hands. He had just turned ten, and he looked so much like his father, it hurt her to think about it. The notion drew her eyes to the mantel, where the family photo sat: Paul, she, and Peter all together. She could barely recall having been so happy, and the picture had only been taken last year.

She dumped the rations into the suitcase, then swept the photo from the mantel and tossed it in too. On the radio, the announcer's voice blathered on with the same thing he'd been saying all day. Now, though, a note of hysteria had crept into his voice, confirming to Dorothy that despite the

Cartel's much-vaunted preparations, something had gone horribly wrong.

". . . all civilians must move out of the city to controlled checkpoints. The following streets are still accessible: Bastion, Bleeker, Haight, North Tower, South Tower, Sterling . . ."

Just twenty minutes ago, they'd been listing the streets that were closed rather than the ones still open. Dorothy knew time was running out.

She checked their tickets once more, tossed on her coat, then pulled Peter to his feet and helped him into his. She took a moment to wipe the tears from his face before picking up the suitcase, taking him by the hand, and racing out the door.

She didn't bother to close it behind them.

Down on the streets, the chaos was worse than Dorothy had imagined. They'd tired of waiting for an elevator and had walked down the thirteen flights of stairs to the lobby, which had been clogged with people trying to get out or perhaps find some respite from the crowds outside.

Not seeing any better option, Dorothy grabbed Peter by the wrist. He held on tight to her too. It almost hurt, but she preferred that to the thought of never being able to hold his hand again.

"Whatever you do," she said to her son, "don't let go."

Peter nodded at her, struggling to put a brave face over the terror gripping his heart. She kissed him on the forehead and pulled him close as she led him toward the doors.

As they reached the exit, the elderly doorman, Mr. Goodman, stepped in front of her to stop them. "You can't go out there, Mrs. Lamb," he said in a pained voice. "It's the end of the world."

Dorothy frowned, wishing that the man would get out of her way and stop trying to frighten them. As it was, she thought Peter might curl up into a ball at any moment.

"I thought they'd give us more notice," she said. "We have to get to the transport. Paul's arranged a spot for us."

"I don't think any more transports will be leaving now, ma'am." Mr. Goodman removed his red cap, looking as if he'd just been told of the death of a respected friend.

"We have to try," she said. She glanced back at her son and then shot the doorman a look that informed him that she would not be dissuaded. "Is it better to sit here and wait for the end?"

"Surely it won't come to that," the man said, but his voice trailed off at the end.

"Many thanks to you too, Mr. Goodman," Dorothy said, showing her true affection for the man. "But you've always been a bad liar. We have to try. For Peter's sake."

She whispered these last words, although she suspected her son heard her just the same. At this point, she didn't—couldn't—care. She just needed Mr. Goodman to move.

The man stood there and stared at her for a moment, then flushed with embarrassment, although for her or for himself Dorothy could not be sure. "Of course, ma'am," he said softly. He unlocked the door and held it open for both Peter and her.

"Thank you," Dorothy said. She surprised herself with how grateful she felt.

"Cardinal watch you," Mr. Goodman said. He tipped his hat to them as he let the door close behind them. "And keep you safe."

Dorothy grimaced at the man, then spun on her heel and ran with Peter into the night.

The side street on which their apartment building towered lay deserted. If not for the wailing sirens and the planes growling overhead, she might have been able to convince herself that it was just another typical night in this Imperial city.

As she and Peter neared the cross street, though, the extent to which panic had gripped the city became apparent.

The streets were clogged with people on foot. Car traffic had gridlocked so badly that people had given up on driving and abandoned their cars where they sat.

A few of the cars had been overturned, and those cars and some others had been set on fire. Dorothy found this strangely comforting, as they provided illumination in the parts of the city in which the lights had gone dead.

People charged back and forth in every direction, seemingly without aim or reason. Dorothy put her arm around Peter's shoulder and pressed into the river of people, angling for a current that would take them in the direction she needed to go.

At one point, she nearly tripped over a fallen man who lay unconscious in the street, possibly trampled to death. She wanted to stop to offer him a hand up, but the crowd pressed her past him before she could try.

The windows of every shop they passed stood shattered, and people stormed in and out of the places carrying food, drink, and anything else they could get their hands on. Some of the looters carried things such as couches and refrigerators, although Dorothy couldn't imagine what use those things would be in times like these.

As they reached the corner of Sterling, Dorothy spied a squad of Imperial soldiers standing atop the back of a flatbed truck, licking their wounds and loading their weapons. One of them sat next to the others, clutching to his head a fistful of gauze that was soaked through with blood.

"Excuse me!" Dorothy said to the soldiers as she and Peter drew near. "Excuse me!"

The troops ignored her, not wanting to be bothered by a woman wandering through the riot with her son. They had bigger concerns, she knew, but she needed their help and was determined to wring it from them.

Shouldering her way across the stream of people, Peter in tow, Dorothy finally made her way to the truck. She pushed her son underneath the truck, where he'd be relatively safe, then climbed up on the back of the flatbed.

"Please!" she shouted.

At first, she thought that one of the soldiers might shoot her. The only thing she could think of was, *Don't let my body fall in front of Peter.* But then the sergeant in charge of the unit came over to speak with her.

"My husband is in the 501st," Dorothy said, shouting over a burst of gunfire that seemed far too close. "How can I get to the family transport point?"

The soldier's face fell. "There's no way," he said. "Serenity Center's been cut off."

"Please!" Dorothy said. "There must be some route we can take."

The soldier scowled, then began barking out directions to her, stabbing with his finger to illustrate how she should proceed. She repeated the plan back to him, and he nodded, then wished her good luck.

She lowered herself back to the pavement and pulled Peter out from under the truck. She kissed him once more, then put her arm around his shoulder again and dived back into the seething mass of people.

14

Dorothy shoved her way through the crowd until she and Peter made it to the far side of the intersection. Then she led him into a darkened alley that snaked around the backs of the buildings. On any other night, she never would have dared enter such a place, but according to the sergeant she'd spoken to, she had no choice.

They emerged from the alley onto Paladine. The towering building before them had gone up in flames, and glowing pieces of it were falling off—or were being tossed—and cascading down from its heights like meteorites. They splattered on the street, sending splashes of sparks everywhere.

A team of medics raced past, bearing wounded soldiers on stretchers. Bursts of automatic gunfire sounded from above, and Dorothy craned her neck to see a brace of heavy machine guns chattering away at something farther down the street, providing the medics with cover.

Peter stopped for a moment, frozen in fear, and Dorothy could not blame him. Determined to get to the transport point, she gave his arm a hard yank and hauled him into the street after her.

As they ran behind the medics, Dorothy glanced back to see what the soldiers were firing at. At that moment, a rocket shot down from the rooftops and sailed overhead.

Dorothy followed the rocket's trajectory and saw it slam

into the street behind her. The explosion illuminated an entire army of mutants marching up the avenue behind them.

The rocket smashed into the lead mutant, a monstrous creature that walked like a man but stood as tall as a giant. It seemed to be made entirely of thickly stacked layers of muscles without any skin to cover them, and it carried a sixteen-barreled rotary machine gun Dorothy recognized as an Imperial Charger.

Chargers were too heavy for a man to carry and usually sat on a reinforced tank mount. Dorothy spotted the remnants of the mount dangling from the bottom of the gun as the monster shrugged off the rocket blast and kept coming.

Behind the great beast marched scores of smaller creatures. Some wore military uniforms, but others were dressed in civilian clothes, and Dorothy spotted a few women and children among them. The most terrifying creatures, though, charged along at either side of the giant mutant.

These two beasts stood on four legs like a horse but had a monster's upper body—including a set of arms and what could only be described as razored bone wings—where a horse's head would be. A reptilian head topped each creature's shoulders at a height of at least a dozen feet, and their eyes burned bright and red at Dorothy. Somehow, though, she was sure the creatures could smell her more than they could see her.

Dorothy screamed and sprinted up the street, pulling Peter after her as fast as their legs would carry them. At one point, they wound their way past the medics, the men in the stretchers slowing them down too much.

They emerged into another intersection. To their right, close to where dead street signals had once flashed, a full platoon of soldiers stood behind a barricade made of wood and barbed wire. They had their guns leveled straight ahead, pointing at Dorothy and Peter.

Dorothy's heart seemed to stop in her chest. Then she realized the men were aiming not at them but over them. She turned and saw a new horde of mutants charging up the street at them from the left.

Dorothy screamed as the soldiers opened fire, heedless of what that might mean to Peter and her, but the great roar of their guns drowned out the sound. She ducked, grabbed her son's hand, and pressed through the intersection as fast as Peter's shorter legs would let her.

As they raced forward, she dropped their suitcase, and it spilled open on the slick pavement. Peter stopped and tried to go back for it, but she refused to slow down or let him go.

"Leave it!" she told him. If they didn't reach the transport in time, they would have no need of any of their belongings, no matter how precious they might seem.

At the end of the street, Dorothy spied their goal: the Serenity Center. They had made it here. Now all they needed to do was reach the roof.

The square in front of the skyscraper stood clogged with hundreds of people struggling to get into the place. Someone had shattered the plate-glass windows fronting the foyer, allowing people to stream in faster, but once they got inside, they had to wait for the elevators to come to pick them up.

Dorothy forced her way up to the front, elbowing aside those who refused to move. A team of well-armed soldiers stood in front of the bank of elevators, refusing to let anyone in. A handful of bullet-riddled bodies lay bleeding on the floor as a testimony to how seriously they took their mission.

"I'm an officer's wife!" Dorothy shouted when she got close enough for one of the soldiers to hear. "My husband serves in the 501st!"

The Imperial soldiers, part of the legendary Blood Berets,

scoffed at her at first. When she produced a pair of tickets, though, their tone changed.

"The transport's about to take off, ma'am," the lieutenant said. "You'll have to hurry."

The crowd protested as the lieutenant escorted Dorothy and Peter past the other Blood Berets and into the elevator, and the desperate souls surged forward. A trio of bursts fired over their head cowed them once more, driving them back.

Lieutenant King opened the gate to a stairwell and ushered Dorothy and Peter inside. "A few floors up you'll reach an elevator," he said. "It should take you right to the top."

"Thank you," Dorothy said, near tears.

King grimaced. "Don't thank me yet, ma'am. From what I hear, it's not much better on the roof. Good luck."

At that moment, the people in front of the building started to scream. Then came an unearthly howl that no human voice could have produced. The whirring chatter of a rotary machine gun accompanied the noise, forming a symphony of death.

"Fucking hell!" King said. He slammed the iron gate shut behind Dorothy and Peter, then charged forward to join his men. The screams only grew louder.

Dorothy grabbed Peter by the hand again and charged up the spiral staircase. After a short, awful climb they reached the elevator lobby, where they found a small car waiting for them, its doors gaping wide.

An instant later, the doors slid shut, enclosing them in the elevator car, and Dorothy felt them lurch toward the heavens. The screams and gunfire faded far below.

Dorothy took advantage of the quiet moment to hold Peter to her once more. "I love you more than life," she said. "No matter what happens, you must know that."

"I love you too, Mum." Peter wiped the tears from his hot cheeks, and she felt him tremble against her.

Before the doors opened, Dorothy's heart fell. She could hear the roar of the people on the roof over the transport's growling engines. When the elevator arrived and opened, the noise went from tolerable to deafening.

Scores of people stood gathered around the transport ship. It could have held only a hundred souls at full capacity, and Dorothy could see by how low it rode on the roof that it had reached that limit long ago. A trio of Blood Berets armed with Interceptor submachine guns stood before the transport's entrance, and they were taking no more passengers.

One of the Blood Berets looked at his watch and gave the signal to the crew aboard the ship to wrap things up. They had to leave, and soon.

Once more Dorothy fought her way to the front of the mob. She hadn't come this far to give up now. She noticed one thing as she shoved the people in front of her aside: Almost all of them were grown men. There were few women and no children to be seen. That alone gave her hope.

As she got closer to the transport, Dorothy realized that it would be impossible for the soldiers there to hear her pleas. The airship's engines roared almost loud enough to drown out even her thoughts.

Even before she reached the front of the mass of people pressing toward the aircraft, the soldier looked at Dorothy and waved her away. He looked like he hadn't slept for weeks, and he wasn't ready to have yet another conversation during which he had to turn people away and let them die.

Dorothy ignored his efforts and pushed on. When she reached the edge of the mob, she realized she had been right. Shout as she might, she couldn't get the man to hear her.

She reached for her tickets and then realized they weren't there. She must have dropped them somewhere after entering the building, but she had no idea where. Even if she'd known, she had no time to backtrack for them. The ship would leave in a matter of seconds.

The soldiers backed up onto the transport, each of them covering the others as they moved. The crowd surged forward, some of them grabbing on to the craft's landing gear, desperate for any sort of ride off the roof, no matter how dangerous it might be.

The Blood Berets fired several bursts of bullets. A few of them went into the air to frighten back the bulk of the crowd. Others, though, made an example of the men who'd tried to cling to the outside of the ship. Such actions might have risked the entire craft's safety, and the Blood Berets couldn't have that.

The transport began to creak into the air, and the three Blood Berets leaped back through the entrance. As they stood there, waiting for the craft to take off, Dorothy made one last desperate plea. Forgetting her own fate, she picked up Peter and held him up before her. The adrenaline coursing through her veins made him as easy to lift as when he'd been a baby.

"Please!" she screamed, even though she knew no one could hear her. "*PLEASE!*"

The last Blood Beret to jump onto the ship handed his weapon to one of his compatriots. Then he reached down and lifted Peter into the safety of the transport.

Peter struggled in the man's arms, squirming about to shout for his mother. "No, no, no!" he said soundlessly, shaking his head so hard that Dorothy feared for his neck.

She looked up at her son, tears streaming down her face. She screamed his name hysterically. "Peter! Peter! Peter!" She didn't want him to remember her in these last moments like this, but she couldn't keep herself together. She knew that at least he would survive, but the terror that gripped her stole that comfort from her heart.

"Mum!" Peter yelled. "Mum!"

"Go!" she finally shouted. She had to be strong for him, she knew, if not for herself any longer.

The transport lurched into the air, and the mob surged ahead. Men shoved forward, desperate for their last chance to live. They climbed over each other and hurled themselves at the ship, grasping at the landing gear and anything else on which their fingers could find purchase.

As the transport lifted off into the air, another overburdened airship came scudding in from down the street. The pilot of the ship carrying Peter did not see it. He must have been too concerned with the scene below him to worry about what might be above.

The higher ship smashed straight into the top of the ascending ship, knocking open its engine compartment. The lower airship burst into flames immediately and then plummeted from the sky like a falling star.

Dorothy rushed to the side of the building, heedless of the danger to herself, the possibility that someone might shove her over the edge. When she got there, she watched the transport plummet toward the street, shedding occupants as it fell.

Then the craft smashed into the pavement below, killing a crowd of refugees who had given up trying to get on the transport and had been looking for hope elsewhere. The fireball that rose from the explosion rolled up the side of the skyscraper until it singed Dorothy's face.

Dorothy stared over the side of the building in utter disbelief. She could not grasp what had happened. Her last hope—her last reason to live—had died with her son. She had nothing left.

She was still there, watching the fire burn below, when the mutants finally breached the locked door at the top of the stairs that reached to the roof. The men nearest the door screamed at the sight of the black-blooded creatures, but not for long. In an instant, the mutants made quick work of them, slicing them into nearly unidentifiable pieces.

Dorothy turned and stood at the roof's edge, waiting for her turn. With Peter gone and Paul probably dead as well, she had nothing left to care about. She no longer wished to live. When death came, she would return its cold embrace.

She didn't have long to wait.

15

Constantine sat in the boardroom alone. The walls had been stripped bare, with only bits of trash and the naked ends of wires curling along the edges of the floor. Of all the rich furnishings that had once been in the room, only the large table and the chairs in which the council had sat for so many years remained.

The world was coming to an end, and it would happen on Constantine's watch. This much was clear. He wished he could have somehow seen it coming.

Since his early years in Capitol's diplomatic corps, Constantine had often wondered if all of humanity stood on the brink of destruction. The launch of the Third Corporate Wars had seemed to confirm that horrible suspicion. He'd done everything in his power to fight against that, to bind together the various corporate factions under the umbrella organization of the Cartel, but they'd reminded him time and again why most people regarded the Cartel as little more than a bit of tissue trying to cover the mouth of a cannon.

Constantine slid open the glass doors that towered behind his chair and stepped out onto the wide stone balcony. He strolled to the tall railing and leaned against it, resting his arms on it as he stared out at the panorama of the city beyond.

New London was an Imperial city, and it showed in the

ornate style of its architecture. More than any other place in the solar system, it was the cradle of Imperial civilization. Although the true seat of power now rested in the Reading Palace on Luna, all Imperials knew that their heritage began here. And here it would soon end.

The Capitol Spire stood burning on the other side of the river, a torch that displayed the destructive powers of the mutant armies to the world. He had watched from his chambers on the floor below last night as a transport had careened into it and set it ablaze.

"Twenty days," Constantine said softly. "The entire planet fallen within a month. How can we hope to stand?"

"You always said that hope was not a plan."

A smile curled Constantine's lips as he turned to see Victoria standing there. She rarely came up to the boardroom, preferring to work her influence in private, far from the spotlight. But with the place empty now, there was nothing to keep her away.

Constantine folded his wife into his arms and held her close to him against the chill wind. He kissed her tenderly and stroked her gray hair.

"When all our plans fail, what else is left?"

She moved to the railing with him. "Truly, there is no hope? None at all?"

"Not for us." Constantine kept his eyes focused on the Capitol Spire. The blaze had exposed the framework of the upper girders, the skeleton beneath the facade.

"Not for me, you mean." Victoria stepped away from her husband and took him in with her eyes. "There's still time for you."

Constantine shook his head, still not looking at her. He reached into his pocket and pulled out a small tin. He opened it and took out a pair of tiny pills that he put under his tongue, where he let them dissolve like bitter candy.

"My health is no better than yours," he said.

"Bullshit. We both know the truth." She reached out and touched his arm. He looked down at her fingers, still unable to meet her gaze.

"You could survive the trip into space," she whispered. A rocket shell exploded at the base of the Mishima Building then, rocking the distant skyscraper to its pagoda-styled peak.

"Not without you," he said. He finally looked into her deep brown eyes and saw the tears she held back there. "I won't leave you here to die alone."

Victoria gestured at the plumes of smoke trailing up into the gray sky from all over the city. A wry, mirthless smile played across her lips. "Darling," she said, "I'll hardly be alone."

Constantine held her tight then and let her bury her face in his chest. She wept openly, not just for them but for the whole of the world, and he joined her unashamedly.

As they let their tears flow, the sounds of war raged all about them. The height of the Cartel's tower muffled much of the gunfire on the ground, but the roar of the fighters and bombers zooming past overhead seemed never-ending.

When they were done, Victoria pulled back and raised her lips for one last kiss. As their lips parted, Constantine held his wife close to him once more and spoke into her ear, making sure she could hear him over the screaming engines all around.

"There's one last thing I have to do," he said.

She nodded. "I'll wait for you."

With that, she strode off for the spiral staircase that would take her to their chambers. It had long been their home. Soon, he knew, it would be their grave.

16

Brother Samuel entered the Cartel's boardroom one last time. He barely knew why he was there, but he had no place else left to go. He had considered trying to get to the local cathedral and offer his support, but the streets were closed, blocked with either battles or bodies.

On the thirtieth floor, the Cartel had opened the bar for one last party. Drinks were free to all, and they were flowing like water, he'd heard.

The Imperial ambassador had asked Samuel to join him there. With the Serenity Center closed off, he had no place to go.

"Why don't you ask one of the other ambassadors for transport?" Samuel had asked.

The man had chuckled. "They won't give it. To make room for me, they'd have to cut loose one of their own, and none of them are willing to contemplate that sort of sacrifice."

The man shrugged. "And let's be honest. We're rivals, not friends. We may know each other better than our wives, but there is no love lost between us. Never has been."

"You don't seem bitter about that, being left behind."

The man grunted. "I'd do the same for them."

Despite the man's affability, Samuel refused to spend his last moments seeking oblivion. He'd spent all his days involved in the Cardinal's struggle for life.

With all hope lost, though, he did the only thing he could think of: He returned to the scene of his greatest failure to fall on his knees and beg forgiveness.

Nothing remained in the boardroom but the table and chairs. Even these had been looted, though, as someone had torn the corporate logos off the head of each of them. Undeterred, the monk went to the foot of the table and opened the Book of Law on it.

He turned to the pages of the First Chronicle, the words of which had been carved into the stone foundations of the Luna Cathedral by Lord Scribe Alexander Horatio at the bidding of Cardinal Nathaniel Durand I. They told of the arrival of the Darkness and the calling of the Cardinal to illuminate the path to enlightenment and safety.

Normally, reading aloud from the Chronicles was a crime, but desperate times called for dispensations. The Cardinal knew what he had to do, and if anyone else in the Brotherhood objected, that would only happen if Samuel failed, and they couldn't make him any more dead.

Samuel knew that the words he read should have inspired him. Instead, he only felt his frustration grow. How had he failed? How had Constantine and his circle of ambassadors been so blind?

He closed the book, the slump of his shoulders telling the story of his defeat. He was a humble man, as all good servants of the Cardinal had to be, but he'd been unbroken. The strength of his faith had carried him through even the darkest times—until now.

Samuel looked over his shoulder at Severian. Sworn to silence, she could not summon any words to comfort him. Despite the fact that his tongue was free, he found that he could not find anything to say to her either.

Samuel glanced at the door at the sounds of gunshots. The battle was getting closer, the mutants working their way up the building, destroying everything story by story.

He wondered if the patrons of the bar on the thirtieth floor were already dead. How could they not be?

"Who would believe in such things?" Brother Samuel said, more to himself than Severian. No matter what, she would not answer. "Who could imagine we should see days like these?"

A voice spoke from the shadows in the rear of the room. Samuel had walked right past them as they'd entered and never even glanced in that direction.

"You should not be here," Constantine said from where he sat at the table.

To her credit, Severian's hand never went to her sword. Whether that was because she'd always known that Constantine was there or because her nerves of steel never let her show surprise, Samuel did not know.

"The barricades are crumbling." Constantine thumbed through a thick stack of envelopes as he spoke. "They'll be here soon."

Samuel nodded. By his estimation, they had only minutes before the entire building was overrun, perhaps more if they bothered to fight.

"When do you leave?" Samuel asked. He failed to keep the bitterness from his voice. His own impending doom did not make him jealous of the fact that this man would live. He would have traded his life a dozen times over to just give the world one last chance.

A mysterious smile crossed Constantine's face. He put his hand over his heart. "The absence of gravity interferes with my digestion. I shall stay."

Samuel raised his eyebrows. He would not have guessed that the man would remain behind and share the world's fate, no matter how responsible he might be for it.

For his part, Constantine seemed to enjoy playing with the monk's expectations. "Perhaps man will get a fresh start on the New Worlds. They don't need this old serpent making the same mistakes."

Samuel nodded. If the man needed to believe that as some consolation as the mutants dragged him off into the long night, why should Samuel argue? Constantine already knew what Samuel believed.

The mutant threat wouldn't stop here. The foul creatures of the Dark Apostles of which the Chronicles spoke would find a way to get off the planet and bring their curse to every planet in the system, every last chunk of dirt on which humanity stood. They'd done it before. They would do it again.

"*Ar dheis Dé go raibh a anam,* Constantine."

Samuel wondered if the man would understand the blessing he'd just bestowed upon him: "May your soul walk on God's right hand."

He turned to go. Severian fell in behind him. As Samuel reached the door, which he'd left open behind him, Constantine spoke.

"Where will you go?"

Was the man truly concerned about this? At the moment, the only destination that seemed clear for any of them was their final reward. Still, the monk chose to play along.

"I shall return to my brothers and sisters and wait for the end."

Constantine nodded. Samuel wished to leave, to put the man behind him, but he sensed that Constantine had more to say. The monk opted to grant the self-condemned man his last wish.

"And how will you get there? The city is besieged on all sides."

Constantine's manner bespoke concern, but Samuel knew it wasn't genuine. He did not understand this man's game, but as he had no better choices, he played along.

Samuel shrugged. "It shall be as God wills."

He hoped that would be a twist of a knife in the man's belly. In the end, Constantine's worldliness had not triumphed. They might all be doomed, but Samuel and Severian would remain faithful to the Cardinal's ideals to the end.

The man nodded as if considering something that had not occurred to him before. Samuel stood ready to debate with the man should he begin to mock his faith—or switch to more persuasive tactics if necessary.

"As God wills, yes, perhaps it will be."

Constantine let the next moment hang in the air between them. Samuel watched the man, not saying a word. He could see that Constantine was savoring this, but he could not say why. Did the man actually enjoy the idea that soon the world would come to an end, and they along with it? Was he really that nuts?

"I have a ship."

Samuel stared at the man. Was this part of some twisted game? To raise false hopes and then dash them again? He'd thought Constantine a fool—at least when it came to dealing with the Enemy—but not so cruel.

Constantine continued, staring out the window as if imagining his ship taking off into the air.

"It won't hold twenty, though. You'll have to make do with less."

For the first time, Samuel allowed hope back into his heart once again. He'd never lost faith—or so he told himself—but he and hope had been strangers for far too long.

The monk's mind began whirring, tackling the many obstacles to his plan. The first trick, of course, would be finding soldiers crazy or suicidal enough to take on such a mission.

He could not depend on finding any of the Brotherhood's elite forces here on Earth. What he wouldn't have given for an Inquisitor, a Keeper of the Art, or—best of all—a Mortificator. He wondered where his old friend Crenshaw was. Undoubtedly scouring the streets of Luna's Ancient Quarters on the Cardinal's behalf.

He would have to rely on soldiers from the megacorporations instead, but he couldn't depend on being able to appeal to their humanity. He'd seen far too little of that outside the monastery. No, he needed something to barter with, but a poor monk like himself carried few coins.

Constantine handed Samuel his thick stack of envelopes. "Take these."

"And what are they?"

"Offworld tickets. They should help you recruit some men for your mission."

Samuel grabbed one of the envelopes and eased it open, careful not to damage the contents. It felt lighter than he had thought it would be. He reached into the envelope and pulled out the contents.

Inside, he found two pieces of paper. They bore the logo of Imperial Skyways and the words ONE WAY.

"Two tickets offworld," Constantine said, his voice low and serious. "Two lives for the price of one. It's a bargain."

Samuel put the tickets back into the envelope as if they were lost pages from the Book of Law. He gathered the envelopes in his hands and placed them atop the Book of Law.

He looked up at Constantine again but did not know what to say. The man's generosity had done more than surprise him. It had humbled him.

He knew better than to question such fortune, but he had to ask. He couldn't help himself.

"Why are you doing this?"

Constantine allowed himself a flash of a smile.

"Most men think they are going to die, Brother. A few of us know it. As I draw closer to my end, I find hope the only investment worth my attention."

Before Samuel could say a word of thanks, a guard burst into the room.

"Sir!" the guard said, terror dancing in his eyes. "The perimeter has fallen. They're hard upon us."

Constantine hesitated. Samuel's heart froze for a moment

as he wondered if the man was about to change his mind. Instead, Constantine favored the guard with a weak smile.

"I'll be staying a little while longer. This is Brother Samuel. He'll be going with you. Take him wherever he wants to go."

The guard reached out to take Samuel by the arm, eager to leave immediately. Severian moved between them, and the guard backed away.

"We have very little time."

Samuel gathered the Book of Law and the envelopes, then stopped and turned to face Constantine.

"God bless you."

The monk had never meant those three words more in his life.

The worldly Constantine responded with a wan smile. "I sincerely hope so, Brother."

Trying to move his passengers along, the guard hustled toward the door. Samuel and Severian followed in his wake. As they reached the door, Constantine's voice pulled Samuel up short.

"Brother Samuel," the man said. "Are you the one? Will you deliver us?"

Samuel's faith had only one answer for that.

"Pray to God that I am."

17

Alone, Constantine went to the table and reached into a drawer that hung close to his seat. He pulled out a single glass and an amber bottle and filled the glass to the very top. Then he strolled out to the balcony to look down at the city.

He thought of going down to be with Victoria, but he suspected that she was already dead. He wanted to remember her as she was, not as a corpse torn to pieces and tossed about their chambers. And if she wasn't dead, he had to confess, he wanted her to remember him whole too.

That assumed, of course, that there would be memories to be had after today. Constantine wasn't sure what lay after the veil of death. He only knew that today he would finally find out.

Below him, the city burned. The entire financial district had gone up in flames, he saw, and the damaged Mishima Building had toppled over, destroying the entire neighborhood to its east. The Serenity Center still stood, as did the Bauhaus Building, but the Capitol Spire had burned down to half its height like a candle lit for too long.

Gunfire echoed from so many different directions that Constantine couldn't hope to spot its source. Screams punctuated the shots from time to time, but these were always cut far too short.

From the far side of the roof, opposite the balcony on which Constantine stood, his skyship roared into the air. He watched it jump into the sky on vertical gouts of flame, then jet off toward the horizon at breathtaking speed. He kept his eyes focused on it until it rocketed up through the dark, roiling clouds and disappeared.

Here and there, other transports escaped into the sky. It struck Constantine that they would have needed a hundred times as many—perhaps a thousand—to have had a hope of properly evacuating the place. People had been leaving Earth behind for countless generations, but there were still too many of them here. Soon that issue would be solved permanently.

On the streets below, mutants stormed through the streets, charging from building to building with impunity. They left nothing but destruction in their wake. The pale, blade-armed beasts seemed to be the most common, but Constantine could see other, larger creatures too.

One of the biggest monsters stood as tall as two or three men stacked atop each other. It was covered with muscles, and its skin was a dark crimson, the color of old blood. A vicious footlong spike ran from the top of its head, and identical spikes shot out from its temples.

The creature carried a rocket launcher that seemed like it must have once been the main armament of a tank. As Constantine gazed down at it, the beast seemed to sense him. It leaned back, took aim with its weapon, and let a rocket fly.

The top of the building was far out of the rocket's range. The missile made it several stories up the side of the building before smacking into the side of it instead of reaching Constantine's balcony.

Despite this, the man did not feel safe. He could hear the mutants fighting their way up the building, taking it floor by floor. The place shook with their efforts every few moments, and for a long while Constantine considered climbing onto the balcony's railing and leaping off.

He wondered if he would pass out before he hit the bottom or stay awake for the whole terrifying ride down.

No, he told himself. He'd spent his whole life facing up to the hard facts of reality. That was how he'd managed to be named the Cartel's chief officer on Earth. He wasn't about to abandon that now. If he was going to die either way, he preferred to be true to himself.

He heard them coming up the stairs. Whether they didn't know how to use elevators or didn't trust them, he couldn't say. Either way, it did not matter. They had all the time in the world.

As night fell on the city, Constantine longed for a final sunset, one last glorious blaze he could watch sink into the horizon. He'd seen his last over a week ago and had not known it. If he had, he would have savored it more, treasuring every last second until the stars shone bright in the open sky above him.

When the mutants broke down the doors to the floor, he heard them come skittering and scratching along the hall, dragging their boneblades across the walls and floor. He might have hoped to hear some more gunfire, but he'd sent everyone else away. Only he still breathed on this, the top floor of the tallest building in town.

He heard them come in through the boardroom. They slashed the table there into pieces. Not once did Constantine flinch at the horrible noises, though, or turn around to see what was making them.

The creatures didn't deserve his attention, much less his fear. They weren't the ones who had killed him, and they would never be. That honor went to the hand of whoever or whatever had put Brother Samuel's horrible machine in motion.

Call it the Enemy. The Devil. Satan. Humanity itself. It didn't really matter in the end.

And this was the end.

The mutants gathered behind him until they filled the boardroom. None of them seemed ready to take the first step out onto the balcony to tear Constantine apart. They were waiting for something, although the man could not know what.

Then he felt it, a larger presence, something indefinable but for one word: *evil*. It was there in the room behind him, and it hungered for his soul.

"Do you even have a name?" Constantine asked. He drained the last of the golden liquid and let his glass fall from his fingers to the pavement far below. He would be dead before it hit the ground.

The mutants behind him hissed their answer in unison, a single word that Constantine seemed to hear in his head the instant before they gave voice to it.

"LEGION!"

18

In a residential neighborhood on the outskirts of the city, Mitch Hunter leaped out of a tracked transport painted olive drab with the Capitol logo emblazoned across the doors. He brushed the road dust off the legs of his dress uniform as he gazed up the street at the gray apartment building that stood there, nestled among others of its kind. The darkening sky to the east gave the only indication that something was terribly wrong—and on its way here.

Mitch had been here before, although not for many years, yet he dreaded the thought of entering the building again. Despite that, he had a job to do, and he refused to shirk it. Even if Capitol hadn't ordered him here, he'd have come on his own. He owed Nathan far more than that.

Mitch slapped the door of the transport to let the driver know he was clear. The soldier would sit there and wait for him until he got back.

As he strolled toward the building, he rubbed his clean-shaven chin. He wondered what she looked like, and what he would look like to her. It had been far too long since they'd seen each other, and he couldn't help being nervous about what he had to say to her.

He laughed a little at himself, a dry and bitter sound. He'd faced certain death more times than he could count, and he would have preferred to go through each one of those experiences again rather than do this.

As Mitch reached the building's door, he turned back to gaze behind him. In the sky above the transport that had dropped him off, he spotted three different sky arks blasting into the heavens, leaving black streaks of smoke in their wakes like skid marks on a road. He wondered why he didn't feel jealous of the people on those ships, the lucky ones who would be able to leave Earth and its problems far behind. Perhaps it was because he didn't feel much of anything at all.

Mitch let out a deep sigh as he walked into the building. He found his way up through the central courtyard—a dilapidated cavity that seemed to push the sunlight away rather than allow it in—letting his legs take him up a path they remembered without prodding. He hesitated for a moment, then knocked on the apartment's door. A moment later it opened, and there stood Adelaide.

She was as beautiful as he remembered her. The years had been kind to her, even if the past week had not. She looked like she hadn't slept in days.

She stared at the man in her doorway for a long moment before recognition dawned in her bloodshot eyes.

"Mitch?"

He nodded. "Yes, ma'am."

The formality grated on him, but he stuck to it. He needed as much distance as possible to make it through this.

"Nathan's not here."

Mitch's heart tumbled into his stomach. Adelaide had spoken as if she expected Nathan to show up at the apartment at any moment, as if he'd gone out to the store to grab a gallon of milk.

The woman stepped back to let Mitch into the shabby apartment, then locked the thick door behind him. The place was small and worn. Although Adelaide had done what she could to make it a home, she'd been fighting a losing battle from the start. The best word Mitch could find for it was *cramped,* although he supposed he might have substituted *cozy* if he'd been in a forgiving mood.

Mitch knew that Capitol didn't pay its officers a lot, even decorated ones like Nathan, at least not compared with what it paid executives of the same grade. That was just another signal from his corporation that money mattered far more than the people who made it. The apartment confirmed it again.

Despite that, the place was large enough for Adelaide and her daughter—and for Nathan when he was home on leave. And during the times he was gone, a place this size could never feel all that empty, Mitch guessed.

The parlor was immaculate, not a trace of dust anywhere nor an item out of place. On one wall hung a picture of Nathan's graduation from the Academy. In the photo, Mitch and he stood next to each other, grinning like the kids they had been, entirely unaware of how their lives were about to be destroyed in the service of their corporation.

Adelaide led Mitch through the parlor and into the tiny kitchen beyond. A girl sat by the window, drawing something. She didn't look up, entirely engrossed in her work.

"I'll make some tea. You've changed. How long has it been? It feels like forever. You remember Grace."

The girl did not look up. Mitch felt relieved at that, then ashamed at his relief. He could hardly bear to look at Adelaide as it was. Grace, who had her father's eyes, would be too much.

Adelaide busied herself with the kettle, then found a small white teacup adorned with colorful scrollwork. She placed it on the counter while she hunted up some tea.

"Yes, ma'am." Mitch peered down at the girl. She was a beauty, much like her mother.

"She's ten now. Ten years old, which means almost five years. Gosh, has it been that long?"

Mitch nodded. It seemed like far longer.

Adelaide was rambling, and Mitch could tell she knew it.

She was holding herself together by trying to construct a veil of normality. She had to know why he was there. He had not been here in five years, as she'd just said, and never without Nathan. There could only be one reason.

"Here's your tea."

He accepted it with a nod, his fingers brushing hers.

"Nobody told you?" He looked straight into her blue eyes as he spoke.

Her voice became tiny. She held her arms against herself. "They won't tell me anything."

Mitch frowned. He had hoped this part of his duty wouldn't fall to him, but there was no way to back out of it now. He started to speak but realized he didn't have the words. He handed the cup of tea back to Adelaide, then fished a laminated crib sheet out of his pocket. He took a deep breath to keep his voice from shaking and read from it.

"On behalf of the Executive Vice President of Personnel, I've been authorized to inform you that your husband, Captain Nathan William Rooker, fell in battle and has been declared missing in action as of—"

Adelaide held her hand up to her face, and Mitch cut himself off in midsentence. Her tears came silent and fast like a sudden rain. Still drawing near the window, Grace never seemed to notice.

Adelaide backed up toward the sofa behind her, unsteady on her feet. Mitch watched her, unable to offer more support. He wanted to take her in his arms, to tell her everything would be all right.

But he didn't. He couldn't. Although Nathan was gone, he still hung there in the space between them.

Adelaide sat back on the threadbare sofa, falling into it. Her face twisted with grief, and the rims of her eyes reddened and burned.

"I have dreams. I see him. They're hurting him. He's still alive," she said. "I know he is."

Mitch put his hand on hers. "Listen. If you think like that . . ."

Adelaide's eyes burned now so that they seemed to glow at Mitch. "And they expect us to just wait here and die."

Adelaide yanked her accusing eyes away from Mitch to focus on her daughter once more. Misery for herself warred on her face with concern for her treasured daughter. Mitch saw now that Adelaide knew more about the war than she had let on and that Nathan had been her only hope through all this. She spoke to him in hushed, choked tones.

"I just don't know what to tell my little girl."

Grace gazed out the window, watching the black contrail of yet another transport arcing up into the sky. The ship's jets rattled the building as it passed them by on its way to parts off-planet.

19

The whiskey hadn't done Mitch any good yet, but he was only one drink into it. *Give it time,* he thought.

The Imperial Heights pub was dark and empty but for the bartender, who was busy packing up the few valuables in the place. Mitch didn't know where the man thought he was going. Passage offworld was rarer than a magic bullet, and he could tell from the ambience that even if the man owned the place, he didn't have enough money to do more than enter a lottery for a ticket.

Still, there had to be someplace better than this. Mitch glanced around. The place stank of cheap beer, old piss, and things fouler still. At the moment, for him, though, that was just fine. He lit a cigarette, then knocked back the last dregs in his glass.

The bartender—a no-nonsense man with long dreadlocks—reached for the bottle in front of Mitch. As his fingers touched it, Mitch grabbed the man's wrist in his fist.

"Leave it." It wasn't just an order. It was a threat.

Without a word, the bartender released the bottle. Mitch let him go. The man stared at him for a moment, then scuttled off to the back room, leaving Mitch alone.

Just the way he wanted it.

Mitch could have kicked the bartender's ass straight out the door of the place and taken every damn drink in it, but the last thing he wanted right now was a fight. He'd had enough of his violent life. Capitol had made him into one damned fine killer in the name of protecting freedom—they'd even called him a hero—and look where that had gotten him.

He'd won the Capitol Order of Valor back in the dunes of Mercury, fighting under Nathan's command. The Mishimans had attacked a Capitol condensation plant at one of the corporate outposts. They figured that if they could cut off the Capitol water supply, they could force the "invaders" off their planet.

Defending the outpost had been tricky. Protecting a place always was. You couldn't move it, and you couldn't abandon it. You could only wait for your foes to make their move and hope you were ready when it came.

The Mishimans had timed their attack to coincide with a sandstorm so vicious that it brought lightning and thunder with it. "Thundersand," they called it. The bolts fused the sand in the air into glass where they struck, and afterward—if you were lucky—you might find one of these frozen artifacts of nature half-buried in the dunes.

Mitch's unit had been on patrol and had gotten pinned down when the Mishiman strike force had attacked. Rather than burying themselves in the sand and waiting for the storm to pass, he and his soldiers had waited for the Mishimans to rumble past them, then come up at them from behind.

At least that had been the plan. The Mishiman commanding officer had trailed after his forces in a heavy battlewalker. It almost tripped over Mitch's unit.

Under the cover of the sandstorm, Mitch tackled one of the battlewalker's legs, then stuffed a grenade into its hydraulic ankle joint. He'd just gotten clear when the leg exploded, bringing the CO down. Without their leader, the Mishimans panicked and aborted the mission.

Nathan put Mitch in for the medal, over his protests.

"You did good, Mitch," he said. "Take some recognition for it."

"What good is a medal on the battlefield?" Mitch asked. He didn't want the attention. He didn't serve Capitol for the glory. There wasn't any in war, and that wouldn't change no matter how many shiny prizes they tacked onto his chest.

"Use it to impress the ladies," El Jesus said. He started to laugh but stifled it when he saw the grim look pass between Nathan and Mitch. "Or not. Put it on your fucking mantel after you retire."

Mitch snorted. "Soldiers don't retire," he said. Nathan arched an eyebrow at him. "Not sergeants anyway."

In the end, he'd accepted the medal and endured the presentation ceremony, which had been mercifully brief. The colonel who'd pinned the damned thing on Mitch's uniform had seemed to hate the whole affair as much as the man he was honoring.

After the photographer had gone, the colonel had said, "You know what that thing's good for, Sergeant Hunter?"

"No, sir."

"Free drinks in the officers' club. Today only."

Mitch had taken him up on that. The whiskey there had been the same as he could get in any local bar. It just came in nicer glasses.

Now he looked down at the drink in his hand again. He didn't give a fuck about the glasses.

After his third drink, Mitch pulled the chain of dog tags from the pouch on his belt and began flipping through them one at a time. With each, he read the name and thought for a moment about the soldier who had once worn it. Then he raised his glass in a silent toast.

A few of the dog tags were too dirty to read, still caked in the mud in which their owners had died. Mitch removed them from the ring, then dipped his fingers in the whiskey in his glass and used the alcohol to dissolve the grime.

Sometime later, the door behind Mitch opened, letting in a chill draft before it slammed shut again. Mitch didn't bother to turn around.

The man who entered the room stopped for a moment to assess the place. Then he strode over to where Mitch sat and stood behind him.

"Sergeant Hunter?" the man said. His voice was low, and he'd phrased his words like a question, but Mitch was sure the man knew exactly who he was talking to.

He ignored him anyway. Whatever the man wanted, Mitch wasn't interested. The spirits that haunted Mitch—both the silent ones of his dead friends and the pungent ones in the bottle before him—were all he cared about right now. He wondered what might have happened to Nathan's dog tags, but he didn't need them. He'd never forget Nate.

"Your name was suggested to me by a soldier in your platoon. Jesus Barrera."

Mitch glanced at the man—the monk. He wore red robes and an expression that mixed condescension and desperation. Brotherhood for sure, and a long way from home.

" 'El Hay-Zoos,' " Mitch said as he went back to his drink. He wondered if the monk would be smart enough to walk away.

"I need soldiers for a mission," the monk said. "A mission to destroy the Enemy."

Mitch snorted. "Which enemy?"

He'd seen enough enemies in his lifetime. In his line of work, *enemy* meant "whoever Capitol wanted him to kill—this week." Megacorporate politics meant that his allies one day were often his enemies the next and then went back to being his allies the week after that. The word didn't mean much to him anymore.

"The Enemy of Man."

Mitch could hear the capital letters in the monk's speech.

"It will be a dangerous mission. I don't expect that any of

us will survive. But it's a chance to save mankind, to save our world. Maybe the last chance."

Mitch knocked back the last of his drink, then looked at himself in the mirror behind the bar. He looked like shit. He'd seen corpses with more life in them. And this man of God wanted his help to do what?

"Fuck mankind. Fuck the world. Fuck you."

The monk didn't flinch, didn't even blink.

"Corporal Barrera told me you would say that. He also said—how did he put it?—you needed a 'get out of hell free' card."

The monk reached into his robes and pulled out a thin envelope. He set it on the bar before Mitch tenderly.

"These won't get you out of hell. But they may put you on the right road."

The monk walked away then, giving Mitch room to wonder what that had all been about. The envelope sat there in front of him as he finished his drink. It was long and white and sealed with red wax stamped with a Brotherhood icon.

The bartender strode back into the room. He tossed a last few bottles into a case on the bar, then latched it. He gave Mitch a final, wordless look. Then he picked up the case and walked out of the bar, leaving the soldier entirely alone.

Mitch stared at the envelope, then reached out and picked it up as gingerly as the monk had set it down. He opened it and, without removing the contents, peered inside at the two pieces of paper hidden there.

Imperial Skyways. One way.

He looked again. There were two.

Mitch closed the envelope and sighed. Here, at least—at last—was something to fight for.

20

Adelaide knew what she had to do, and she went about the horrible process of doing it. She'd heard the reports. Mitch had confirmed the worst of them. The echoes of the shelling near the front lines of the battle rumbled like thunder in the sky, and they came closer with every passing hour.

If she'd had only to think of herself, Adelaide might have tried to leave. She could have packed a duffel bag, put on a pair of hiking boots, and struck off in the opposite direction from the shelling. Still, she knew she never would have been able to outrun the mutant advance on foot, and the roads were closed to civilian cars.

Looking out the window, she saw yet another transport lifting off in the distance. She knew that she and Grace could have made it there, but they had no money to pay for tickets. Even in the best of times offworld travel was expensive, but on days like this tickets wouldn't be available at any price.

She could have taken one of Nathan's rifles from his locker under their bed. The top of the building would be the perfect vantage point to snipe at the oncoming hordes as they marched up the streets like a growing tide of dead flesh.

But she had Grace to think about.

Adelaide might—*might*—have been willing to subject herself to those terrors, to fight bravely against the mutants until they tore the last breath from her chest, probably along with her heart. But she couldn't bear to think of Grace's last moments being so filled with fright.

She put another pill into the cup and ground down on it with the spoon until it cracked and then was crushed. Then another and another and another, until the entire bottle was gone.

What would Nathan think of her? she wondered. If the Brotherhood was right, if there was an afterlife in which they might meet, would he accuse her of cowardice or applaud her bravery? This was the hardest thing she had ever done, and she kept having to wipe away her tears so she could see to do her awful work.

According to the Brotherhood, of course, suicides went to hell, and those who murdered their children deserved no less, even if they meant to save the innocent from a fate far worse than death. The Cardinal's view of the world had no room for such shades of gray. There was good, and there was evil, and the line between them was razor thin.

Where would Nathan go upon his death? If he was dead, that was. Mitch's words still echoed in her head, telling her to give up such silly notions. But the images from her dreams were too powerful, too real for her to ignore.

In them, she saw Nathan hovering near death's door, bleeding from a dozen fatal wounds. Instead of crimson, though, he bled a tarry black. The mutants, which she could see too, tortured him with scalpels and syringes, cutting and poking him, violating him with their blades. He screamed and screamed, and when he finally stopped, he coughed up the same black stuff she saw flowing through his darkened veins.

Every time Adelaide closed her eyes, the dreams came back to her. She hadn't slept for more than a few minutes at a time in the past three days. She'd started to hear Nathan's screams while awake—or so it seemed. They echoed in her ears, and from them she could find no escape.

Having finished her work with the pills, Adelaide pulled a bottle of milk from the apartment's small refrigerator and poured it into the cup. Her fingers shook as she did, and she had to hold the bottle with both hands to keep it steady. She filled the cup nearly to the top and then put the bottle aside on the counter, not bothering to recap it and put it away.

She used the spoon to stir the milk, mixing in the pills. Soon the mixture seemed ready, and she brought it to her nose to sniff it. It smelled bitter, so she added a spoonful of sugar to blunt that terrible edge.

Grace walked into the room then. Adelaide had told her they were about to leave on a trip to go see her daddy. The girl had squealed with excitement and gone to put on her best dress.

Seeing her daughter standing there—so sweet and beautiful and full of life as she twirled about in her pink dress, making the skirt flare—Adelaide nearly lost her nerve. She'd spent the girl's entire life trying to protect her. How could she end it by her own hand?

You are protecting her, Adelaide told herself. She couldn't let Nathan's fate befall their little girl. She knew that Nathan would have done the same thing for her, and that thought offered her some cold comfort.

"Look at you," Adelaide said. She wiped the last remnants of tears from her face and steeled herself for this. If she meant to make Grace's last moments happy ones, it wouldn't do for the girl to see her mother cry.

Adelaide stood before her daughter and brushed her beautiful hair from her face. In many ways the two were best friends. They spent most of their days in the apartment, sealed away from the troubles of the rest of the world, with only each other for company. That was the way they both liked it best.

Nathan had wanted it that way too. When they'd moved into the place, just after Grace had been born, it had been a place full of hope, somewhere they could store and build their dreams. Now it housed only her nightmares.

"It's perfect," Nathan had said on their first night in the place, as he held Adelaide in his arms.

"It's like nothing I've ever known."

"That's why it's perfect."

Adelaide had been born on Luna—practically in the shadow of the Sacred Dome—the child of freelancers, people who lived outside the shelter of the megacorps and owed them no allegiance. She had met Nathan when he'd been stationed there.

She'd been working as a nurse in a private hospital. He'd carried Mitch into the ER. They'd been in a running firefight with a squad of Bauhaus Blitzers, and Mitch had taken a bullet in his shoulder.

"You should see the other guys," Mitch had said, laughing right up until she'd started to pry out the bullet.

The man she'd seen today, who'd come to tell her of her husband's death, seemed nothing like the Mitch she'd known back on Luna. In those days, he'd had, if not a purpose, a sparkle in his eyes, one that she'd once found irresistible. Then, of course, it had all gone sour, and she'd seen precious little of him since, so little that she'd fallen hard for his more stable friend and married him instead.

Despite their breakup, Mitch had always been there for Nathan, both on the battlefield and in the barroom. He'd been Nathan's best man at their marriage, and he'd been happy for them both, or so it had seemed.

Adelaide had never been religious. Her parents had studiously avoided becoming enmeshed with the Brotherhood, a tricky feat on Luna, which the Cardinal practically owned. Looking at her daughter now, though, she couldn't help but thank God for bringing Nathan to her and this darling girl to them both.

"You are such a pretty girl." Adelaide knew she told her daughter this several times a day, but it grew truer with every hour. Just when she thought she couldn't possibly love the girl any more than she already did, Grace would find a way into her heart again and make it stretch even farther.

Grace smiled at her mother, showing all her teeth. "Is it time yet?"

The girl was so eager that she could barely contain herself. Her legs and fingers fidgeted every second. She hadn't been this excited since her last birthday.

"Almost," Adelaide said. She stood up and looked at the cup sitting on the counter where she'd left it, then glanced at the clock.

Should she do this damned thing now, before the mutants got too close? Or should she try to treasure every precious moment with her little girl and risk having her plans for a peaceful end foiled? She looked at Grace again and didn't know how much longer she could go without breaking down in front of her.

Better to do it soon. She reached over and picked up Grace's hat and handed it to her. Then she went to take the flowered cups and the merciful murders they contained.

As Adelaide went to the counter, she heard someone walking up the outside hall. With most of the rest of the tenants having evacuated the place already, she wondered who it might be. She'd been dreading such a noise for days, ever since she'd last heard from Nathan. She'd had no idea that Capitol would send Mitch to bring her the bad news.

Was it more humane to hear about her husband's death from a friend? Or would it have been better to have had some unknown officer bring her the details of Nathan's doom?

She'd wanted to fall into Mitch's arms, to let him hold her as the grief took her and wracked her with sobs, but she'd not let herself. Innocent as it would have been and as much as she needed it, it would have felt like cheating on Nathan, and that thought was more terrible to her than having to bear all the rest on her own.

The sound in the hall mystified her. For an instant she froze, thinking it had to be the mutants. But such creatures wouldn't move so softly, would they?

As Adelaide was about to pick up the cups, she noticed a pill on the floor. It must have fallen from the table as she'd crushed the others. She knelt down and picked it up, deciding that she would swallow it with her drink to make sure the poison did its job.

Then a sound from the door made her head turn. She saw an envelope slip through the mail slot and flop down on the floor.

The postman had run off, and the mail hadn't come for over a week. Suspicious of a trap, Adelaide crept over to the door and looked down at the envelope. It was long and white, and it had two words stamped on it in black block letters. They were the two most amazing words in Adelaide's life since Nathan had said "I do."

They read: EVACUATION PASS.

Adelaide snatched up the envelope and clutched it to her for a moment. Then she opened it and pulled out two tickets bearing the Imperial Skyways stamp. Across the top of each, she read the words ONE WAY.

Adelaide put her hand to her mouth and finally began to cry. All the grief and everything else she'd kept bottled inside for fear of crumbling in front of her daughter came streaming out, soaking her face in tears. She had no idea how long she was there before Grace came to check on her.

"Mommy?"

The little girl stood near the threshold, staring up at her mother with uncertain eyes. Clearly she needed to know what could be so wrong with the adult around whom her life revolved.

Adelaide turned around and scooped Grace up into a tight embrace. She held on to her so hard for a moment that she had to peel herself away to make sure the girl could breathe.

Grace brushed away Adelaide's hair so she could look into her mother's eyes. Adelaide forced a smile at her through the tears, then realized that the smile wasn't fake at all.

"Guess what," she said to her daughter. "We get to go on a rocket."

21

It felt good to be back in the monastery, even if only for a while. Brother Samuel knew, though, that his stay there would be all too short. He'd finally gotten his team together, but they were a mess, a collection of individuals.

In fact, they were the farthest thing from a team in anything but name. Hailing from four different corporations, each of which had its own philosophy and fighting style, they were used to working against one another, trying to kill each other. Now he would have to meld them into a unit on the fly. Every moment they wasted meant more people dead, added to the Enemy's forces. They had to move soon.

The soldiers sat in the pews of the abbey's church before him, assembled like the professionals they were. They looked straight ahead, each of them having already sized up the room and the people in it.

They were still short one man, but the time had come to begin. Standing at the altar, Samuel spoke, assuming the role of teacher that fell so naturally to him. All eyes in the room moved toward him.

"The Chronicles foretell the release of the Enemy, the ruin of our world, and the final days of this age. But they also prophesy the survival of man—that Neachdainn the Deliverer shall walk reborn among us and redeem us from destruction."

The door in the back of the chamber slammed open, and Mitch Hunter sauntered in, a duffel bag over his shoulder.

Samuel breathed a silent sigh of relief. He had grown tired of waiting for Hunter and had begun this briefing without him. He'd begun to wonder if the man would bother showing up at all, and he didn't have the time or resources to spend chasing him to ground.

None of the others had absconded offworld with the tickets Samuel had given them. Captain MacGuire, in fact, had refused them entirely. It had been a matter of honor for him to not accept payment for saving humanity. *We should be saving men like him,* Samuel thought, *not sending him to hell.*

He'd known it had been a risk to offer such things to dangerous people with only their ethics to keep them from running off with their precious fees, but he'd chosen these people not just for their ability as warriors but also for their loyalty to humanity. He suspected that the trials they would face might require more than bullets to solve, and he wanted to make sure he had the right sort of people at his back when he needed them.

Despite being late, by showing up Hunter had proved himself to be just such a person.

Hunter surveyed the others as he walked in. Something passed between him and the oberleutnant from Bauhaus, Max Steiner. Samuel couldn't identify it for sure, but these men knew each other, and not in a kind way.

Despite that, Hunter ignored the Cog and walked over to sit down next to his friend Barrera.

"How's the leg?" Hunter asked his fellow Capitol soldier.

"It's good." Barrera almost seemed embarrassed at the question. To cover this, he took another chomp out of the apple he'd been eating.

Samuel cleared his throat and resumed, not bothering to start over for Hunter.

"It is in the service of this prophecy that we are now irrevocably bound. You are no longer fighting for profit. You are fighting for the survival of Man itself. Brother?"

Brother Fredrik, the head of the monastery's Fourth Directorate—the Administration—stepped forward to speak. Although Fredrik was an intelligent soul, he was unused to having to speak with people and nervous about handling such an important briefing. He pushed his spectacles back on his nose before he spoke.

"Six weeks ago, in an artillery exchange between Capitol and Bauhaus, the Great Seal created after Neachdainn defeated the mutants the first time was broken open, and the Machine beneath it was activated once again."

Barrera nudged Hunter and nodded at Steiner. "There's your friend," he said.

Samuel didn't know just what kind of history might exist between Hunter and Steiner, but he hoped they would be able to put it behind them. Most of the soldiers in the room had fought against each other, if not personally, then at least on opposite sides of a battle. If humanity was to survive, they would have to look past such petty concerns to the danger that threatened to kill them all.

Fredrik continued, showing no sign he'd noticed the exchange. "In the ruins of the Imperial city of Canaan, catacombs lead to tunnels to the Machine. You will travel along these tunnels, find the Machine, and blow it up."

The soldiers stared at Fredrik patiently. None of them wanted to be the first to speak to the monk, each of them hoping he would continue of his own accord. Samuel considered prodding the monk, but he wanted to see which of his soldiers would force the issue first.

Captain MacGuire spoke, asking the question in his understated Imperial manner and accent. "Is that all? We'll just blow it up?"

Brother Fredrik nodded emphatically, then added something he'd forgotten to mention before. "We have a device."

"Device," said MacGuire. It was not a question but a prompt.

Fredrik meant the graven disk surrounded by swords, Samuel knew, the one that had sat beneath the Book of Law in the chamber high above the monastery's chapel. Samuel had always regarded the device with a mixture of attraction and fear. The idea of using it to destroy the Enemy appealed to him, but he'd always hoped that such a duty would fall to another brother, not to him.

He had not been so fortunate. Still, this was a burden he was ready to bear.

"From the first Brotherhood battle," Fredrik said about the device. "Ripped from the Machine."

MacGuire pursed his lips. "So it's a bomb."

Fredrik did not flinch. His years in the monastery had robbed him of any sense of irony. "We don't know, but we think it is."

Steiner scoffed at this. "You think so?"

Fredrik hastened to explain his theory. He'd studied the contents of the vault ever since he'd arrived at the monastery a dozen years ago. No one knew it better than he, but his knowledge had huge gaps in it.

"The Chronicles have a set of ancient schematics, not an instruction manual. The device is as ancient as Neachdainn himself."

MacGuire ignored the implication that he could not understand the device and focused on the details. At forty-something years old, he was by far the most experienced of this group of veterans. You didn't survive to such an age in this line of work without being both skilled and cautious, Samuel knew, and it made him value the man's contributions that much more.

"How safe is it to transport?" MacGuire asked.

"Does that matter, MacGuire?" Steiner did not bother to keep the disdain from his voice.

MacGuire arched an imperious eyebrow at the oberleutnant. "You may call me 'Captain,' Steiner, and yes. Bombs don't get stable when they get old. I want to know we can move it without blowing up."

Brother Fredrik piped up with the answer before the bickering between the two men got worse. Samuel had expected some friction like this, but he appreciated the monk's efforts.

"It's a two-stage device," Fredrik said. "You carry the trigger independently. Without it, the bomb's just dead weight. You then turn it with a key, which we don't have."

Fredrik held up a page from the Chronicles. It showed a long rod with a half circle cut out of its tip. "It looks like this, and it should be in the Machine."

"What if we can't find it?" asked Duval.

Fredrik became even more serious. "Then the mission will fail, and every man, woman, and child on this planet will die."

The soldiers all fell silent as they absorbed the gravity of the monk's words. The big man from Capitol spoke up then.

"Why not just drop it down that big fucking hole?" Barrera said.

Steiner nodded, impressed with the directness of the question.

Brother Fredrik grimaced as he tried to explain. "The Machine is ten thousand years old. It's survived earthquakes, wars, plate tectonics, and worse."

"Then why the fuck the fucking bomb?" asked Barrera. Despite the coarseness of his language, he bore no tone of anger in his voice, only irritation.

Samuel came to Brother Fredrik's rescue.

"Because, Corporal Barrera, one of us is going to put the bomb inside the Machine."

" 'The Deliverer,' " Duval said. This time she had no trace of sarcasm in her voice.

"That's right." The fact that she'd made the connection

impressed Samuel. It meant she'd been listening and thinking about what he'd said, not just tearing it apart.

Barrera shook his head in mock dismay. "Who drew that *pendejo*?"

"I did." Samuel said the words with as little emotion as he could. He didn't know for sure that he was the Deliverer, although he suspected that was the case, but he was willing to don that mantle either way.

Samuel looked at each of the soldiers in turn and saw new respect for him in their eyes. He'd gone from being the man who'd hired them to being their leader, and unlike their corporate masters, he'd shown he was ready to lead from the front.

Sensing he had a prime moment to finish his briefing, Fredrik began speaking again.

"We've interpreted key passages in the Chronicles, and they correlate to an archaeological site here, in Canaan." He pointed to a spot on a large map, right at the eastern edge of a large and wide sea. "We believe there's an entrance to a series of caves, and these caves lead to the Machine. Kind of a back door."

Barrera grinned at the words *back door*. Samuel decided he didn't want to know what kind of double entendre the man was enjoying.

MacGuire craned his neck for a better look at the map, then turned to Fredrik. "That is a very handy book, but I'll hazard we'll do some killing on our way down. Does your Chronicle offer any suggestions there?"

Fredrik started to shrug, but then one of the soldiers answered MacGuire's question.

"I can," said Oberleutnant Steiner.

22

Mitch already hated this. The monk—Brother Samuel—had talked a good game, but the operation stank of failure. They hadn't even left the damned monastery yet, and Mitch could already see it going a dozen ways wrong. Now the Cog from that first night against the mutants, the one who had tried to slice him to pieces with a knife, was leading him and the rest of their motley crew down into the monastery's frozen bowels, deep in the heart of the mountain.

The Brotherhood had paid a handsome price for his services, though, and Mitch wasn't about to back out of the deal. At first he had wondered if this all was too good to be true. Two tickets for offworld transport landing in his lap, just when he needed them? And all he had to do was save the world—or die trying.

The tickets had seemed real enough, although Mitch hadn't had a way to confirm that before he'd had to leave. The best he could do was leave them with Addy and hope that she managed to get to the transport in time. He'd watched from the shadows of her building's central courtyard as she'd opened the door to look for him. Failing to find him, she'd broken down on her threshold and wept. She knew what the tickets were and what they meant. She'd get Grace to safety if there was a way.

Now, though, Mitch wondered if he hadn't gotten the raw end of the deal. It was one thing to risk his life for a paycheck—he did the same thing for Capitol every day—and another to throw it away. At least his superiors at Capitol made some attempt at having a workable plan. Brother Samuel seemed to have only hopes and prayers.

That and the Brotherhood's connections. Capitol had granted Samuel's request to second Mitch to his task force without hesitation. What the Cardinal wanted, the Cardinal got, especially when it only involved giving up a corporal and a sergeant for this fool's errand. Mitch suspected that no one at Capitol thought Samuel had a chance in hell of success, but it wasn't worth angering the Cardinal over a couple soldiers' lives.

Steiner called a halt as he reached the door to a cell. They'd passed several like it on the way here, but this was the one he wanted. Brother Fredrik hustled forward with a set of keys and fumbled with them for a minute before managing to unlock the door.

"Courtesy of the Bauhaus Corporation," Steiner said as he held the door wide.

The team filed in past Steiner. El Jesus had to duck to avoid hitting his head on the door. Mitch felt tempted to lean into the Cog with his shoulder as he passed him, but he resisted.

Inside, Mitch couldn't tell the size of the room. A circle of light pooled on the ground several feet into the room, cast by a single lamp set into a barred fixture in the ceiling. Beyond that lay only darkness and who knew what. They could have been standing in a cavern or a closet.

No one said a word. Mitch watched how they moved: padding in on stealthy feet, spreading out in either direction. They might never have worked together before, but—with the exception of Fredrik, who hung back behind the open door—they were all professionals. They knew what they were doing.

"Keep to the near wall," Steiner said.

As the words left the oberleutnant's lips, a mutant warrior lunged out of the darkness and into the pool of light.

Juba had his pistol out before any of the others even touched their weapons, and he had a fistful of bullets in it before they could cock their guns. He stepped forward as he fired, his shots hitting closer to the monster's center as he went.

The slugs slammed into the mutant and ripped huge chunks of flesh from its bones. It kept charging, not slowing for a moment or noticing a thing. Only the chains around its arms and neck finally brought it to a halt inches from Juba's face.

Mitch had seen the mutants on that night when they'd lost Nathan, but they'd been like sharks in the sea of mists. He'd never gotten more than half a glance at any of them. Here, under the light, he finally got a good look at one of them, and he wanted to vomit.

It looked like a man—probably once had been one—but only in a twisted, horrible way. Its eyes were black, as if the pupils had exploded and splattered across their insides. It was bald, and its skin looked greasy and gray.

Something black flowed in the mutant's veins—or sat there unmoving. Mitch could see the dark lines of the violated blood vessels snaking beneath the monster's hide.

Both of the mutant's forearms terminated not in hands but in boneblades, much like the one Mitch had chopped off this creature's cousin on that dark and hateful night. In the light, it looked like the blades had grown straight out through the mutant's flesh, and the tarry black stuff showed where the blades had punctured through it. The edges of the blades were serrated, and both were covered with dried dark red blood.

Mitch had expected the mutant to show all the emotion of the dead. Instead, its features were twisted into a waxy mask of rage. It didn't want to just kill everyone in the room. It wanted to slaughter them and tear them apart into unrecognizable pieces.

Pulling on a metal gauntlet, Steiner stepped up and gestured toward the thrashing mutant like a carnival barker at a sideshow. He showed a strange mixture of pride and revulsion tempered with an infectious curiosity like that of a biologist explaining his latest dissection.

"As you see, individual bullets are largely useless."

To punctuate his claim, Steiner punched the mutant across the face with his armored fist. Chunks of the creature's cheek splattered onto the floor, but it did not seem to notice.

"Mutants don't feel pain or go into shock."

Mitch scowled. He didn't like being this close to the mutant, and the way Steiner abused the creature turned his stomach. He saw Samuel look away.

Duval leaned in close to the mutant and cocked her head to one side as she peered at it. The creature was close enough for her to feel its fetid breath on her face. She stared at its wounds, at the places where the flesh had been blasted away, a question forming on her pouty lips.

"How can they move at all?" she asked.

The mutant kept up the pressure on its chains, straining tirelessly against them. The links creaked with the effort of keeping the creature in check.

"There's changes to the mitochondria which boost myofascial release," Steiner began. He cut himself off when he noticed the blank looks on the faces of everyone in the room but Fredrik, who still stood half cowering behind the door.

Steiner scowled for a moment, searching for the right phrase in his lightly accented English.

"Cut a chicken's head off. Watch it dance."

The others nodded their understanding, although few—perhaps none—of them really got it. The answer was too pat for Mitch. If you cut the chicken's head off and ripped off parts of its wings, it couldn't move its wings. Something else was going on here, something Steiner's Bauhaus scientists couldn't quite explain.

Of them all, Mitch noticed, only Brother Samuel seemed to have no questions. As a man of faith, he already had all the answers. Mitch just hoped they were the right ones.

"How'd you capture this thing?" MacGuire asked.

Steiner rubbed his hand against his gauntlet, warming to the subject. "Our scientists requested a subject for tests. We went out with shocksticks and nets. The sticks were useless, and those blades tore our nets like paper." He allowed himself a small smile. "We finally pinned this one under a tank."

MacGuire shook his head in disbelief. He spoke in a voice filled with reverence. "How many men did you lose?"

"Didn't count."

The Cog's dismissal of the price his men had paid to bring him this prize disgusted Mitch. Steiner reminded him of a big-game hunter he'd met in the Venusian jungles once. The fat pig of a man had taken great pride in the giant hunting cats he'd felled, but he never mentioned the number of people who'd died flushing the damned things into the open for him.

"What's the fastest way to kill them?" Duval asked.

"Catastrophic tissue damage," Steiner said, ticking the recommended methods off like a list. "Automatic small-arms fire, usually a clip or more. Explosives."

El Jesus patted his shotgun. "Willy-petes?"

The Cog raised his eyebrows at the corporal's peculiar choice in specialized shells for his weapon. "White phosphorus? Of course."

Steiner would have gone on, probably at great length, but the groaning of the mutant's chains finally twisted to a scream as the main length, which anchored all the rest to the far wall, snapped.

The mutant lunged forward, and the soldiers scattered. They all went for their guns, and Mitch wondered if the greatest danger in the room would be from the mutant or from the soldiers shooting at it and hitting each other.

Duval blocked the mutant's first attacks with her armored forearms, parrying the mighty blows. But the force of the slashes knocked her back and finally off her feet.

Before any of the others could squeeze off a single shot in their defense, though, the grim and silent monk with the swords—Mitch thought he'd heard Samuel call her Severian—skinned her blades. They flashed at the mutant faster than the eye could follow, and the creature dropped to the ground.

Both of the mutant's arms and one of its legs lay separated from its body, which writhed among its pieces on the floor.

"And swords," Steiner said, finishing his checklist.

Severian spun her blades, flinging the oily black gore from them, cleaning them with her speed. She sheathed them with the same smooth motion she'd used to draw them, then fell silent again, like a clockwork toy that had completed its preprogrammed routine.

Mitch knelt next to the mutant and prodded the creature with his pistol. He half expected the thing to bound up on its remaining leg and try to bite him. Or for the severed limbs to snake back to its body and reattach themselves.

Instead, the fire in the mutant's eyes died. As the black sludge flowed from its wounds, its pupils returned to a human color, and the rage melted from its face.

Then its mouth worked open, and it said something in a horrible whisper.

"Help me . . ."

Mitch stared at the man dying before him, trying to grasp what all this meant. He knew one thing for sure, though. "This guy's still alive."

23

It wasn't that Mitch hated churches—just the people in them. He had nothing against the buildings themselves and could appreciate them for their architecture and decor. He knew that a great deal of thought and care went into evoking the proper symbolism in every element of the monastery's chapel. The color of the carpet, the angles of the pews, even the height of the altar—it all meant something.

He just didn't give a fuck about it.

He watched from the back pew in the chapel as the other soldiers all knelt before the altar. A monk named Brother Henrik presented El Jesus with a bit of communion bread, then continued down the line.

For a moment Mitch felt a tinge of jealousy. He wanted to be up there with the others, joining them in the sacrament, in the community that it helped build between them, but he couldn't bring himself to do it.

It would have been easy to fake it, to take his place in line and mouth the words that the others all spoke in unison. He'd known many soldiers who did that before every battle. He'd once asked El Jesus how he could believe in the Cardinal's teachings after everything he'd seen. The big man had shrugged and said, " 'Cause I fucking do."

Nathan had chipped in then. "You don't see the beauty in the world anymore, Mitch?"

"There's plenty of beauty outside of a church. I don't need a dusty old book to show me that." He'd shot Nathan a surprised look. The two of them talked about many things, but they usually managed to avoid the subject of faith.

"What the hell you talking about anyhow?" Mitch asked. "You're a condom converter."

"The fuck?" said El Jesus.

"He converted so he could get married and quit wearing rubbers."

Nathan gave Mitch a grim look at that, and Mitch wondered if he had not only crossed the line but pissed on it as he went by.

"Don't give me that," he said to Nathan. "I knew you before. You never saw the inside of a church unless you were chasing someone into it."

"That doesn't mean I didn't pray."

"We all pray in the trench," El Jesus said.

"Not your top," Nathan said.

"No shit?" The big man sized Mitch up once more. "Bullshit! He just keeps his mouth shut when he does it."

Mitch had laughed it off then, let it slide. But Nathan had been right. He never did pray. He had no one to pray to.

The problem wasn't that Mitch couldn't fake it. He didn't want to. He took religion as seriously as anyone else. He wanted to believe. He just couldn't.

"You do not receive the sacrament?" Brother Samuel said from behind him.

Mitch didn't jump. He'd heard the man padding up behind him. He didn't look back either.

"I'm not hungry."

Samuel sat down on the pew, next to Mitch. He rubbed his face and eyes and blew out a deep sigh. Mitch sensed that the man had a tremendous amount on his mind and probably could have used someone to talk to.

He supposed that was what the monk had his god for.

"The man?" Mitch asked. He didn't have much hope for him. He'd tried to bind up the ex-mutant's wounds with strips torn from Brother Fredrik's robes, but not too many men could survive a triple amputation, not to mention whatever had been done to him to turn him into a mutant.

"He died."

Mitch nodded, still not looking at the monk. "He say anything?"

He didn't know what he was looking for. Perhaps some sort of explanation for what had happened to him and how someone might stop it.

Samuel worked up a grim smile. "He asked forgiveness."

They let the silence sit between them for a moment while the soldiers at the altar finished their communion.

Finally, Mitch turned to the monk, a question forming on his lips as he gave voice to what had been churning in his mind. "Do you think, inside every one of those things . . . ?"

Samuel shrugged inside his heavy robes. "I do not know. We can only pray that God is merciful."

Mitch suppressed a bitter laugh. "No days like that."

With the sacrament finished up front, the soldiers stood and began to mill about. El Jesus stood looking up at the Brotherhood icon over the altar, and Mitch knew the man was offering up some last-minute private prayers of his own. He wondered if his soul was on El Jesus's list.

MacGuire strode up the aisle and stood in front of Samuel. He was all business. Mitch wondered if the man was ever off duty.

"Brother Samuel."

"Captain."

MacGuire fished a slip of paper from his breast pocket and handed it to the monk. Samuel unfolded it, revealing a series of items written in a clean, steady hand.

"Please give your abbot this list," MacGuire said. It

wasn't an order but was more than a request. "We'll need them as soon as possible."

Samuel scanned the list and nearly choked. Mitch had an idea about what was on it. MacGuire had already approached him about it.

"Any last requests?" the Imperial had said.

"World peace."

"We're working on that. Anything the brothers here can provide?"

"What do you mean, like for a last meal?"

"It's a tradition for the condemned."

"Glad to know you have such high hopes for our mission."

MacGuire had smirked at that. "This is my fifth final meal."

"This year?"

MacGuire had pursed his lips and then shaken his head. "Ever, of course."

Mitch had nodded. "You Imperials sure have it easy."

Brother Samuel, in contrast, didn't seem to find the list so amusing. He tried to give it back to MacGuire, but the Imperial would not accept it.

"This is a house of God," Samuel said, as if that ended the argument before it started.

MacGuire refused to back down. "And we're going to die doing His work."

Samuel shook his head, feigning regret that he could not help the man out. "There is no alcohol here."

Mitch snorted. "You telling me that God doesn't drink?"

Samuel glanced at Mitch, then followed the other man's gaze to the tabernacle behind the altar. Brother Henrik was opening it to get the supplies for the next mass's communion. There had to be hundreds of dusty bottles of wine shelved inside it.

Samuel looked back at Mitch and stared at him for a long

moment before understanding what he meant. His chin set in grim determination.

"That is for communion."

Mitch smiled, knowing he'd win the argument. "This is communion."

24

Mitch stifled a groan as the monk stuffed the paper into his robes and walked up to the front of the chapel.

"I don't mean to bore any of you," Samuel said.

Then quit talking, Mitch thought. The monk glared at him as if he could read the soldier's mind.

"I realize that history lessons sometimes don't seem relevant, especially to men and women of action. However"—Samuel gazed into the eyes of each of the soldiers—"if I were you, I'd want to know what I was fighting for."

"Been fighting for Capitol for three years now," said El Jesus. "Ain't bothered me yet." A nervous twitter started through the room, but Samuel shut it down with a frown.

Mitch rubbed his eyes and leaned his head back against the seat of the pew. He'd listen, but only because he didn't want to bother plugging his ears.

"Millennia ago, something landed on Earth, something that did not belong here," Samuel said.

"The meteor that killed the dinosaurs?" Juba said.

Samuel raised an eyebrow. "Not that long ago." He cleared his throat and continued.

"This thing brought a horrible evil to our world. It is that evil against which the Brotherhood has always stood. It is the evil we were founded to fight."

"The Brotherhood isn't that old." Steiner spoke respectfully. Even if he didn't believe the monk's words, he'd clearly drunk the Brotherhood's wine. He gave Samuel his due for his robes alone.

Samuel nodded. "Cardinal Nathaniel Durand the First founded the modern Brotherhood not so long ago in terms of the age of the world, but the roots of the Brotherhood stretch back much farther than that.

"The ancient Druids knew the secrets of the Enemy before anyone else, and they led the war to seal the mutants away the first time they came. They inscribed that knowledge in a book they handed down to their heirs, from generation to generation, should the mutants ever return."

Samuel put his hand on the leather-bound book attached to him by a chain around his wrist. "The Druids were the forebears of the Brotherhood. They prophesied its rise but did not directly create it. Like most people, they believed that even if they did not live forever, their institutions would.

"They built some things to last. Like this book"—he patted the cover—"and the Great Seal."

"Which we blew up," Mitch said, sitting up. He pointed over at Steiner. "When we were fighting them."

Every eye in the place whipped toward him. Samuel's frown deepened. "You were in that battle?"

El Jesus leaned forward, his face gone white. "Fuck me gently with a chainsaw."

"*Fickmich.*" Steiner looked like he might throw up.

Samuel put his hands on his face for a moment, as if he were praying into them. Then he wiped them down his cheeks. "The Enemy has been active for centuries."

Duval nodded. "These mutants, I've heard rumors of them before. They crop up in big battles all the time."

Mitch had to confess that he had too. He'd usually chalked them off to the insane ramblings of shell-shocked soldiers. But had they been nuts to start with, or had the experience driven them mad?

He wondered how long the bureaucrats in charge of each

of the megacorporations had known about such creatures. They had to. Yet they kept sending people into battle, risking stirring the damn things up.

"But we're talking more than a few mutants in a trench this time," Mitch said.

"Reports of these creatures have come in from around the globe," MacGuire said. "From across the worlds. They have not limited themselves to battlefields.

"The foot soldiers tend not to use weapons. Their boneblades are usually enough, and they don't seem to have any means of supply. However . . ."

Mitch hated "howevers." There always had to be a "however," and they rarely made anything better.

"They come in a far wider variety than most know. Nepharites. Razides. Ezoghouls. Necromutants. Zenithian Soulslayers. Calistonian Intruders. Praetorian Stalkers. The grunts are known as Legionnaires."

"From what legion?" Juba said.

"The Dark Legion."

"Fucking kidding me," El Jesus said.

"You said these things are on other worlds too?" Mitch wanted to be sure he got this right.

Samuel grimaced. "The Brotherhood has located citadels on every settled planet. These are usually in places so remote that few have seen them. Some are underground. Others are as large as mountains."

"But the Brotherhood monitors them?" Steiner said.

"It is part of our mission."

Mitch asked what everyone else had to be wondering. "How bad is it?"

"On the other worlds, the citadels have not launched any new attacks. On Earth . . ."

The man looked like he wanted to creep into a hole and die.

"The Cartel believes we have less than forty days."

"Before what? Before the Cartel's offices fall?"

Samuel shook his head. "Before we are overrun."

"Fuck fucking me," El Jesus said.

"So," Mitch said, "what happens then?"

"When what?" Samuel said.

"When we fuck it up."

Everyone stared at Mitch coldly, even El Jesus. He shrugged. "All right, *if* we fuck it up."

Samuel grunted. "It won't end here. The citadels on the other planets will react. The people there will have no way to defeat them. One by one, the worlds will be overrun."

"How can you say that?" Duval said, panic creeping into her voice. "How would the other citadels even know?"

"The mutants work together across vast distances. They are communicating with each other somehow, through their Dark Symmetry."

"So?"

Samuel nodded toward Mitch. "If they can get a signal across the continent, perhaps even the planet—"

"Then they can reach across worlds, too," Mitch interrupted. He got up and walked over to the tabernacle again.

"What are you doing?" Samuel said.

Mitch ignored him and opened the tabernacle's doors. Inside stood scores of bottles of wine racked in dusty unlabeled bottles. He took one out, cradled it in his hands, and blew the dust off it. Then he tossed it to El Jesus, who plucked it from the air.

"Use it or lose it, *hermano*!" The big man grinned.

25

That night Samuel knelt before the altar alone. He'd left Severian in her cell to prepare herself for the battle tomorrow. He'd never wished more that she could talk with him, but he knew she'd given up her voice to God many years ago. She wasn't about to abandon that for a prebattle chat—even if it seemed like the battle might presage the Apocalypse.

The monk lit a solitary votive and watched the flame flare for a moment before settling down for a slow burn on the blackening wick. The scent of the incense from the earlier mass still hung in the air and carried Samuel back to his youth on Luna, where he'd served as an altar boy in the cathedral.

More than once, Samuel had been given the honor of serving a mass officiated by the Cardinal. Standing in the man's sacred presence filled Samuel with wonder at the mysteries of God. He'd almost missed his cues twice and once had spilled a bit of sacramental wine on the Cardinal's sleeve.

At that point, Samuel had felt that if a column of flame didn't strike him down for his incompetence he might fall over dead on his own. The Cardinal, though, had favored him with a serene smile and put his hand on Samuel's shoulder. At that moment, Samuel knew that everything would be all right.

The next day, he had announced to his parents that he would be entering the Brotherhood to become a monk. They couldn't have been prouder. None of them, of course, had known what that would entail.

After years of study, Samuel had decided to devote himself to entering the Second Directorate, better known as the Inquisition. He had a fire in his belly for rooting out evil, and he aimed to put it to good use. His analytical mind and flair for ferreting out the truth would serve him well, he knew, and his instructors had agreed.

He'd worked hard and been selected to become a Mortificator, one of the Brotherhood's elite cadre of black-robed assassins. As part of his apprenticeship, he'd been paired with Sebastian Crenshaw, the greatest Mortificator of his time. Crenshaw had been a brutal instructor, fair but unyielding. He'd seen the worst effects of heresy and corruption firsthand, and there were few limits to what he would do to protect humanity from them.

One night, late in Samuel's apprenticeship, he and Crenshaw and an Inquisitor named Nikodemus had gone out to hunt down a prominent heretic known as Lucente. They'd flushed the man from his hole of a headquarters, a cavity in the underbelly of Luna filled with the horrible filth of a pernicious cult dedicated to the Dark Apostle Semai, the Lord of Spite.

Lucente had run like a rabbit forced from his burrow, and the three Inquisitors had given chase. "He's too valuable as a source of information about his fellow cultists," Crenshaw had said. "We need to take him alive."

As they closed in on the heretic, he became more and more desperate to get away. When it finally looked like he was cornered, he gunned down a young mother and plucked her infant child from her stroller. His back to the wall, Lucente put his still-smoking pistol to the wailing child's head.

Crenshaw sent Samuel to the right to angle for a clear

shot while he tried to talk the man down. Nikodemus had fallen behind during the chase and was nowhere to be seen.

"You've no place to run," Crenshaw said. "Put down the child, and we can make this painless."

Lucente just laughed, knowing he had the upper hand. "That's why humanity is doomed. You brothers are too weak-minded. You put barriers up before you that limit your actions. That's why the darkness will always triumph!"

The man started to cackle madly and lifted the baby before him to gloat. As he did, a flat crack sounded from somewhere above, and the child was blown to pieces in the man's hands.

At first Samuel thought the heretic had killed the child, perhaps by accident, but Lucente seemed as shocked as anyone. While Samuel still stared, shocked at the mess that had been made of the child, Crenshaw stepped forward and knocked the man flat with a single, sharp blow. Lucente offered no resistance.

A few moments later, Nikodemus arrived, his Mephisto sniper rifle slung over his shoulder.

Crenshaw spat at his fellow Inquisitor as he finished up. "That was unnecessary. We had the situation under control."

"You could have lost him," Nikodemus said, no trace of remorse in his voice. "How many more would have died or been influenced by his heresy had that happened?"

It was then that Samuel realized what Nikodemus had done. Enraged, he charged at the man. A moment later he found himself flat on his back, clutching at a broken nose.

"That was an innocent child!" Samuel said, spluttering through the blood running down his face.

Nikodemus gave Samuel a flat, empty stare and said one thing before leaving him and Crenshaw to escort the heretic to an interrogation cell: "There are no innocents."

The next day, Samuel put in for a transfer out of the Inquisition. Despite Crenshaw's disappointment at losing such a promising protégé, he joined the Mission instead, and he had been a part of the Third Directorate ever since.

The Curia, the powerful committee that worked under the Cardinal, hadn't been happy about Samuel wasting so much of his training. To make an example of him, they assigned him to this remote outpost on Earth, the backwater of the entire solar system.

Here Samuel had quickly become one of the top monks in the monastery. Since many of the other monks had been banished from Luna for various offenses, that meant he often felt like one of the inmates in charge of the asylum. Still, the fact that the monastery housed the original material for the first Chronicle as well as the device designed to destroy the prophesied Machine of the mutants meant that he never lacked a sense of purpose.

For most of his years here, though, Samuel had felt like little more than a caretaker. The prophecy had lain fallow for so many years that he felt sure he would never be called on to help fulfill it. He never used that as an excuse to be slack in his duties—he took pride in his work and that of the brothers who worked with him—but he had to admit he'd been as surprised as anyone when word of the mutant invasion had come through.

Now, tomorrow, he would lead a crew of mercenaries into the heart of the Enemy's citadel in a suicidal attempt to destroy it and save the world. He wondered for a while if he was ready for this but then realized that it didn't matter. He was as ready as he was going to be, and now he had to place his faith in God and do the best he could.

That would have to be enough.

26

Mitch always hated these nights, the last few hours before embarking on a new mission. He'd done as much as he could to prepare. Now it was a matter of killing the hours before the real action began.

Sitting in a shadowed corner of the hall the monks had opened for them, he took a slug of wine straight from one of the bottles he'd liberated from the tabernacle. The alcohol helped take the edge off. No matter how sloppy he might get tonight, he knew he'd have plenty of dead time on the transport tomorrow to sleep it off.

Having a hangover on a rattling deathtrap of a plane wasn't any fun, but Mitch was long past caring about that. This might be his last hangover ever, and he was damn well going to enjoy causing it.

An old cylinder player in the corner cranked out music. Mitch hadn't seen one of them in years, but he figured the monks lived too far from a radio station for them to get any of the regular stations.

"Can we shut that shit off?" El Jesus said. The younger man took a long pull from his latest bottle. After knocking the last drops out of it, he tossed it back over his shoulder. It shattered against the wall behind him, the shards joining the remnants of the other bottles already thrown there.

"The monks don't have anything else," Juba said. The Mishiman savored his wine from a pair of glasses he'd hunted up for himself and Duval. He'd taken the time to pick through the dusty bottles to find an excellent vintage and was determined to enjoy it properly, no matter how many of the others were happy to swig their wine straight from the bottle.

"They all sound like dirges," MacGuire said. He'd spent most of the evening with the two other men from Imperial, who hadn't said three words between them all day, at least not in front of Mitch. MacGuire did all the talking for them.

"Don't you find that appropriate?" Steiner called over from where he and the two other soldiers from Bauhaus had spent the last hour or so playing chess. He'd won the last three games straight and didn't seem to think much of his competition. None of the other soldiers had seen fit to challenge him to a game, though, so he kept trouncing the other Cogs, more out of boredom than anything else.

El Jesus stared at Steiner as the Cog strolled over to stand over him. He tried to focus his eyes for a few seconds, then gave up. "What I find it is fucking depressing. I got enough dark shit rolling around in my head without that magnifying it. We'll all be crying in our boots by the end of the night."

"You may," Steiner said. "The men of Bauhaus do not weep for themselves. Only for our foes."

El Jesus rolled his eyes at the man. "Ha, ha, ha, mother-fucker."

Steiner suppressed a sneer. "In Bauhaus, the enlisted men do not speak to the officers in such tones."

"Well," El Jesus said as politely as he could, "fuck lucky me."

Mitch sized up the situation. Steiner was a loudmouth from a society that prized such bastards, and he had two junior soldiers to witness the disgrace of this Capitol corporal showing him disrespect. Fortunately, he'd taken off his hol-

ster when he had sat down to play chess, and that put his
gun on the other side of the room.

Mitch sat up, letting his chair scrape on the floor. As he
did, he took a long drag on his cigarette, enough to make
the tip glow like a furnace. Steiner's gaze flicked in Mitch's
direction and caught there for a moment. The Cog had gotten the unspoken message. If he decided to mess with El
Jesus, Mitch would stop him cold.

Steiner looked back at El Jesus to find the drunken corporal grinning up at him, daring him to do something stupid.
If he'd been Steiner or MacGuire, Mitch would have stood
up and chewed El Jesus out for screwing around with men
who were supposed to be his teammates, like them or not.
But he just didn't give a fuck.

Let the sheep butt heads. Let them knock each other silly
trying to prove who was the better man. El Jesus was a
grown man. He could take care of himself.

If Mitch had been inclined to worry for anyone, it would
have been Steiner. Even drunk, El Jesus could likely take the
man in a fight. He had several inches and at least forty
pounds on Steiner, and he was too wasted to know when to
quit.

A shot rang out, and the music player splintered into
dozens of pieces. Steiner whipped around to see MacGuire
holding a smoking pistol.

"The young man is right," the Imperial said in his clipped
tones. "It was getting on my nerves."

MacGuire didn't point his gun at Steiner, but he didn't
have to. The Cog understood what MacGuire meant: *Leave
it alone. We'll need all the soldiers we can get.*

Steiner's nostrils flared for a moment. He hadn't seen
MacGuire go for his gun, and the shot had startled him. The
adrenaline pumping through his veins told him he should
do something—something violent—to tip the scales back in
his favor.

Mitch slid his pistol from its holster and held it ready under the table in front of him. He didn't think he'd have to use it, as MacGuire could drop the oberleutnant before he got anywhere near his own weapon. The other Cogs worried him more than Steiner did. If one of them or both decided to come to their commander's rescue, this bullshit argument could turn into a bloodbath.

Mitch glanced at the Mishimans to see which side they might take. The Imperials would back MacGuire's play no matter how batshit crazy they thought he might be to get in the middle of a Capitol-Bauhaus row. The soldiers from Mercury were the wild card.

Juba sat watching the entire display as if he had a front-row seat to his favorite play. He took another sip of wine from his glass and rolled it around on his tongue. An amused smile played on his lips.

Duval seemed to be ignoring it all. She had something brown in her hands, and she'd buried the lower half of her face in it. When she noticed Mitch looking at her, she put it away, but not before he saw what it was: a teddy bear.

Steiner, whose eyes were as sharp as Mitch's, put his tongue in his cheek for a moment as he gauged his chances. Then he tossed back his head and laughed.

"Isn't this the way it always is?" he asked with a grin. "The tensions run so high, we are like dogs in a kennel. Unable to reach our foes, we turn on ourselves in our frustration."

El Jesus smirked. "I know you didn't just call me your bitch."

The entire room burst into laughter, some of it more nervous than heartfelt. Either way, it was all real.

Smirking, Steiner waved off El Jesus's joke and returned to his game, which had become more interesting to him than yanking El Jesus's chain. The Cogs sitting with him continued with the match as if nothing had happened, at least nothing their commander would care about.

Juba raised a glass to MacGuire. The Imperial snapped a

quick salute to the Mishiman before holstering his weapon. Mitch knew the man would start to clean it as soon as the barrel cooled. The other Imperials watched his back as he returned to them, just in case Steiner decided that the conversation wasn't over yet.

Brother Fredrik burst into the room then, a pair of tinted goggles pushed up on his forehead and an acetylene torch burning in his hand. He stopped after he entered and stared at the scene.

"I heard shots," he said.

"Shot," Mitch said. The man gave him a confused look. "Singular."

Fredrik seemed unable to understand what Mitch meant. Then he spotted the broken music player, and his jaw dropped.

For an instant Mitch feared that the monk would break into tears. Then a wide smile cracked his face, showing all his teeth.

"It's about time someone put that thing out of its misery," he said. Satisfied, he turned to get back to his work. As he left, he shot over his shoulder, "That's just the kind of teamwork you're going to need."

This time, nobody laughed.

27

Mitch had the worst dreams that night. He saw Nathan strapped down to a horrible machine, stripped naked and violated with nails and needles, boneblades growing from his arms and legs. Behind him, Adelaide and Grace struggled and screamed as the mutants tossed them onto the rack of their monstrous machine.

He knew he was sleeping—dreaming—but he couldn't stop the images from coming, filling his head. He screamed for someone, something to wake him, but no one heard.

In his dream Mitch couldn't move a muscle. It seemed as if every muscle had been strapped to an examining table that had been elevated so that he could see all the horrors inflicted on his friend and his family. He couldn't even close his eyes.

As the machine began putting holes in Adelaide, he struggled harder and harder, but nothing happened. Sooner or later, he knew something had to give. He wondered if it would be him.

Mitch's eyes snapped open. He lay on a bench in the same hall in which he and the other soldiers had drunk the night away. His tongue felt as dry as an old scroll found in a desert cave, and his head pounded from the morning light streaming in through the slitted windows.

Samuel stood in the doorway, surveying the soldiers and

the self-inflicted damage they'd done. When he spoke, his voice was quiet but his words were firm.

"It's time."

A pair of monks scurried in after him with a meager breakfast for the soldiers. Mitch drank as much water as he could stomach and chewed on a bit of bread. The monks didn't have much more to offer, but that was all he really needed.

Most of the others didn't look much better than Mitch felt. El Jesus looked like he might weep at the first loud noise. MacGuire had to be hurting, but he still had the grim, officious look he always wore. Only Duval seemed like she might not be hung over, but she wore a private pain on her face instead.

After breakfast, Samuel spoke. "If you will follow me," he said.

The game was over, Mitch sensed, and it was time to show his hand.

Samuel led the ten soldiers up through the monastery, with Brother Fredrik bringing up the rear. The monks they saw along their path scurried out of their way. Whether they were terrified of the strangers or simply didn't want to interfere, Mitch could not say.

As they went, they passed a window that looked out on the postage stamp of a landing pad that sat atop the only level hunk of rock in front of the monastery, on the other side of a massive stone bridge. An airship sat out there, warming up in the icy cold, smoke billowing from its burners.

Mitch spied the pilot giving the airship a once-over while a monk on a ladder scraped ice off the craft's windshield. The copilot, a serious man with a stiff gait, followed after him, double-checking everything.

Mitch wondered if the ship would be ready for them to take off in conditions like this. The Capitol Ground Forces wouldn't have let something like bad weather stop them, but these looked like civilians used to flying a private craft for a wealthy man. They might have other ideas.

Mitch trusted that Brother Samuel would motivate them. If the man could get together a team of soldiers like this, he could certainly light a fire under a couple of pilots. Of course, in weather like this, lighting a fire sounded like a fine idea.

Samuel opened the doorway to a spiral staircase and led the procession up to a vault high above. Severian waited there for them and opened the door with Samuel's help. She stood there with her sword drawn and ready while the others filed past her, crowding into the room.

Snow-colored light spilled into the room through a high skylight, cascading down onto a circular sword rack filled with blades. Their exposed steel gleamed softly in the dim light. At Samuel's gesture, the soldiers lined the rounded wall of the tight, circular room and stood there wordlessly.

The air in the vault smelled stale, and cobwebs hung in every corner. Despite that, the place resonated with reverence and mystery, and even Mitch could feel it.

Severian, who looked as fresh and ready as ever, removed one of the swords from the rack. She held it flat in her open palms, presenting it as if it were a delicate treasure.

"Juba Kim Wu." Samuel intoned the words like a prayer, although Mitch couldn't tell if it was meant to be an offering or a petition. The Mishiman stepped forward and accepted the weapon with a gracious bow.

"Maximillian von Steiner."

Steiner stepped forward and took his sword. He hefted the blade, feeling its weight and balance and admiring its craftsmanship. Then he stepped back to join the others as they waited for their weapons.

"Valerie Chinois Duval."

The Mishiman woman paced forward and stood stone still. Severian repeated her ritualized movements for Duval and presented her with a sword. Duval's eyes glittered with excitement. Most Mishiman warriors were trained with the sword from a young age, and Duval clearly was no exception.

"Jesus Alexandro Dominguin de Barrera."

The fact that Samuel not only remembered El Jesus's full name but pronounced it correctly impressed Mitch. He watched Severian repeat her ritual, then wait for the corporal to accept his blade.

Nothing happened. El Jesus failed to step forward. Mitch glanced over at his corporal and saw that the man was asleep on his feet.

Mitch gave him a firm nudge.

"What?" El Jesus said, careful to temper his irritation as he opened one eye. He knew better than to chew into his sergeant.

Mitch jerked his head at the large two-handed sword that the kneeling Severian held out for the man. El Jesus looked at the blade for a moment, then at Severian. With a sheepish look on his face, he accepted the sword.

Samuel and Severian continued with their ritual, naming each soldier and presenting him or her with a sword. Every one of the others accepted the blade with honor.

Samuel came to Mitch last. Mitch wondered if that had always been the plan or if the monk had decided not to risk another incident like the one with El Jesus until he had no other choice.

"John Mitchell Hunter."

Mitch watched Severian go through her silent sequence one final time. When she finished, he strode up to where she knelt and took the sword from her. He ignored the blade and locked eyes with her instead.

Despite the austerity of the monk's life, Mitch could see the beauty in Severian. On Luna, she might have been a model—or just another aspiring actress waiting tables. In her gaze, he saw immense intensity and pain, and he wondered what might have driven such a woman not only to hide herself away in the ass end of the world but to take a vow of silence as well.

Severian's eyes searched Mitch's as he looked through hers. It struck him that she had no other way to communicate. Gestures only went so far, although hers were always elegant.

Although the woman piqued his curiosity, Mitch respected her choices and what she had done with them. He saw her for what she was, not what she wanted to be or had once been, and he accepted that without comment or reservation.

Severian looked away.

Mitch hefted the sword. He was ready to go.

28

The day dawned bitter and cold, and the icy wind bit through the soldiers as they walked out to where the transport sat steaming at one end of the rocky runway. Captain Michaels waited for them at the door, greeting them each as they climbed up the short steps into the main cabin. He recognized their type: killers one and all.

Better to be with them than against them, Michaels thought. He'd taken a job as Constantine's private chauffeur to get away from people like this—he'd seen enough of them in his days in the Capitol Navy—but he still appreciated that there were times you needed to have someone around who knew how to kill. These days, with the mutants overrunning the planet, they were in serious demand.

Still, Michaels fucking hated this, and he'd spent most of the morning telling Hodge all about it.

"Why the hell can't someone else save the world?" he'd said as they had run through the preflight check for the third time. "When I signed on with Constantine, I figured I'd put all this bullshit behind me. You know, drive the big bus through the air for the man with all the money. A man who wouldn't send me into a warzone or up against a horde of damned mutants."

Hodge snickered as Michaels went about his rant. That irritated Michaels as much as anything. After about five minutes of laughter at his expense, he turned on his copilot and said, "What's so damned funny?"

"You," Hodge said with a sly smile and an Imperial accent. "You who think you have it so bad."

"You call this paradise?" Michaels flung his arms at the wintry world around them.

"I've seen worse," Hodge said. "And so have you."

"And I've seen a whole lot better. I've gotten used to it!"

Hodge ran a hand over his face in an attempt to wipe away his nervous grin. "Sure you have. It's been wonderful, hasn't it, working for a man like Mr. Constantine. Why, I'll bet the worst trouble you've had over the last five years was wondering when they might ask you to fire up this old bird next."

"You're full of shit." Michaels didn't like the way the conversation was turning against him.

"Am I? I was right there with you. The biggest trouble we had in Mr. Constantine's service was boredom."

Michaels shook his head. "Well, we certainly don't have any issues with that anymore, do we?"

Hodge giggled. "No, I suppose not, but you finally got what you wanted, didn't you?"

"You're cracked. Who in his right mind would want to fly a pack full of mercenaries to Canaan? I didn't sign on for this shit."

Hodge stuck out his lower lip. "But you wanted it. You've always wanted to be a hero, haven't you?"

"You call this being a hero? More like the hero's chauffeur."

Hodge let a faint smile show his rotten teeth. "And is that so bad? We're pilots. We move people around. Now we get to move around heroes instead of well-heeled fucks. Sounds like a step up to me."

Michaels laughed despite himself. "Sure. Except I'm the pilot around here."

"And I'm perfectly comfortable with that, with being the chauffeur's sidekick."

"Why's that?"

"Heroes die. Chauffeurs fly away."

As he greeted the so-called heroes Brother Samuel had put together, Michaels sincerely hoped that would be so. Given what he knew about the mission, though, he didn't think it all that damn likely.

A hawk circled overhead as the soldiers boarded the ship. The major in charge of the Imperials spotted it and stopped dead in his tracks to watch it. Then he pointed it out to the Mishiman woman, who'd nearly run into him.

"Didn't know there were any left," he said.

Of course not, Michaels thought. *You don't get too many large, free-roaming birds out in the asteroid belt.* He craned his neck back to look at the bird. He wasn't too sure the damned thing wasn't a vulture, but he decided against sharing that with the Imperial.

As the two soldiers from Capitol strode up through the snow, the bigger one looked at the other man's sword. "Ever use one of these?" he asked.

The Capitol sergeant laughed. "On a bet a few times."

They didn't inspire confidence.

Once everyone was inside, Michaels went through and did a preflight check of the main cabin. The last thing he needed was for one of the soldiers to get hurt on the way to their destination. He and Hodge had assigned seats to the passengers on the basis of a loose estimation of their weight and their intimate knowledge of the peculiar balance issues of their craft.

Brother Samuel got the seat of honor in one of the niches. None of the seats were what Michaels would call comfortable, but this one was the best and gave the brother a view of all the others.

Hodge and Michaels had spent all day yesterday tearing the various luxuries out of the airship so they could fit more people in it. The way Constantine had made it, only six people could travel in the airship, although they did so in style. With all the junk torn out, though, they could fit in the ten soldiers and their gear in the main cabin, plus Brother Samuel and Severian, while he and Hodge drove and the two stokers in the compartment above kept the engines blazing hot.

Michaels gave the Capitol corporal's seat one last check. The poor corporal had been selected to sit on top of the velvet bag that held the device he had heard the monks talking about.

"How come I gotta sit on the fucking bomb?" the soldier asked.

Michaels patted the man on the shoulder. "That's the best seat on the plane."

"How you figure that?"

"If it blows up, we're all dead." Michaels smiled, showing all his teeth. "This way, you won't feel a thing."

"Thanks a fucking lot," the corporal said.

Michaels couldn't tell if he was serious. He snapped off a quick salute and then headed for the cockpit, shouldering his way past Severian, who stood in the doorway.

Hodge, who stood in at the copilot's controls in the booth behind the cockpit, had already begun the preflight routine, and Michaels joined right in, barking back and forth at the man. Sometimes Hodge rode in the machine gun pod on the top of the ship, just for the spectacular view, but he wouldn't find his way up there until they were well under way.

Although Constantine had modified much of the craft, he'd left the gunner's position alone and kept it in tip-top shape. A wealthy man like that was always a target, and he'd believed in peace through a preemptive show of force.

The familiarity of the preflight process comforted Michaels. He might not have flown a ship of soldiers into a warzone before, but he'd been through this part of flying the craft countless times.

"Boiler one redline, boiler two redline," Hodge's voice said in Michaels's headphones. They'd spent a good chunk of the morning stoking the burners, and their efforts against the icy weather had paid off. "We're ready for launch."

"Sound all clear," Michaels said.

Somewhere, Hodge pushed a button, and a warning siren began to howl outside the ship. If any monks had been tinkering around near the landing pad, they now knew to get the hell away.

Michaels flicked the last few switches to bring all the ship's functions online. The altimeter needle stuck, but a few quick taps with his finger freed it. He grabbed the controls and shouted into his microphone.

"Throttle up one and two."

"One and two, aye," Hodge said.

"Throttle up three and four."

"Three and four, aye."

Michaels saw a young boy in a monk's robes running up to the airship with a slip of paper in his hand. The boy stopped on the stone bridge, far enough away that he would be safe. Michaels thanked the Cardinal he'd bothered to use the siren in such a godforsaken place.

Michaels pushed down on the accelerator and leaned back on the wheel. A vast cloud of smoke and steam swallowed the airship, and a moment later the craft began to rise on a column of the same stuff. Freeing himself from the greedy gravity of the ground always gave Michaels a thrill, and this time was no different. He felt like he had been born to wrestle rockets into the sky, and he gave thanks that he'd been able to do it once again.

It didn't occur to Michaels until the ship was rocketing into the sky that the boy's message might be for someone on the airship. If so, he hoped it wasn't anything vital. It was too late for him to stop now.

29

Mitch had always hated flying, but he'd gotten used to it. He hated a lot of things in his life. Flying was just one more.

Of course, flying in a converted pleasure ship on his way to save the world from a machine that made killer mutants out of human beings—that was something else. He felt comfortable hating this even more.

He kept his eyes wide open as they launched into the air on the ship's three vertical rockets. Then those rockets swiveled horizontal, and they went zooming out toward the tops of the mountains. He peered through one of the small portholes in the side of the ship and watched the monastery grow tiny behind them, then disappear behind the ship's exhaust.

Mitch glanced at Brother Samuel during the takeoff. The monk spent most of the time with his eyes closed, muttering prayers that no one but him could hear over the engine noise. He clutched his big leather-bound book to him as if it were a baby, even though it was chained to his wrist.

Mitch didn't see the value in carrying a book like that around with you. He knew that Samuel had probably memorized every last passage in the damned thing. Keeping something that large chained to yourself only guaranteed it would get in your way.

Soon the ship punctured the thick layer of snow-laden clouds and broke through into the sunshine above. The vessel's vibrations tamped down as it leveled out, and the soldiers settled in for the long ride.

MacGuire unbuckled himself from his harness and began poking around the cabin. The other two Imperials slept, and Steiner and one of the Cogs played cards in the cabin's rear. The other read a book he had pulled from his gear. Severian sat near the cockpit, dividing her attention between the pilot and Brother Samuel. El Jesus shot the shit with Juba and Duval in the dead center of the cabin.

MacGuire chatted with each soldier as he moved about the cabin. The man seemed to have appointed himself the commander of the mission, the morale officer, or both. Still, Mitch had to admit he was effective, a solid leader.

Eventually, MacGuire made it over to Mitch and sat down next to him. He had a knowing look on his face.

"You fought with Capitol's 101st in Africa, under General Bishop."

The man had been talking with El Jesus a moment before. "That's right," Mitch said.

MacGuire smiled. "I was on the other side. Imperial Eights."

Mitch remembered that campaign. Capitol had triumphed, blasting the Imperials off the continent, but at the cost of many lives. It had been a waste of ordnance and lives, all because executives in both companies had decided that the played-out diamond mines in the southern part of that blasted land might still have some value in them.

Once Mitch had been transferred out of that unit, he had never wanted to come back to Earth again. Up until the latest conflict, he'd been able to make good on that promise to himself.

"Good times," Mitch said, not a trace of irony tainting his tone.

MacGuire smiled gamely. "I'm glad to fight beside you on this one, Hunter."

The noise had gotten to be too much. Hunter could

barely make out a word of what the Imperial officer was saying. It seemed like a good excuse to cut the conversation short.

"Huh?" He leaned closer to indicate he couldn't hear.

"I'm glad we're on the same side," MacGuire shouted.

"What?"

MacGuire shrugged at him, giving up.

Mitch had absolutely nothing to say about MacGuire's sentiments. If the man thought they could bond over an old battle in which they'd fought like punch-drunk boxers blinded with swollen-shut eyes, he was wrong, especially considering they'd been trying to kill each other and their friends.

Mitch only reluctantly soldiered. MacGuire was a professional born into Clan MacGuire, one of the most powerful of the Imperial families, and he had a tradition of countless generations of warriors to live up to. If he didn't actually enjoy battle, he still embraced it. The two would never see eye to eye, and Mitch wasn't inclined to explain why.

Eventually the Imperial took his leave. As he stood, he clapped Mitch on the shoulder. Mitch ignored him and looked over to see what El Jesus was up to.

The big man sat sketching in his notebook. He carried paper and pencils with him everywhere he went, even into the trenches of war. The process seemed to calm him, giving his life a center to which he could fall back.

Mitch followed El Jesus's line of sight to see who he'd chosen as his subject. It was Steiner, who sat oblivious to it, or maybe he just chose to ignore it. The Cog was sharp enough to have noticed, Mitch knew.

One of the Imperials who'd been sleeping next to the big man had woken up looking as pale as a mutant. El Jesus noticed and handed the man his helmet, upside down. The soldier nodded gratefully, then vomited straight into the bowl. Then he cradled the fouled helmet in his lap as he prayed for it all to end one way or the other.

Juba fished around in his shirt and pulled out a stick of gum. He handed it to the ill Imperial, who accepted it with a sincere nod of thanks. He looked afraid to open his mouth again because of what might come out but managed to stuff the gum between his lips and start chewing.

The gum wouldn't cure what ailed the man, but it might help get the taste out of his mouth. Mitch noticed one of the Cogs starting to turn green around the gills at the scent of the puke, and he hoped this wouldn't turn into an even longer trip than it was supposed to be.

Mitch spotted Duval staring at Juba, and he wondered what the connection might be between the two or if there was one. The megacorporations held sway over millions of lives under their individual banners. The fact that two people worked for the same company didn't mean they'd ever heard of each other before.

Juba noticed Duval staring at him and offered her a stick of gum.

"No, thanks," the woman said. Despite declining his offer, though, she kept staring at him.

Even Mitch found this odd. In some ways, she acted like a child. She stared at the world with wide-open eyes, taking it all in, much as if she'd just seen it for the first time.

Still, she was a soldier, and Mitch assumed she was a good one. On a mission like this, there was no room for dead weight. He was sure Brother Samuel wouldn't have settled for warm bodies to put on the few seats on this ship.

However, he'd have needed to find people desperate enough to take on a suicide mission or who at least needed those tickets of his badly enough.

"What?" Juba finally said.

"Your fish."

She pointed toward the tattoos that covered one of the man's arms. They showed a shark chasing a school of fish. Each of the fish bore a date and a corporate logo. Mitch even spied a few Brotherhood tags mixed in with the rest.

The man had turned his arm into a leather belt on which he'd cut notches for each kill. Mitch wondered if that represented all of them or if there were others hidden on covered parts of his skin.

For a long time, Mitch had known the exact number of people he'd killed and could remember the details surrounding each incident: the date, the face, the method. He'd long since given up. During his stint in Capitol's military prison, he'd had to do some horrible things to keep the same things from happening to him, and he'd done his best to put every bit of that out of his mind. The kills had started to go along with those moments too.

He might still be rotting in that prison if Capitol had not decided he was more useful to them killing people instead. He suspected Nathan had had a hand in making that happen, although his friend had never said a word about it, and he had never asked. Of course, by the time Mitch had gotten out, Nathan had asked Adelaide to marry him, so Mitch hadn't had too many grateful thoughts for the man right then.

"You like my fish?" Juba asked Duval.

"It's beautiful."

Juba popped his gum. "Thanks."

Duval looked into his eyes. "You're the shark."

Juba shook his head and smiled. "Death is the shark. I'm just a guy with a gun."

30

Mitch glanced through the closest porthole. In the distance, a transport rocketed into the sky. It looked like a falling star going the wrong way.

El Jesus stood up and leaned over Mitch's shoulder. He gave a bitter chuckle, then said, "There goes all the money. Looks like we got on the wrong fucking shuttle."

The corporal backed up as Mitch turned around. The transport was already out of sight.

"You were born on the wrong fucking shuttle," Mitch said to his friend.

The big man grinned, then slipped into Spanish. The others in the ship might speak it too, but chances were better that they didn't.

"*¿Qué se arrastró su culo y murió?*" El Jesus asked. "What crawled up your ass and died?"

"*Tu mami.*" "Your mother."

Oh, ho. El Jesus smiled. "*Mi mami es gorda. Pero mi hermana cabrá. Ella es fina como una chingada comadreja.*" "My mother is fat. But my sister could manage. She is skinny as a fucking weasel."

Mitch laughed and made a mental note to avoid the man's mother and look up his sister the first chance he got. Just for grins.

The cabin fell silent after that. The others seemed to be put off by the use of a language they didn't understand. The

Cogs had been chattering in German the entire trip, but that hadn't bothered anyone. Perhaps that's because no one expected any better from them.

Mitch sat back and closed his eyes for a minute. When he opened them again, he spotted MacGuire. The man had finally taken a break from acting as the team cheerleader and sat down to have a moment to himself. He stared at a worn photo, his eyes warm yet dry. After a moment, he noticed Mitch looking at him and flashed it at him.

The photo showed a pretty woman of MacGuire's age. She smiled back at him so hard he could see her love straight through all the years and miles that separated them. MacGuire gave the picture a quick kiss and stuffed it back in his shirt.

As MacGuire put his photo away, Steiner shook his head at the man. He clearly had no space for sentimentality in his life. He'd trounced his men in cards, just as he had in chess the night before. Mitch wondered if Steiner was really that good or if the other Cogs had long ago learned to let him win.

The games were over now, and Steiner had spent the last hour giving his weapons one more going over. Now he'd switched to loading loose rounds into spare clips in anticipation of the coming battle. Like all Capitol troopers, Mitch never carried ammo that wasn't in a clip, and doing so seemed like an antiquated affectation.

Across the aisle, Juba worked at his rifle barrel with a bent-bristled toothbrush. The thing already gleamed, but Juba seemed bent on making it shine like chrome.

Mitch understood the sentiment. In battle, the only thing you could rely on was yourself and your equipment, and only if you'd taken the time to check and service the equipment yourself. Others failed, intentionally or not, but that was their problem, not yours.

You took care of yourself and your gear and did your job

the best you could. That's all anyone could ask. That and maybe a little luck.

Duval turned to Juba. "So who got them?" she asked.

"What?" The man had no idea what she was talking about, and neither did Mitch. She'd changed the subject without notice.

"Your tickets."

Juba inclined his head so he could look down his nose at the woman. "Why do you want to know?"

"Suicide mission. We're going to die together. That's an intimate thing."

Never one to miss a straight line, El Jesus barged into the banter at that point. He leered at the woman. "You make it sound like we're gonna fuck."

Duval gave the corporal a mysterious glance. "You can fuck a lot of people. You only die once."

That sat the man back in his seat and furrowed his brow. It took him a moment to wrap his head around it, like wrestling with a Zen koan. Then he pronounced his judgment: "That's fucked up."

The conversation stopped as Hodge's voice came crackling over the intercom. Mitch had barely seen the gunner throughout the trip except for a quick walk the man had made through the cabin at one point to stretch his legs. He had not said a word to anyone besides the pilot, just stood by the cockpit for a few minutes cracking his back before returning to his post.

"Multiple contacts bearing oh-oh-four and oh-one-five," Hodge said.

Michaels, the pilot, answered, a tinge of jealousy in his voice. "Escape transports. Getting the hell out of here."

He'd been a bit friendlier than Hodge, at least while they'd been on the ground. As soon as he had gotten behind the wheel, though, he'd been all business, and the soldiers hadn't seen him since.

Mitch noticed Duval staring at him, and his gut clenched.

Normally, a beautiful woman looking at him wouldn't have bothered him a bit, but he knew this was nothing like that. It was just his turn to be the object of her curiosity. The first words out of her perfect lips confirmed that.

"What about you?" she asked.

"What about me?" He wasn't about to make this easy for her.

"Your tickets."

Mitch grimaced, then stood up and made his way toward the cockpit, ignoring Duval's wide eyes. He didn't want to tell them about Adelaide and Grace. Particularly, he didn't want to tell El Jesus. Not yet.

He leaned in the doorway and peered over Michaels's shoulder. Mitch had never been in a transport this small before, but the controls looked pretty much like they did in the bigger jobs. In a pinch, he could wrestle the wheel around long enough to put the ship in for a landing, but he was glad to have a dedicated professional piloting the beast instead.

"Stand behind the line," Michaels said without glancing back.

"Just looking." Mitch wondered if the man always had such a sunny disposition when flying or if MacGuire had somehow pissed him off with one of his visits.

"Look all you want." Michaels glanced around, checking the various clusters of instrument dials. "Get in my way while I'm flying, you're gonna lose something."

The pilot said it not as a threat but as a factual statement. Mitch decided to believe him.

"Where are we?"

"Close," Michaels said. "Crossing the median. Start our descent into Canaan in a couple. Canaan's bad."

"It's bad all over this world, no matter where you go." Mitch realized he didn't like Earth much, mother planet or not. Life here was a bitch for all involved.

Mitch glanced around the cockpit, past the instruments. This wasn't just a place to sit. It was Michaels's office.

A picture of a pretty woman sat tucked into the edge of one of the windows. Every time the man looked to his left, there she would be. To the pilot's right, a small figurine of a saint sat right above the altimeter.

Charts and logs lay about the place. There were many of them, but each was fastened down separately and clearly had its own place. Mitch supposed that when working for a man like Constantine, you always had to be prepared to head off anywhere at a moment's notice. He wondered what kinds of stories the ship could tell, but he figured he'd have to settle for the pilot instead.

"So after we drop, you what?" Mitch asked. "Off to Luna? Mars? Outer reach?"

The pilot shook his head. "Already used up too much fuel to make orbit, much less break it."

That surprised Mitch more than he had thought it would. "So you're fucked like the rest of us."

Michaels finally looked back at the soldier. "How do you figure that?"

Mitch shrugged.

Michaels snorted and turned back to the controls. "Don't see how you're fucked, seeing you volunteered for this. You must have had a reason."

The man had a point. Whereas Mitch had sold his services—and probably his life—to Samuel for those two tickets, Michaels had stood by his employer instead. He could have just taken the ship and flown away. No one would have blamed him. Instead, here he was, flying a pack of mercenaries straight into the heart of hell.

"You like flying?" Mitch asked.

"It's my life."

"What if your life was killing?"

Mitch realized his hand had wandered to the chain of dog

tags in the pouch on his belt. He forced himself to quit playing with them.

Michaels showed a rueful smile. "Man does everything for a reason. Even if they don't know it themselves. Because otherwise, what are you? No different from those things. Just another demon."

31

El Jesus had given his tickets to his mother and his sister. They'd hugged him and praised his name to the Cardinal. He'd never felt so much like a hero in his life.

Samuel had found him at their home. El Jesus had gone there on leave to wish his family a final goodbye. They'd all been weeping about how fucked up everything was when the priest had shown up, tickets in hand.

Before accepting the deal, though, El Jesus had taken Samuel aside and spoken with him in the kitchen alone.

"I can't do this," he had said quietly. "I want to, but it's suicide. I can't go fucking get killed while my mami thinks I'm going to hell. It'd kill her sure as a bullet."

Samuel had frowned. "You're a soldier, Corporal. Surely your mother has come to terms with the fact you could die at any time."

El Jesus had shaken his head. "I always swore to her I'd come back alive."

"And she believed you?"

"To this day."

"Can you not swear to her again?"

El Jesus had frowned. "Those other times, I figured I'd probably make it. Not so much this time."

Samuel had thrown up his hands. "We need you, Corporal. With your help, we can save the world."

El Jesus had nodded. "I understand that, Padre. I really

do. And I appreciate the tickets. *Muchas gracias* for those. But I—I need one more thing from you."

Samuel had waited silently for the corporal to go on.

"I need absolution."

Samuel had regarded the corporal coldly. "Are you sorry for your sins?"

A lopsided grin had appeared on the big man's face. "Not really, Padre."

"Then there's nothing I can do."

"But Brother, you have to. I need you to." He had looked toward the kitchen door, out toward where his mother and sister were sitting in the parlor, chatting excitedly, thrilled that they had hope again—hope and a chance to live. "Please."

"I cannot lie for you."

"You're asking me to die for you," El Jesus had said. "Just tell my mami you've set it up so I go to heaven. What's a little lie?"

"It's wrong."

El Jesus had rubbed his chin. "What's worse, Padre? Lying about a sinner's soul or making his good mother miserable because you won't?"

Samuel had considered that for a moment. He had looked at the tickets in his hand. El Jesus could tell he had been thinking that those bits of paper should be enough. The corporal had to sweeten the pot.

"You do it, I'll tell you where to find my top, too," he said. Samuel's eyes lit up at that.

"Sergeant Mitch Hunter," El Jesus said. "Best NCO I ever seen. Real hero material."

Samuel nodded and sighed. His shoulders sagged, and El Jesus knew he had him.

"All right," he said. "For humanity and the fate of the world."

Samuel placed a hand on El Jesus's shoulder. "The responsibility for this sin lies within you, son."

El Jesus grinned, his eyes brimming with tears. "I think I can live that that, Padre, as long as Mami thinks I'm going to a better place than this shithole."

Samuel smiled at that. "For that, we'll certainly pray."

Now Juba took advantage of the break in the conversation to slip in a question to Duval. "Who got yours?"

"I have two children."

Juba raised his eyebrows at that. "You're a little young."

"I started young." She wasn't going to say more about it, El Jesus could tell.

"*Mierda,*" El Jesus said. He was impressed in an awful way.

Juba ignored the big man. "What are their names?"

Duval smiled at that. Like any proud parent, this was something she was happy to talk about. Mitch wondered if she'd given up being a soldier to become a mother. If so, would she be rusty? Or would fighting for her kids' sake make her deadlier than ever?

"Jack's seven, and Constance is five," she said. "Getting on the ship, you'd think they were going on a ride. They were so excited. End of the world."

She smiled, and El Jesus could feel the warmth in her from across the cabin's aisle. For a moment no one said a word.

Finally, Juba spoke, answering Duval's question.

"There's this girl. I don't know her name. She works at the Pearl, across from the barracks." He grinned at the memory of her. "She's got this walk. Pure Sin City. Eyes you drown in."

El Jesus could not believe what he'd heard. "You gave your ticket to a woman, and you didn't even fuck her?"

Juba winked at them all. "I said I didn't know her name."

El Jesus laughed. "So you fucked her then!"

It struck the corporal that Juba might be lying about the girl, but he didn't care. If it was a good enough story, the truth of it didn't bother him. It never had.

32

Michaels cursed to himself as they drew closer to Canaan. He'd been flying for so long that his ass had gone numb, but he was too close to the destination to put the ship on autopilot and go for a stretch. Instead, he tried stretching his legs in his seat. It was better than nothing.

Hodge's voice crackled over the intercom.

"Another contact at three-four-three . . . This one's closing."

Michaels peered out through the windshield but knew he wouldn't be able to see the newcomer from there. He wasn't ready to take evasive action quite yet, but this close to Canaan he wanted to be cautious.

"Give them a heads-up," he said.

A moment later he heard Hodge speaking over the radio. The man kept his tone clean and controlled at all times. Michaels might have given Hodge hell every now and then, but the man made a damn fine copilot.

"Attention Transport *HMS Tango-Six,* you are encroaching on a military vessel. Break off your current route, come around to your heading oh-three-eight, copy?"

The only thing Michaels heard for a reply was blank static. Whoever was on that ship either couldn't hear them or didn't care to reply. He decided to try them with a more forceful tone.

"*HMS Tango-Six,* come around to your heading oh-three-eight, do you copy?"

His tone made it clear that this was not a request but an order. Still there was no response, and the airship kept straight on its heading toward them.

Michaels tried to shake off the bad feeling he had about this. "Plumbers flying planes," he said.

He turned to Hunter, who was standing in the cockpit door, looking morose. He could understand why the man wanted to escape from the cabin—mercenaries made terrible talkers in his opinion—but it was time for him to go.

"Strap in," he told the sergeant, "I'm going to put her through some paces."

He gave Mitch a few seconds to hustle back to his seat and give the others the heads-up. Then he announced his actions over the intercom.

"Changing course to two-eight-five."

"Two-eight-five, aye," Hodge said. The man sounded like a hollow echo.

Michaels brought the ship's nose around toward the new heading, not bothering to be gentle about it. If the people in the back thought that little turn was rough, he was about to give them the shock of their lives.

"Diving to fifty thousand feet."

"Fifty-angels, aye."

Michaels leaned forward on the wheel, hard. The ship lurched forward into a steep dive.

Michaels suppressed a smile as anything not tied or held down in the cabin smacked against the ceiling. He wondered if the sick Imperial had managed to dispose of the contents of his helmet yet, but it was too late to care.

The ship began to shake like she wanted to fall apart. The speed was more than she could bear, but Michaels didn't plan to push her that hard for long. When he felt like the fillings might rattle out of his teeth, he pulled back on the wheel and leveled out. As he did, he allowed himself a quick smile.

"That oughta to do it," he said. If that hadn't shaken their silent friends, something was seriously wrong.

Hodge's voice cracked as he spoke over the intercom. "They're changing direction. They're on an intercept course."

Michaels reached up to the cockpit's ceiling and lowered an intricate scope that unfolded from its housing there. He peered through the magnifying lenses and let one piece of glass after another drop into place, focusing them on the fly. As he did, the civilian transport came into view and then grew bigger and bigger in his vision.

It looked just like any of the dozens of other ships Michaels had seen rocketing into the sky over the past few days. If it hadn't been coming about to charge straight at him like a drunk teenager bent on playing chicken, he would not have thought much about it.

Michaels's eyes grew wide. He barked an order at his copilot.

"Take your station."

Hodge balked at first, just as Michaels knew he would. "That's a civilian ship—"

Michaels didn't have time to argue with the man about it. "Take your station!"

Michael glanced back and saw Hodge climb a nearby ladder through a hatch in the ceiling that led into the ship's weapons turret. A moment later he felt rather than heard the power-assisted gimbals on which the massive pair of recoilless rifles sat spring to life as Hodge took control of the gunner's pod.

Michaels checked the position of their attacker again, for that was what he now knew it to be. No one with benign intentions would point one ship at another like that. He spied it dead ahead. It seemed to glow in the sunlight, and it grew brighter as it came closer.

"HMS Tango-Six," Hodge said over the radio, "break off or you will be fired upon." The horror showed in the man's voice. This wasn't something he wanted to do.

Michaels decided he didn't want to have to deal with the problem that way either. Far better to outfly the bastards than outgun them.

"Hold on!" he shouted into the intercom as he prepared to put the airship through its paces.

Inside the cabin, he knew the passengers had to be straining against their flight harnesses. He hoped they'd all managed to get themselves strapped in well or they were going to have a very painful flight. He couldn't tell for sure, as enough loose equipment was rattling around the place to drown out anything else.

Michaels swung the airship left, right, then left again, up and down a few times, and then came around to their original heading. He peered through his scope to see what fruit his efforts had borne.

He saw the civilian transport right there in front of him, only closer than ever. It rode a rocket of flame straight for them.

"Repeat," Hodge said, his voice as shaky as the plane had been, "you will be fired upon." Michaels could hear the ache of conscience in the man's tone. *"Tango-Six,* do you copy? You must break off now."

Nothing came back over the radio. Michaels felt his heart start to pound and his palms begin to sweat. He was a good pilot—he knew that—but he'd not been involved in air combat for years, certainly not in a transport like this. His hands ached for the controls of a Capitol fighter, not this damned pleasure boat.

Hodge begged the other ship to stop. *"Tango-Six,* break off, break off, break off!"

Michaels swept left, right, up, down. The transport out there kept matching his moves. There was no way he could shake her without ripping Constantine's ship apart. He wondered if he should give it a try anyhow, but then the proximity alarms went off.

The sirens told the passengers what Michaels and Hodge already knew: They were in serious trouble. Some of the soldiers in the back started to panic, but most of them held steady. The veterans had to have seen worse before—or at least thought they had. No one, including Michaels, knew just what they were up against.

"Fire!" Michaels shouted at Hodge. "Fire the guns!"

Hodge had signed on as Michaels's copilot because he'd suffered shell shock in the Imperial Defense Forces. He had not fired a weapon since leaving the military, which perhaps made him a poor choice as the ship's gunner. Maybe Michaels should have sent Hunter or one of the other soldiers into the turret, someone with less compunction about possibly killing a ship full of innocents.

"Break off, break off!" Hodges said. *Don't make me do this,* his tone cried.

They had no time left. The transport was right there, and she was going to hit them. The only chance they had was to blow her from the sky. Michaels twisted the wheel in a vain attempt to slip his ship out of the way, but he knew it would never work.

"Fire!" he said.

Hodge yelled into the intercom and pulled the trigger on his weapon. The twin recoilless rifles spat fire, alternating their attacks at the target.

The civilian transport sailed past them then, just missing them. Michaels glanced down at his radar screen, a red disk on which a pair of thin brass arms moved a brass marker. He'd heard of electronic screens being used in ancient times, but such things hadn't worked in centuries. Only the Cardinal knew why, he supposed.

He saw the transport coming around for another pass and angled the ship so that Hodge would have a clear shot at her. The sky outside spun madly as Michaels tried to make the ship move in ways she had never been built to move. They wound out of it with the ship half in the clouds, which swirled around them in white and gray.

Hodge let loose at the transport with another barrage of lead, but it went wide again. Perhaps some of it found the transport's tail, but if so it didn't slow the craft down.

Michaels glanced down at the radar screen again, but the marker wasn't there anymore. He tapped the display, but the little brass ball did not come back. It was as if the transport had disappeared.

Had Hodge downed her? Michaels doubted it. He refused to let hope rise within him.

"Captain," Hodge's voice said, "I've lost them!"

Michaels heard the gimbals spinning around over his head as Hodge searched the skies for the transport. The copilot's labored breath filtered through the intercom as he hunted for his prey.

Michaels wondered who was hunting whom. He looked forward just in time to see the civilian transport emerge from the clouds right there in front of him.

The last thing Michaels saw—in the blink of an eye, right before the impact—was a blood-drenched mutant sitting at the transport's controls.

He couldn't tell for sure, but he'd be damned if it didn't look like the thing was laughing.

33

Mitch had been through a lot of rough rides in the Capitol Ground Forces but never anything like this. The ship had bounced through the sky like a yo-yo on a string, the sirens deafening everyone aboard, and then had pitched and yawed so hard that he could barely tell which way was down.

The impact had shaken every person in the plane to the bone. Then everything became strangely quiet for a moment. The sirens stopped, and the ship's engines ceased working. For a split second, the plane seemed to hang in the air like a mortar shell at the top of its arc.

Then, just like a shell, it came plummeting down.

A hole had appeared in the cabin ceiling right where Hodge's turret used to be. It was gone now, and Hodge along with it. The cabin depressurized through the ragged gap, the horrible wind sucking out everything that wasn't bolted to the floor.

In the engine compartment—which sat on the top of the ship, just behind the gunner's pod—one of the boilers burst open and spilled into the passenger compartment below. Boiling coal tar burst onto the men seated near the plane's tail. Four soldiers—two from Bauhaus and two from Imperial—were caught in the lethal mess, their bodies incinerated before they could scream. Mitch realized then that he'd never even gotten their names.

The river of boiling tar tore off the tail of the plane and pulled the dead men out into the open air along with it. MacGuire began to unbuckle his harness and shouted at the others over the unbelievable roar of the icy wind. He pointed to a hatch in the floor near what was now the back of the ship.

"Get to the escape pod!" the Imperial yelled.

Mitch was sitting right next to him and could barely hear him. Still, he had to admire the man's leadership. He'd just lost two of his men. He could have just raced for the pod and left the others to figure out what he was doing and then follow as they were able. Instead, he instantly shoved aside his grief, took charge, and worked to save everyone he could.

"What?" Duval asked.

Mitch wondered if she'd been injured in the crash. If so, more than her hearing must have been affected. Any properly trained soldier knew what to do in an emergency at this height. They had scant minutes before the burning hulk would reach the ground, but that was enough time to get the hell out of it if they moved fast.

"Escape! Pod!" MacGuire stabbed toward the rear of the cabin, punctuating each word.

Mitch wondered if Duval didn't know about the escape pod. It wasn't standard issue on every ship, but he'd recognized the shape of it from the outside as they'd boarded the craft.

The time for thinking had passed. He had to move fast or die.

Mitch waited for El Jesus to get moving in front of him, then released his harness and half walked, half crawled after the big man down the aisle of the wrecked ship. The others did the same, falling into line as soon as they could.

Every foot along the aisle felt like a mile. Inertia shoved Mitch toward the ceiling, making it hard to get any traction on anything. As he got farther along, though, air screaming past the missing tail section yanked him toward the back of the plane, in the direction of the escape pod.

Steiner had been sitting next to the men who'd been burned to death by the burst boiler. His face and hands were still red from his own close shave with the steam and tar. He reached the escape pod's hatch first and managed to wrench it open. After that, he tumbled half inside and held the door open for the next soldier to come along.

Duval dragged herself into the pod next, and Juba slipped in right behind her. El Jesus yanked himself over the hatch's lip, and Mitch fell in straight after.

Mitch looked back to see Severian hauling Brother Samuel along after her, his precious book clutched under his free arm. He was shaking his head and shouting at her, but she couldn't hear him over the noise.

Mitch reached out and helped pull Samuel the last few feet toward the hatch. As the monk fell into the pod, he could finally be heard.

"The bomb!"

El Jesus, who'd been sitting atop the thing, pounded a fist against the pod's shell. "Fuck!"

Samuel ignored him and shouted at Severian. "Get the bomb!"

Severian nodded, then raced back toward El Jesus's seat. The spinning craft buffeted her about like a leaf in a storm, but she moved like a dancer through the chaos.

Mitch wondered how close the ground was now. Then he decided he didn't want to think about it.

Severian yanked the red velvet sack from beneath El Jesus's seat. It had been too well secured to be torn free during the cabin's depressurization.

El Jesus pushed past Mitch to get his hands back on the bomb. Mitch understood. The man had left the payload behind, and now he wanted to make up for it. He knew that El Jesus wouldn't make the same mistake again—if he lived long enough to have that chance.

Mitch glanced around. The others had jammed themselves into the cramped pod and had started to strap their bodies into the harnesses that lined the walls. Sunlight shone in through small windows above and below.

To the top, Mitch could see black smoke trailing out of Constantine's wrecked airship. Through the window under everyone's feet, the Earth grew closer by the second.

Severian shoved the sack into El Jesus's hands and slipped by him into the pod. The big man put the bomb under his arm like a football and then reached out and slammed the hatch shut.

"Let's go!" El Jesus said, spinning the wheel to seal the pod away from the doomed ship. He clambered down into the only free seat, the bomb clutched tight to his chest.

"Is that everyone?" MacGuire asked.

"Fuck, yes, it's everyone!" El Jesus said. The corporal put the bomb on his lap and started to buckle himself in.

MacGuire nodded at Juba. The Mishiman reached over and opened a little door labeled POD RELEASE. He reached inside the recessed compartment beyond and flipped a switch.

Nothing happened.

Juba toggled the switch back and forth, again and again. Still nothing.

"Circuit's been cut!"

Mitch had been afraid something like that might happen. The escape pod was usually the last thing maintenance crews bothered checking. If it didn't work, who the hell would be alive to complain about it?

Even if it had been in top condition at the start of the flight, a direct collision like that meant all bets on the integrity of any system on the craft were off. Escape pods usually were used in less catastrophic circumstances than this. Engineers who thought up scenarios like this would have assumed everyone was already dead.

Without a word, Mitch made his decision and climbed

back up toward the hatch. He peered through the glass set in the hatch at the cabin beyond. He spied what he was looking for and began to wrestle with the wheel

Steiner stood up too. "What are you doing?" the Bauhauser asked.

Mitch didn't look down, just concentrated on the task at hand. "Manual release on the other side of the hatch."

"You'll be killed."

Mitch kept working at the wheel. "Yeah."

Steiner reached up and helped him turn the wheel. Opening it was far slower going than sealing it, but they kept at it, working as a team.

Mitch felt the locks holding down the hatch click as they finally fell out of place. Before he could shove the hatch open, though, something heavy fell against it.

Mitch looked up to see Michaels looking down through the window in the hatch, his face a red ruin of glass and blood. After the head-on crash, Mitch had counted the pilot as gone for sure. The man had pulled himself all the way from the shattered cockpit to reach the pod, dying every hard-fought step of the way.

Michaels looked down at Mitch through the glass, a defiant snarl on his battered face. He snapped off a final salute to Mitch and those below him. Then Michaels reached out and pulled the manual release.

34

The escape pod broke free from the airship and zipped off into the sky. It arced away from the ship to find its own path back to Earth. Mitch watched Michaels and his ruined ship shrink almost to nothing in a matter of seconds. As he looked, he tightened the hatch's wheel once more.

By the time he'd finished, the plane had fallen out of sight. Mitch gave the pilot a mental salute, then flung himself back into his seat and struggled to strap himself in.

As an airworthy vehicle, the escape pod made a good brick. Being in it felt like riding a barrel over a never-ending waterfall. Mitch didn't know if he'd have been able to secure himself in his seat if El Jesus hadn't used his free hand to hold him down.

Once he got the final strap down, Mitch looked at the others. They stared at each other wordlessly. He knew that many of them wanted to start screaming in fear, but they impressed him by holding back, at least for now.

Juba kept his gaze locked on an altimeter embedded in the wall near the nonworking release switch. The big hand on it spun like a roulette wheel, with the smaller one, which ticked off feet by thousands, chasing it hard.

"Silk should pop at five thousand," Juba said. He had to shout over the wind noise but kept his tone calm and measured. "Here we go—"

A huge jolt shook the escape pod, and Mitch wondered if

everyone in the place had sustained a concussion. He shook his head to clear his vision, then looked straight down. The ground seemed to be zipping up at them as fast as before.

"We're still falling," MacGuire said. For the first time, Mitch noticed a note of true panic in the man's voice.

"We're too heavy," said Steiner. The Cog shook his head in a way that shouted, *Shoddy Imperial workmanship.* "We blew the chute."

MacGuire scowled and reached out with his hand, pointing at a toggle switch over El Jesus's seat. "The backup," he said. "Hit the backup!"

El Jesus reached for the toggle with his free hand. He'd held on to the bomb like a vise throughout the fall and the jolt from the first chute. Keeping the bomb under his arm made the reach a little too long for him, but he stretched his fingers as far as they could go.

"No!" Juba shouted, finally ready to panic.

El Jesus's hand froze just as it touched the switch over Juba's head. The big man gaped at the Mishiman. "No? Fuck no! Yes, motherfucker!"

Mad and scared as he was, El Jesus didn't hit the switch quite yet.

"We pop it now, we'll shred it like the first! We open low, it'll slow us down before we hit, before the silk rips apart!"

El Jesus stared at the man as if he'd just told him to get out and sprinkle fairy dust on the outside of the pod. When Juba moved to put his own hand on the switch, though, El Jesus let his drop.

Mitch looked to MacGuire. The Imperial stared at Juba and bit his lip.

What the Mishiman had said made sense. It gave them a choice between a hard landing and a fatal one. The only trick was it would require perfect timing and nerves of steel to pull it off.

The altimeter passed two thousand feet and kept dropping. No matter what happened, they wouldn't have to wait long for the results.

"Do it," MacGuire said.

Juba ignored him and kept his eyes on the altimeter. Mitch wondered if MacGuire would pull his pistol on the Mishiman and order him to hit the switch. Of course, the threat of death wasn't much use in a situation like this.

"Fifteen hundred."

Juba sounded as if he'd just hit his personal best. He narrowed his eyes as he waited for the exact right moment. MacGuire put his hand on his sidearm. Mitch shot him an angry look to make him stay put. Did he think he was going to shoot the switch instead?

"Okay, here we go!" Juba shouted. "Here we go!"

Brother Samuel began to pray loudly. The rest of them clung to their straps. Mitch glanced over at the altimeter, which was spinning like a racecar's wheel.

Through the windows below, Mitch could see nothing, just clouds. Then the escape pod broke through.

Below, Mitch spied a rain-soaked city that had the black, wet look of a doused campfire. No lights burned in the dank, abandoned buildings, not even in the burned-out skyscraper at which the escape pod hurtled.

"We're gonna crash!" he shouted at Juba. "You better pull that fucking chute!"

"Juba's right," Duval said. That didn't comfort Mitch in the least.

El Jesus wrapped himself around the bomb and closed his eyes. A hard enough impact might set the thing off, Mitch guessed, even without the trigger. At least they'd make a big crater then.

"You'd better be right about this!" Mitch said to Juba. "You'd better be right, you son of a bitch!"

Juba reached up to pull the switch that would release the chute. Before he could do it, though, the escape pod smashed into one side of the skyscraper's top, which seemed to reach up to snatch it from the sky.

Mitch felt like the jolt might jerk his bones right out of his skin. He almost passed out from that alone.

Bits of the skyscraper shot through the sides of the escape pod like bullets. Blood exploded from somewhere, and someone screamed in pain.

The steel shell smashed through wall after wall and floor after floor so fast that Mitch couldn't count them. Then the pod burst free from the building's sleeve, into the open sky, and careened toward the open ground below.

The chute popped open then. It slowed them down, but not by much. Would it be enough?

Mitch bent his head down and braced himself as he stared at the ground zooming up at him. Even at the last moment, he couldn't bring himself to pray.

35

Mitch had been sure he was dead. No one could survive a fall from forty thousand feet and walk away from it. But the two chutes had slowed the escape pod, as had the multiple floors of the skyscraper they'd shot straight through like a massive bullet.

Mitch felt like hell, but he hadn't ended up pancaked on the floor of the pod, his flattened remains mixed in with those of the others. They'd left the monastery with sixteen people: ten soldiers, Samuel, Severian, Hodge, Michaels, and the two stokers above. Only eight of them had made it into the pod.

From the distinct smell of blood, he doubted if all of them would make it out.

Mitch undid his straps and spilled out of his seat. He seemed to be the first to free himself, but he could tell by the groans all around him that he wasn't the only survivor.

A weak light filtered in through the window in the pod's hatch, although Mitch couldn't see anything through the haze that seemed to cover it. He reached up and felt the wheel still there. Gritting his teeth against the pain he felt in every joint and muscle, he started to turn it.

Before long, Steiner got to his feet and lent Mitch a hand. Between the two of them, they made fast work of it, and soon the locks on the hatch clicked open.

The thing didn't want to open, but Mitch and Steiner got

their hands on it and shoved upward. The metal around the opening had bent, crimping the hatch on tight.

"Put your back into it," Steiner said.

Mitch resisted the urge to put his fist into the Cog. Instead, he channeled his irritation into shoving upward with all his might. Steiner did the same.

With a high-pitched groan of twisted metal, the hatch finally gave way. It moved slowly at first, then pitched upward and over. It fell off its broken hinges and tumbled away. Mitch heard a soft splash as it smacked into the rain-soaked ground.

Mitch pulled himself out of the pod first and slid down the still-steaming metal to the land in mud up to his knees. It had been one more bit of luck that they'd landed on such soft ground. Hitting a slab of concrete might have killed them all.

Steiner landed right next to Mitch, splashing him with even more mud. He was beyond caring about such things.

A groan from inside the pod made him look back. He saw El Jesus squeezing his way out, carrying a black bag with him. He stomped back to the pod and helped the big man down.

El Jesus must have found a bag of supplies in the pod and repurposed it. From the shape and weight of the bag, Mitch knew it contained the bomb.

Juba slipped out of the pod next. Duval followed him, and the Mishiman turned around to help the woman down. She ignored him and landed like a dancer in the mud, which barely seemed to touch her.

"Captain's fucked," El Jesus said in a flat, quiet voice.

Mitch hauled himself back up the side of the capsule and slipped inside, feet first. Severian sat there at one side of the Imperial while Samuel knelt next to him on the other side and prayed over him.

Blood soaked MacGuire's pants and had pooled in the bottom of the pod. Mitch saw where a strut had separated from the side of the capsule's frame and gone straight through the captain's leg from the seat below him, pinning him there.

Mitch's breath caught in his chest. The man didn't have much of a chance. Maybe in a place where there were doctors and hospitals, he might have been fine, but as it was, he was fucked.

Even if they could get him free and bind his wound, he wouldn't be walking anywhere. He'd hold back the entire team, or at least as many as decided to stay behind to take care of him. Either way, Mitch didn't plan on leaving him there, so it was time to get to work.

"We'll cut you loose," he said, peering more closely at the injury.

MacGuire shook his head and spoke through gritted teeth. "It hit the artery. You pull it out, I'm gone."

Mitch had seen enough wounded soldiers to know the man was right. Much as it pained him to admit it, there was nothing they could do but leave him there, probably to die.

Brother Samuel finished his prayer and made the sign of the Brotherhood on MacGuire's forehead. He'd been giving the man his last rites.

"*Ar dheis Dé go raibh a anam,* John Patrick MacGuire. Amen."

"Amen." MacGuire said the word as strongly as he could, but his voice still cracked.

Samuel lay his hands on MacGuire's head for a moment and offered a silent petition. Then he turned and climbed out of the escape pod without another word. Severian followed him, offering not even a salute to the man.

Mitch squatted down next to MacGuire. He had no words for the captain, but they didn't need any. They both knew there was no good way out of this, and there was no need to emphasize that with pointless complaints.

Mitch waited with the Imperial for a while, until he was ready. Despite his initial dislike of the man, he'd come to respect him as a good and decent leader. Outside of Nathan, Mitch had seen damn little of that in battle, on either side. He deserved to exit on his own terms.

"Sergeant Hunter," MacGuire said, his voice raw but controlled, "can I ask the borrow of a grenade, please."

Mitch reached into his pack and pulled out a grenade. He handed it to MacGuire, who clutched it to him like a talisman that could keep the shadows away, at least for a little while.

"Thank you. Good luck, Sergeant."

Mitch squeezed the man's shoulder.

MacGuire nodded at him. "Yeah," he said through teeth gritting in pain.

Mitch climbed up and out through the hatch. Outside, in the gray light of the overcast day, the others worked at cleaning their weapons off the best they could. Steiner rinsed the barrels of his guns in a deep puddle of murky water. Juba held his weapons up in the rain, twisting them in awkward ways to help the weather remove the mud.

Off to the side, El Jesus pissed on his shotgun. It was crude, but it worked.

Duval and Juba unlimbered their rifles and kept them at the ready. The way they carried them, with the straps off their shoulders and wound around their forearms, Mitch knew they were ready to roll.

In his free hand, Juba held a map as he surveyed the land around them. "Off by four leagues," he said. "North by southwest."

The Mishiman looked down at the map. "Gotta go through the city like the old monk said."

Mitch pulled out a cigarette and flicked open his lighter. As he brought it to the cigarette in his mouth, a loud *WHUMP* sounded from inside the escape pod behind him. He paused for the barest moment, then went back to lighting his cigarette. He never looked back.

El Jesus picked up his shotgun and started thumbing shells bearing yellow and red stripes into it.

"White phosphorus?" Juba asked in an uncertain tone. He knew what the shells were. He just wasn't sure anyone should be using them.

El Jesus grinned and pumped the gun to chamber the first rounds into each of the barrels. "Conchita here, she's a real spitfire."

Steiner grunted as he rigged the duffel bag around the bomb into a sling and shrugged it onto his back. "Just make sure you're not near me when that thing blows up."

The Cog readied a pair of Hellblazer machine pistols and stuffed them into a tanker rig that hung them high across his chest. He nodded at Mitch, as prepared as he was ever going to be.

Severian and Samuel carried only their swords. Mitch might have questioned the wisdom of that—he preferred to do his killing from a distance—but he chose not to argue. He'd seen what Severian could do with her blades and knew she'd be fine. At least you never had to worry about running out of ammunition with a sword.

As for Samuel, Mitch wasn't sure the brother would be able to handle his blade without cutting himself. He might have been a hard-ass at one point in his life, but a decade or two of monastery life would take the edge off anyone—except a bodyguard like Severian, of course. The best Mitch could say about Samuel's choice of weapon was that he wouldn't have to worry about the man accidentally shooting him.

Mitch hoisted his M50 in his hands, slid off the safety, and put his finger over the trigger guard. The pod still smoking behind them, they started off toward their ultimate goal.

36

Canaan turned out to be a dirty slice of hell. The buildings had been burned out and abandoned for decades, if not centuries. Mitch couldn't tell how far the destruction extended around them, but his eye hadn't seen an undamaged structure since they'd come crashing down.

It seemed as if it had been raining here since just after the buildings had burned. Mud caked everything and in someplaces ran in rivers down the cracked and broken streets. Mitch felt a chill that had nothing to do with the shitty weather.

Mitch had taken the point as they moved out. He dashed from cover to cover, careful to avoid wide fields of fire or places for an easy ambush. The others followed him at a distance, each giving the others plenty of space. If they were spotted, a sniper or a joker with a rocket launcher might be able to take out one or two of them but not the whole group at once.

Mitch stopped at the corner of a mostly whole building and waited for the others to catch up. When a few of them did, he took a deep breath and prepared to move out once more. Before he could, though, Juba grabbed him by the shoulder and hauled him back.

Mitch resisted the urge to club the man in the chin with the butt of his rifle. As he glared at Juba, the Mishiman pointed to something moving in the distance.

Mitch squinted and spotted a pack of mutants loping down the street. The creatures hadn't seen them, but if Mitch had gone charging out into the street, they would have for sure. Mitch nodded his thanks to Juba, then pointed at Duval and motioned for her to take point for a while.

Duval waited for the mutants to disappear around a distant corner and then moved out. Mitch and the others followed her, once more a few seconds apart.

They chased Duval through the streets of the city, working their way closer to their goal. As they went, the buildings became newer but no less abandoned. On several corners, Mitch spotted handbills with the faces of missing people. He felt sure none of them would ever be found.

Eventually, Duval signaled for a break.

"Check your targets," she said. "Hey, your two." She pointed just off to their right.

Duval squatted on her knees behind a truck overturned in the middle of the street. Juba came up behind her, then Mitch and the rest. He wondered if they were all as tired as he. The trip from the monastery had been long and brutal, and the crash landing had taken a lot out of him.

If anyone had gotten the worst of it—other than Mac-Guire—it was Steiner. The Cog panted heavily as he lugged the bomb along, still in the bag on his back.

"Need a hand with that?" El Jesus said.

"No, thank you," Steiner said with a little laugh. He almost sounded human.

Juba held up a hand. "Quiet."

Sounds of movement came from up ahead, on the other side of the car. Mitch craned his neck to see a pack of figures racing down the street away from them.

Juba swung the barrel of his gun around the side of the truck and took aim, but Duval pushed the gun away. Mitch spotted what Duval had seen. These weren't mutants. They were living people.

"Refugees," Mitch said. "Where the hell they going?"

The locals rounded the nearest corner and disappeared. Mitch left the cover of the truck to follow them. Then he heard gunfire coming from that direction, and he moved faster.

Mitch knew he was going in the wrong direction. He didn't care.

"Hunter!" Duval shouted his name as if the sound of her voice might stop him in his tracks. She might have been a mother, but he wasn't anything like her kids, he was sure.

37

Mitch rounded the corner cautiously and ducked straight into an open square in the center of the city. A transport ship sat dead in the middle of the place, belching smoke and steam. A crowd of supplicants surrounded it, begging and pleading with a pair of armed men standing at the foot of the transport's ramp.

The men fired their machine guns into the air again. This time the mob fell into a terrified silence, and an aisle opened to the north.

A man in an expensive suit and a gorgeous woman in a beautiful coat made their way up to the ship via the aisle. Behind them a porter pushed a pile of luggage on a huge cart.

Some of the people protested as the wealthy couple boarded the transport, but they quieted when the bigger of the two men, a chubby bastard who made El Jesus look tiny, leveled his gun at them. Still, the women and children in the crowd wailed and begged for the guards to let them on the ship. Their cries fell on ears that weren't deaf but blocked by greed.

Mitch wondered why the people didn't call the guards' bluff and charge the ship. Then he spotted the stack of bodies scattered about the foot of the airship's ramp. The guards apparently had no compunction about firing on innocent people pleading for their lives.

The rest of the squad slid up behind Mitch. He didn't

turn to acknowledge them as they watched the guards at work.

While the big guard kept his weapon trained on the crowd, the other—a tall, skinny man who reminded Mitch of the Grim Reaper—barked out an announcement.

"The current bid is two gold watches, a diamond necklace, and ten thousand gold talents!" He flashed a smile that nearly split his face in two "Going once . . . Twice . . ."

The crowd surged forward a foot, but the big man shouted them down with his bellows and the threat of his bullets.

"Keep back! Keep back, by God!" he said.

The skinny man grinned even wider and pointed a long, thin finger into the crowd.

"Sold! To the skeleton in the monkey suit."

A man so ancient he looked like he might fall over dead on his way up the ramp started forward. A beautiful young woman at his elbow helped him along, and another porter lugged a tower of luggage behind them.

The skinny guard took the goods from the old man and let the woman aboard the ship with a grotesque leer. Then he shoved the old man back into the crowd.

"One ticket, not two!" the guard said with a cackle.

The old man sputtered in protest. "I bought it."

The fat guard let loose an evil laugh at that. "And she'll show her gratitude by shining my crack all the way to Mars!"

"Unless you want to buy another ticket," the skinny guard said with a lustful look nearly as awful as the one his fat friend had given the girl. He glanced at his friend, and the two cackled with glee.

"That's all my money!"

The fat guard snarled. "Then fuck off!"

The old man stepped toward the fat guard. "Do you know who I am?"

The fat guard shot the old man through the chest. He flew backward into the crowd, which backed away as if death by bullets was contagious, leaving him to collapse in a pool of his blood.

The fat man spit on the corpse. "That's who you are."

The skinny guard crowed in delight. "Ass, stash, or cash!" he said. "Nobody rides free! The next seat starts at five thousand talents!"

"We need to cut through here," Juba said to Mitch as much as to the others. He pulled out his gum and stuck it on his helmet, then pointed to a break in the buildings on the opposite side of the square.

Duval shook her head. "Good place for an ambush."

"Can't be too many mutes," Juba said, gesturing at the crowd. "There's too much easy meat."

Steiner scoffed at that reasoning. "All the more reason for them to come."

Duval pointed toward the break in the buildings that Juba had noted, then circled her arm to show how they could proceed around the mob. "We go through the square, this street here's a lot harder to get pinned down."

Mitch shouldered his rifle. Like the others, he'd strapped his sword to it for easy carrying. The tip of the blade jutted out past the barrel of the gun like a bayonet. He had to make sure he didn't jab himself with it.

He started forward, heading for the crowd. If the team wanted to cut through the square, that was fine with him. He meant to take the direct route, though.

Steiner said something filthy in German, then called after Mitch. "We don't have time for this."

"Make time," Mitch said.

As he neared the crowd, the people parted before him, opening a clear path straight to the ship.

"Hunter!" Steiner said.

Mitch ignored him. He figured their chances of saving the world were next to shitty, but if he could make some sort of difference here at least, he meant to do it.

The fat guard was still waving his gun at the crowd,

snarling and cursing. "I will shit on the next whore who shoves her brat in my face!" he said. A woman near him fell back, wailing in fear.

The skinny guard kept up his auction patter, delighted both with himself and with how much money he stood to make. "The bid stands at seven thousand talents and three bottles of very old Scotch whiskey . . ."

The man's voice trailed off as Mitch stepped out of the crowd and stood over the cooling body of the wealthy man the guards had cheated.

"Let them on," Mitch said.

Hopeful that the newcomer wasn't the trouble he seemed, the skinny guard grinned. "You making a bid?"

Mitch didn't laugh. He unsnapped the flap over his pistol's holster. "You take the kids first. Then the women. Then the men, if there's any room left."

The two guards glanced at each other, confused for a moment at the size of the intruder's balls.

"Hey, soldier boy," the fat guard said with as much menace as he could muster. "Ship can only carry so much weight."

"Well, what do you weigh?" said Mitch. "Two seventy-five?"

The fat guard swung his rifle up and put the end of the muzzle right against Mitch's skull. "Three-ten."

Mitch nodded, a grim smile on his lips. By putting the gun that close to him, the jackass had made this almost too easy.

Snake-fast, Mitch tilted his head to the right and slapped aside the fat man's rifle with his left arm. At the same time he brought up his gun-filled right fist and blasted a crater in the man's head.

The fat guard's body collapsed to the ground without a twitch.

Mitch half turned to the crowd. "Three-ten. That's two women, two kids, right there. Come on, let's go."

Two young ladies, each with a young child clutched in her arms, pressed forward and squeezed past Mitch. At a look from the soldier, the skinny guard let them by. He looked like he would piss himself if Mitch took a step toward him.

"How much do you weigh?" Mitch asked as he sized up the man with his eyes.

The skinny guard swallowed hard before answering in a croak, his throat gone dry. "Very little."

Mitch fingered his pistol. "Dump the luggage. Take them all."

The skinny guard nodded his agreement. Behind Mitch, one of the women reached down and grabbed the fat man's rifle. She'd make sure the guard kept his word.

Mitch turned to leave, and a wide aisle opened in the crowd before him. No one said a word of thanks, but he didn't expect any. They just stared after him in awe.

When he got back to the squad, the others looked at him in a new light. He realized he'd just blown his image of not giving a fuck, but he didn't care about that either.

"You figure out where we're going yet?"

Juba grinned at Mitch out of far more than his pride in being able to read a map in this shitty weather and this hellhole of a town.

"Good."

Without consulting anyone, Mitch took point again. The squad fell into place behind him without any objections.

Steiner caught up with Mitch and fell into step just behind him.

"Endanger the mission again and I'll shoot you myself." Steiner showed no anger. He only stated a fact.

"Why wait?" Mitch asked.

He picked up the pace then, leaving Steiner behind. If the Cog meant to shoot him in the back, he might as well give the bastard a good target.

38

Mitch glanced up and saw the cold sun fighting to peek through the angry clouds above. He wondered if its bluish color was the product of some kind of pollution or something else they could blame on the mutants and their Machine.

Mitch had long thought that humanity had done a perfectly fine job of killing itself off. He'd never guessed there might be something else out there capable of doing it better. He wondered what would happen if they managed to put a stop to this mutant threat the way Brother Samuel seemed to think they could. He figured they'd all be back at each other's throats within a matter of weeks if not days.

He glanced back at Steiner. Perhaps minutes instead.

The moon vanished behind the spires of a Romanesque church. The place's central dome—what had once been its roof—thrust up from the belly of the wrecked city, lying half-buried in the mud.

Mitch looked back for Juba. The Mishiman pointed straight at the place and nodded. They were there.

The center of the dome had a large hole in it, fashioned there when the place had been built centuries ago. Mitch couldn't imagine it let in much light, but in the days before electricity it had probably been the best thing going.

Juba and Duval unspooled a pair of nylon ropes from their packs and set about anchoring them to two stone pillars. They then dropped the other ends down the hole in the dome. Mitch heard them slap onto the ground below with a splash.

All the soldiers clipped their harnesses to the slender strands. Mitch led the way, working his way to the hole, not trusting the ancient dome to hold his weight until it proved itself. It ended up being as sturdy as the earth.

As he peered down through the hole, the light didn't show much. Mitch fished out a flashlight and shone it into the vast chamber below. The beam of light reflected off a vast, shallow pool of rainwater that had collected on the floor, running off to the south in a wide rivulet. Otherwise, the place seemed empty.

His pistol in one hand, Mitch put his feet on the rim of the hole and tied a Munter hitch around the carabiner on his harness. Then he leaped off the edge.

As he fell, Mitch let the rope play out as fast as he dared. Once he got within a story of the pool below him, he pulled hard on the rope with his brake hand and came to a sharp halt. He swept the room with his pistol, but nothing came at him out of the darkness or made any kind of sound except for the steady patter of rain through the hole above.

He lowered himself the last few feet and found his boots ankle deep in the chilly water. The place smelled of must and mold but not of fresh death.

Mitch unhitched himself from the rope and gave the all-clear to the soldiers above. They zipped down next to him, one after the other, in a matter of seconds. As they came, he surveyed the edges of the place with his flashlight.

Once down, Duval poked around a bit on her own. In the beam of her light, she found a statue of a hooded monk with his arms crossed in front of him in the form of an X. Instead of true arms, though, he had boneblades.

"Christ," she said. "What sort of church is this?"

No one answered.

A moment later El Jesus touched down on the wet floor. "How do you lose a city?" he asked.

The water from the puddle ran off toward a tunnel to the south. When the others were down and ready—with their own flashlights on, either in their hands or attached to their guns—Mitch motioned for them to head out. He took point once more. He looked back at Juba for direction, but the Mishiman shrugged helplessly.

Samuel nodded at Mitch to go forward. "The catacombs lead down to the lost city," he said.

Mitch grimaced, then prowled down the corridor, his pistol before him the whole way. The paved sides of the arched tunnel soon gave way to a series of interlocking bones. The path ran directly through the ossuary, it seemed, a place filled with human skeletons stacked tight and deep for untold generations. Mitch wondered how far back from the tunnel walls the bones went, but he had no real desire to find out.

Duval spoke first, in a hushed, reverent tone. "There must be thousands."

"Millions," Samuel said. "Each new age builds upon the bones of the old."

"How many times have they come before?" Duval asked. By "they," she meant the mutants, Mitch knew.

Samuel frowned as he shook his head. "They didn't do this. We did this. We've always excelled at killing one another." His voice got louder as he warmed to his subject. Mitch suspected this had been the source of more than one of the monk's sermons back at the monastery. He instantly started to tune it out.

"Perhaps that is the Enemy's greatest offense," the monk said. Try as he might, Mitch couldn't avoid listening. "He would challenge our supremacy as the architects of our own end."

As Mitch glanced back at the monk, he spotted Severian cocking her head to the side, listening for something.

"Halt!" Steiner said in a harsh whisper.

Brother Samuel bit his tongue, and he and the others stopped moving. From somewhere behind them, back toward the church proper, the sound of rocks falling echoed down the tunnel. It happened only once, then stopped.

Mitch held up a hand to signal for everyone to wait and remain silent. It could have been the wind knocking something loose from the rim of the hole down which they'd descended. Probably no one had been in this place for a long while, and even the footfalls of the soldiers might be enough to jar something loose. Or the transport might have passed overhead finally, leaving the world shaking in its wake.

Or someone might be following them.

Mitch counted off a full minute. If they had picked up a tail, it was being careful, patient.

Mitch put a finger to his lips and looked hard at Samuel and Duval. This wasn't the time or place for a lecture, no matter how inspirational the surroundings.

Samuel grimaced, but Mitch was more irritated with Duval. She was supposed to be a professional and should have known better. Her cheeks flushed with embarrassment, and her lips tightened into a short line.

Satisfied, Mitch signaled for them to move out. He took point once more.

The ossuary turned out to also be a labyrinth. Passages split off the main one over and over, often, he guessed, leading to dead ends. Getting trapped in one of them could be disastrous if someone was following them, and making choice after choice put Mitch on edge.

At each intersection he glanced back at Juba and Samuel. Most times Juba silently indicated the proper direction, based on his calculations. Sometimes he motioned for the monk to consult with him in whispers so soft that Mitch couldn't hear them.

Each time they chose well, never winding up facing a blind tunnel filled with bones. Mitch noticed that they consistently were moving lower and lower through the maze, deeper and deeper into the earth.

As he rounded one corner, Mitch hauled himself up short. He turned and beckoned for Samuel to come forward.

As Samuel joined him, Mitch examined the tunnel before him. It widened out into a chamber at least the size of an aircraft hangar. The sides to the left and right fell away, and the far wall was the steel and concrete face of a modern skyscraper that over the centuries had sunk into the ground or been buried.

Mitch and Samuel led the team into the room, working their way over the fallen rubble. "The city of the ancients," Samuel said. "Buried five hundred years ago in the Black Winter."

"Holy shit," Duval said.

Steiner padded after them, bringing up the rear. "We're being watched," he said.

Mitch knew that but didn't see what they could do about it. Their only choice was to move forward as fast as possible and hope that whatever was hunting them wouldn't keep up.

The room's vaulted ceiling rose high over their heads, exposing three full floors of the building before them. The glass that had once filled the panels of the building's skin had long since been shattered and knocked away, and ancient, faded graffiti covered much of what was left.

Mitch stared at the scrawls and picked out the faces of mutants, demons, and things far worse: creatures made of stacked muscles torn from their victims, others with skin made of jagged razors. Images of blood covered everything, and Mitch could not tell if the red came from paint or was real.

There seemed to be five different sections, each dedicated to a different sort of depravity. He picked out words, names: Ilian, Semai, Demnogornis, Muawijhe, Algeroth.

The last name appeared over the row of empty windows

set at ground level next to an illustration of a massive beast with horns jutting from its insane head in three different directions. The eyes of the artwork seemed to glow with hate and followed Mitch no matter where he moved in the room.

Below the demonic creature someone had used blood to paint a crude sign in Latin. It read, RELINQUES TOTUS SPEC FORNICATORES MATRIS.

"Brother," Mitch said, trying to keep his voice steady. "What's it say?"

Brother Samuel looked more determined than ever as he translated the words aloud. "Abandon all hope."

He paused for a moment.

"Motherfuckers."

Behind them, El Jesus gasped, stunned. "No shit."

39

As the soldiers gaped at the skyscraper's violated facade, the sounds of stones scraping reverberated down the tunnel behind them. Each of them crouched at the ready, their weapons pointed back the way they'd come.

They stayed that way for a long moment, but nothing happened. Nothing came charging at them out of the darkness, howling for their blood. No mutants, no demons, nothing. Not even another sound from the tunnel's depths.

Mitch knew one thing for certain, though. That sound hadn't happened by itself. Someone had made it.

Steiner was right. They were being followed.

"Fuck," El Jesus said, summing it up.

Samuel pulled out the Book of Law to consult the Chronicles. Mitch leaned over the monk's shoulder and saw an engraving on one page that depicted the skyscraper's facade exactly. Someone had drawn an arrow that pointed into the dark maw of the lowest bank of shattered windows. Samuel tapped it with a thick finger. That was where they had to go.

Duval took point this time, her rifle at the ready. She moved like a lioness, heading for the window and the hallway of stone and steel beyond. The others followed close behind her. In those tight quarters, they would have to worry less about being clumped together and more about being separated and picked off.

As Mitch and the others joined Duval in the building, she

played her flashlight around the interior. On one surface opposite the windows, the bright beam revealed the golden shapes of demons carved in bas-relief. They looked like half-buried fossils emerging from the facade.

"What are these?" she whispered.

Samuel moved close and examined the shapes, almost brushing his fingers across them. Mitch half expected them to leap off the wall and try to strangle the monk, but they stayed there, trapped in the wall.

"I have no idea," the monk whispered back.

Juba pointed the team down a long hallway and signaled that they would eventually need to keep going down. Duval led them into it. They moved in single file, each of them ready to snap into action at the barest sound.

At the end of the hall, Duval entered a room and moved to the side, covering the others and letting them push in after her. The walls were covered with ornate carvings and gold trim that had long since tarnished with the grime of untold centuries. In the wall opposite the entrance stood a set of rusted elevator doors.

Juba stepped up and pressed the down button to call the elevator car. It crumbled to dust at his touch. He looked over his shoulder to see El Jesus gaping at him. In response, he just shrugged.

The time for the subtle approach was over, Mitch decided. Whoever was following them knew they were there. If they stayed there too long, their pursuers would eventually decide to attack. Better to move along before that happened.

Mitch stepped up and gave a vicious kick to the center of the elevator doors. The bulk of them disintegrated into rust-colored dust on contact, and the few remaining shards tipped over into the shaft beyond.

An elevator car hung there, stuck between floors, caught halfway down to their floor. Mitch grabbed the edge of the car's floor and gave it a good tug. It held.

Satisfied that he wouldn't be cut in half, Mitch knelt down and poked his head into the shaft beneath the car. There was plenty of room for them to slip underneath it, even Steiner, who still carried the bomb on his back.

A rusty cable snaked down past the car, disappearing in the darkness below. Mitch spit into the shaft but never heard it hit.

Mitch pulled himself back into the room and nodded at the others. Severian handed each of them a winch they could attach to their combat harnesses and to the cable. Mitch had used one of them before and suspected the others had as well—except Brother Samuel—as it came with most megacorps' basic training. With it, they could control their rate of descent and even winch themselves back upward in a pinch.

The trick to all this, of course, was making sure no one dropped the elevator car or anything else on top of them as they slipped down the shaft. While on the cable, they'd be easy targets with nowhere to go.

"We don't want them coming down on top of us," Mitch said. The other soldiers were professionals. They knew a call for a volunteer when they heard it.

"I got it," Juba said.

It was a dangerous assignment, everyone in the room knew, but Juba seemed to have a good handle on it. He walked up to the shaft and tried to pry the elevator's inner doors open with his bare hands. Normally, he might have been able to manage it, but the rust made it nearly impossible.

El Jesus came over to give him a hand. They each took one of the pair of sliding doors in their hands and, on the count of three, pulled.

The doors groaned open, loud like a scream. Everyone winced at the sound, but it couldn't be helped.

Juba tossed his pack inside the elevator car, then hauled himself into it. The car juddered for a moment, shaking with the Mishiman's weight. Mitch heard him hold his breath. Hell, everyone else did too. They only let it loose once the shaking stopped.

Mitch craned his neck up to get a good look into the car. A full third of the floor was missing, a huge hole open straight down into the shaft below.

Juba got to his knees and began to pull bits and pieces out of his pack and lay them in a row on the floor, positioned so they could not roll away. Mitch recognized the metallic parts as augmentations for the man's rifle. Mishima always excelled at weapons customization, and Juba seemed a fine student of that art.

From what Mitch could see, the man had a belt feed, a bi-pod, a water-cooled barrel, and a grenade launcher to trick out his rifle. When he was done with it, he'd have a whole new gun, one that would be perfect for blasting away at hordes of mutants from a locked position. He applauded the Mishiman's forethought.

El Jesus hadn't moved from his spot since Juba had climbed up into the car. Mitch wondered if the big man thought he could pull the Mishiman out of the car if it started to fall. More likely he'd kill himself trying.

"Not the safest place to be," El Jesus said to Juba.

Without a smile or even a glance away from his task, Juba responded. "Gotta pay for those tickets sooner or later." He screwed the last pieces in place and finally allowed himself a ghost of a grin.

"*Verdad.*"

Juba and El Jesus hit fists.

Once Juba was ready, Mitch leaned in under the car and secured his winch to the thick, rusty cable. He gave the clamp a good tug. Despite the rust, it held tight.

"Brother," Mitch said.

The monk came over and knelt next to Mitch at the mouth of the shaft. He had an oil lantern with him to light their way. Mitch didn't care much for relying on an open flame while entering an unknown area underground. All it would take was one loose gas main to ruin their whole day.

Samuel looked down the shaft and swallowed hard. Mitch could tell from looking at the man that he'd never done something like this before, but he wasn't going to let that stop him.

Still, Mitch planned to go down before Samuel, and he didn't want the man coming down on top of him and knocking them both to their deaths. It was time for a quick lesson.

Mitch attached his winch and then swung his legs out over the pitch-black abyss. He tested the harness once more, then slipped off the edge and lowered himself a little way down the shaft. Severian helped Samuel get into his rig just above Mitch.

Juba poked his head in next to him. "Jesus, that's deep."

"Sixty stories," Samuel said. He looked down at Mitch. "We'll go first and let the others find the way."

"What he said," Mitch said to Juba. He reached up and pointed at his winch. It was a simple bit of machinery, but you still had to know how it worked to not kill yourself with it.

"All right, Brother. This is the brake. Lift it up and let yourself down. Punch it in and you stop. That's it. Take it easy."

The monk reached out to thumb a small lever. "And this?"

Mitch shouted a warning, and the monk's hand froze.

"That's the quick release." Mitch grunted. "Don't touch anything."

Samuel nodded, then blew out a long breath. He wouldn't admit it, but the words in the tunnel had shaken him. The shaft was all he'd needed to push him over the edge.

"All right," Mitch said. He kept his voice as calm and

easy as he could, as if they were headed down to the park for a quick walk. "Let's go."

Mitch put his hand on Samuel's arm and slipped over the edge of the shaft. As he went, he pulled the monk down with him. Their winches whined, their handles spinning like mad, as the two men dropped down into the unknown.

40

Mitch looked up to make sure Samuel was all right. They came down at a good but controlled clip, and the monk seemed to be handling it all right.

Light streamed in through the gated openings from the other floors into the shaft. For a moment, Mitch wondered where the light could be coming from, but he figured he might be better off not knowing—or alerting anything that might have put the lights there.

"Twenty," Samuel said, counting off the floors.

Mitch groaned. "How fucking deep is this thing?" He knew Samuel had said sixty stories, but it didn't seem possible.

Above, as a silhouette framed in the small rectangle of light streaming in from the elevator lobby, Severian leaned into the shaft and attached her winch to the line.

El Jesus came soon after her, then Duval, with Steiner behind her. They came down as fast as the winches would safely let them, staying a good length apart. Mitch breathed a sigh of amazement when he saw that the cable could actually hold six fully armed people, including one carrying a bomb, not to mention Juba, still stationed up in the car.

"Ah, it's getting hot down here," said Mitch. He wiped the sweat from his brow with his sleeve.

"Forty," said the monk.

The shaft kept going and going, with no end in sight. The

lights from the sides of the shaft stopped, and they had nothing but darkness ahead.

"Fifty-five," Samuel said.

A moment later the monk muttered to himself, "How far?" Then he called out, "Stop."

Mitch thumbed the brake on his winch gently and slowed to a stop. He hung there, suspended in the darkness. Samuel shoved his brake all the way over and came to a hard stop that shook the cable up and down its entire length. He growled in pain as his back bent over the wrong way.

Mitch looked up at the monk. It looked like his fall might have jerked the clamp of his winch loose from the cable.

"Sixty."

"We're running out of rope here," Mitch said.

"We've gone too far," Samuel said, his voice shaking with both effort and concern.

Mitch tried to peer into the blackness around him and realized he could see nothing. "It's dark. God, it's dark."

"Something's not right," Samuel said, his voice thick with pain.

Samuel pulled something out of his pack and put the end of it into the flame burning in his oil lamp. The flare burst into fire, emitting a dazzling light that cast the monk in a reddish hue. He dropped the flare, and it tumbled past Mitch into the darkness below.

Mitch swung his head around to see where the flare had gone. It kept falling, tipping end over end and growing smaller and smaller until all that was left was a tiny spark in the distance.

Mitch looked up to see Samuel's face sag as he watched the flare keep going.

"It can't be," the monk said.

Mitch growled. "Got anything in that damned book?"

"What have I missed?"

Mitch gritted his teeth as Samuel pulled his leather-bound book from where he'd tucked it over his heart, inside his robes. He fumbled with the book and nearly dropped it as he brought his lamp up high enough to read by its light. He flipped through the pages with frantic speed, looking for a passage to provide them guidance.

From far above, Mitch could hear the others talking.

"Don't fall behind, Steiner," Duval said. "It's a long way down.

"Yeah," Steiner said, "all the way to hell."

The cable started to vibrate in Mitch's hand, and he looked up past Samuel to see Severian and the others on their way.

Then he heard something shuffling in the darkness below him. He couldn't tell how far away it might be. He only hoped it didn't know he was there.

"Weird sounds down here, pal." He did his best to keep his voice calm despite the fact that he wanted to reach up and rip the book out of the man's hands. This was not a library, and they needed to get out of the shaft as fast as they could.

Samuel ignored Mitch entirely, concentrating on the book. "It has to be here. Fifty-five, sixty floors down. There should be a ledge. It says so right here. It has to be."

The cable started to shake harder and faster as the others drew closer. The sympathetic vibrations knocked Samuel's winch again and again until it finally popped free.

Mitch didn't even have time to curse as the monk tumbled past him. His hand darted out and grabbed the book by the binding, right around the place at which the chain was anchored to it.

As Samuel fell, the chain snapped taut, and the monk's sudden weight threatened to rip Mitch's arm from its socket. Worse yet, the winch meant to hold Mitch to the rusty cable—one fully armed man—now held two. It groaned loudly over Mitch's head, and he knew it would only be seconds before its clamp's grip gave up, just as Samuel's winch had.

"Do not let me fall," Samuel said, his voice straining with pain. The shackle from the book's chain cut into his flesh, even as it kept him from falling to his doom.

"Brother," Mitch said as he tried to keep hold of the man swaying below him, "I'm trying."

Mitch could feel the links on the chain start to stretch and give way. The chain had been forged to hold a book to a man, not a man to a book.

Mitch tried to pull the monk up. He reached for him with his other hand in a desperate attempt to reach him before the chain broke. Doing that and keeping his balance on the winch proved nearly impossible, but he meant to try.

He leaned back as far as he could, and Samuel reached up for his hand. They were still more than a good foot apart when the chain snapped and the monk tumbled into the darkness.

41

Mitch started to shout in protest, but he never had a decent chance. Just as he was about to curse the monk, the chain, the cable, and everything else in the whole damned world, Brother Samuel stopped falling.

The bottom of the lift shaft ended up being right below them, just out of sight. About half of the floor had collapsed, though, into what seemed like a bottomless pit. When Samuel had thrown the flare, it had gone straight into the pit, but when he'd fallen he had landed on the part of the floor that was still there.

Lying on his back, bruised and aching but alive, Samuel looked up at Mitch in stunned silence. Then the monk threw back his head and laughed. Mitch was so relieved, he couldn't help joining in.

"Brother," Mitch said, wiping the tears from his eyes, "you are one lucky son of a bitch."

Samuel sat up and recovered his lantern. "God provides, Sergeant," he said as he got to his feet. "God provides."

He was going to say more but cut himself off when the light from his lamp fell on a mutant standing right next to him on the ledge. His tongue froze in his mouth as he tried to twist away from the creature lunging at him, slashing with its boneblade.

He was a hair too slow. The blade sliced through his robes

and cut into his side. It glanced off his ribs, though, rather than cutting through them.

Mitch thumbed over the quick-release lever on his winch. He slid straight down the rope and landed on the mutant, smashing it to the ground. Unfazed, it struggled like mad, trying to throw him off.

Mitch pumped two rounds from his pistol right into the thing's chest, but he might as well have kissed it. It snarled and twisted under his feet, tossing Mitch toward the nearest wall.

As the mutant stood up, Mitch lashed out with his foot and kicked it back toward the pit. As it fell, it grabbed at the cable and snagged it. It used its momentum to swing around the rusted line and come back to grab the pit's edge.

Mitch swore under his breath and prepared to empty an entire clip into the thing as it climbed up from the pit again. He had no idea if that would stop it, but he intended to try.

Before he could pull the trigger, though, someone grabbed him from behind. Mitch wound up inside another elevator lobby with Samuel hauling him in. Together they flung themselves forward and slammed shut the elevator gate just as the mutant leaped up to attack. It slammed into the other side of the metal bars, trying to batter them down, but the gate held—for now.

The two men leaned their hands against the doors, keeping them wedged closed as they caught their breath. As they did, someone opened up with automatic weapons fire far up the shaft.

It could only be Juba, Mitch knew. That meant the mutants had finally caught up with them from that direction too.

"They're bottled up in there," Mitch said. He couldn't leave the others in the shaft to die. With mutants coming at them from both directions, they wouldn't stand a chance.

Mitch drew his sword and prepared to open the door. He hadn't had a lot of training with long blades like this, but he figured it couldn't be much worse than a knife fight. He'd been in plenty of those.

"Wait!" Samuel grabbed Mitch's arm before the soldier could pry open the doors.

Mitch snarled at the monk and tore his arm free. Then, by way of explanation, Samuel smashed the glass of his lantern against the steel elevator doors. Burning oil dripped out of the center of it as he handed what was left of the lamp to Mitch. He nodded at the monk, finally understanding the man's plan.

Up above, the gunfire suddenly stopped. Mitch winced. Had the mutants brought Juba down? Would they come sliding down into the shaft any second now?

Then the barrage of bullets started again. Apparently Juba had just needed to reload. That meant he was still alive, although Mitch wondered how much longer that would be true.

Over the racket from Juba's gun, Mitch heard El Jesus yammering, "We got an ugly down here!"

Mitch held the broken lantern in one hand and his sword in the other. He nodded at Samuel to move, and the monk hauled open the doors.

From somewhere up above, Steiner said something, but the creaking of the door drowned it out.

As soon as the elevator doors opened, the mutant leaped at Mitch and the monk. Mitch smashed the broken lamp into the mutant's face, and the creature burst into flames.

The burning oil didn't seem to hurt the mutant at all, but at least the fire blinded it. Mitch dived at the creature with his sword, hacking away at it.

Above him, he heard Duval say something, the same word Steiner had used. It sounded suspiciously like "Grenade!" Between the chatter of Juba's gun, the horrible acoustics of the elevator shaft, and the blazing mutant slashing at him, though, he couldn't be sure.

The mutant circled warily, listening for the sound of

Mitch's footsteps as Mitch swerved around the room. As he went, he swept Samuel along with his free arm, keeping himself between the monster and the monk. Taking the hint, Samuel moved back into the elevator shaft, getting as far away from the fight as he could.

Mitch ducked beneath a wild slash of the mutant's burning boneblade, then stood up and delivered a two-handed blow to the creature's neck. Its head went spinning off into the corner. Meanwhile, its body kept flailing about, not seeming to give a damn about the fate of its cranium.

Mitch gritted his teeth and started hacking away at the mutant in earnest. His first cut removed the creature's left arm. The next sliced through both its legs at the knees. Then he brought his blade around in a mighty swing that chopped the creature's chest in half.

The mutant collapsed in pieces at Mitch's feet. It still twitched like mad but was no longer any kind of threat.

Mitch glanced over at Samuel and saw the man peering back at him from inside the shaft. It was then that he remembered what he thought he'd heard Duval shout. He started toward the shaft, even though he knew he'd be too late.

Samuel looked up then and flinched as he saw the grenade coming at him. He put up his arms in a pointless attempt to shield himself.

Mitch could hear the grenade's timing coil whining. It was just about to detonate.

Just as the grenade was about to smack into the monk, a hand snaked down from above and seized it. The fingers clamped down on the timing coil, stopping it and keeping the grenade from going off.

Mitch dashed to the shaft to see Severian and her arm attached to the hand that held the grenade. She hung upside down from her harness, her winch groaning from the strain. She must have slid down most of the shaft at top speed to be able to have caught the damned thing in time. Her winch glowed red hot from the friction.

El Jesus whizzed to a braking stop just above her. "*Chingame!* Girl, don't you drop that match."

Still silent, Severian reached up and popped the release on her winch's clamp. She flipped over as she fell, landing next to Samuel with the grace of an acrobat, the grenade still clutched in her fist.

Mitch stared at the grenade and saw how little of the timing coil was left. If Severian hadn't snagged it, it would have killed them both for sure.

The woman crept to the edge of the pit and hurled the grenade down it with all her might. Mitch peered over the edge to watch it as it fell. Not even twenty yards down, it exploded, lighting up the floor below.

Mutants covered the floor from one side to another, and the grenade had barely hurt any of them. Once the initial surprise at the explosion wore off, they looked up and spotted Mitch and the others looking down at them.

The mutants knew they were there.

42

Juba had not had a good day. He'd thought he'd known what he'd ordered up for himself when he had volunteered to take up this defensive position, but even his worst fears had been horribly naïve. He figured that with his gun he was the best equipped of the soldiers to hold off a pack of mutants.

He just hadn't counted on a whole damned horde.

As the others had slipped down the shaft on their whizzing harnesses, he'd waited silently, listening for any hint of an intruder. He'd heard the noises following them as they'd made their way through the ossuary and then in through the building to the elevator lobby. He knew they were coming, but he hadn't imagined how many.

After waiting for half of forever, Juba had heard the sounds again: scritching and scratching down the long hallway that separated the elevator car from that horrible entrance into the building. He had imagined the mutants sharpening their boneblades by rubbing them along any piece of metal they could find, unable to stop themselves, like a dog licking an open wound. When the sounds had gotten close enough, he had lit a flare and chucked it down the hallway as far as he could.

It had landed in front of a wall of mutants that stretched back down the hall as far as he could see.

That was when Juba had started firing.

The bullets slammed into the mutants and through them, picking them apart bit by bit. He wondered if he shouldn't have gone with high-explosive bullets or at least dum-dum cartridges. They would have had more stopping power, but they were almost impossible to find in belts. He'd opted for more instead of better bullets. Quantity over quality.

It seemed the maker of the mutants, whoever or whatever that might be, had made the same choice. Juba's storm of slugs chipped away at mutant after mutant, eventually putting down each one that charged into his field of fire. As each one fell, though, another charged forward to take its place.

When the belt had run through, Juba's hands were vibrating so much that he felt like the gun was still firing. Without a word, he reached down and grabbed the end of a second belt from his bag. He fed it into the gun as steam rose from the glowing barrel. Water-cooled or not, he had to take care or his weapon would soon jam. Until the crushing wave of mutants coming down the hallway stopped, though, that would be the least of his problems.

By the time Juba ran through the second belt, his arms hurt from hosing down the oncoming horde. He'd blasted them back a bit farther this time, and he hoped that would give him more time to reload. He set the butt of the gun down on the elevator floor and reached down into his pack to grab the third and final ammo belt.

Before he could start to feed it in, though, he heard a scratching on the roof of the car. He had just enough time to take up his gun before the mutant dropped down through a hole in the ceiling to land next to him.

With no bullets in his gun, Juba fired the gun's attached grenade launcher instead, but the tight quarters of an elevator missing a chunk of its floor made that difficult. As he squeezed the trigger, the mutant knocked the long barrel upward.

The grenade punched through the ceiling of the elevator

car. Juba held his breath, then looked into the blood-mad eyes of the mutant standing before him. It had no idea what was coming next.

The grenade exploded above the car. The blast severed the cable holding the car in the air, and it began to slide straight down the shaft.

In free fall, the car plummeted, sending up a shower of sparks every time its sides scraped the inside of the shaft. Despite the insane danger, the mutant kept fighting. It leveled a savage blow at Juba that sheared through his gun's red-hot barrel and sliced into his shoulder beneath.

Dropping the rifle, Juba wrestled out his sword and smashed the mutant in the face with the hilt as he freed it. As he struggled with the beast, its foot knocked over his pack, and a box inside of it tipped over. The lid gave way, and a dozen grenades tumbled out.

The sword was too long to use properly in the elevator, so Juba half-sworded it, gripping it about the blade. The razor-sharp steel went straight through his skin and cut his fingers to the bone, but he ignored the blood and pain.

He parried another slash of the mutant's boneblade, then smashed it back with his blade. Every blow was agony for him, but he kept on fighting, refusing to surrender. He was going to die either way, but he'd be damned if he'd let this bastard kill him.

Despite his efforts, the mutant stabbed him in his shoulder with its boneblade again, and he dropped his sword. The creature slashed down at him again, and he reached up and caught the blade flat between his palms.

The mutant stared at him, surprised. In a heartbeat, he had his sidearm out.

The mutant came at him with its boneblade again, but he caught the creature's elbow with his hand. Seeing his chance, he stuffed his pistol up into the mutant's armpit and fired, blowing the creature's arm clean off. While it stared in dumb amazement, Juba reversed the now-free arm and jammed the tip of it right through the mutant's mouth, pinning the creature to the wall behind it.

Still falling faster than ever, Juba glanced down the hole in the car's floor. There he saw the bottom of the shaft choked wall to wall with mutants. He smiled and prepared to say hello to his ancestors, knowing they would welcome him with open arms.

This would be a good death.

43

As Juba gunned down row after row of mutants from the elevator car high above, Mitch and El Jesus stood at the edge of the hole in the bottom of the shaft, doing the same to the creatures trying to crawl up through it.

Mitch fired burst after burst from his M50, picking his targets one at a time. He tried to hit the ones that stood atop the shoulders of others, hoping that he could knock a whole line of them off the wall at once. They rarely came off more than two or three at a time, though.

He stuck to the top and right side of the wall while El Jesus took the bottom and left. The big man's shotgun created craters wherever his white phosphorus shells struck, raining burning destruction down on anything below.

Still, the bastards kept coming.

Just as Mitch was about to exhaust his clip, he felt something land behind him. He glanced over his shoulder to see Duval unhitching herself from the cable. A moment later Steiner landed next to her and did the same.

With those two clear, it was time to go. The only one left up top was Juba, and he would have to survive on his own. Mitch hoped the man would find some way to escape from all this alive. If not, he hoped Juba sold his life dearly.

Duval and Steiner moved into the lower elevator lobby first, then unlimbered their weapons and prepared to lay down covering fire. Mitch backhanded El Jesus on the shoulder, and the two of them dashed back toward the lobby to join the others. Mitch stuffed a fresh clip into his gun as he turned around.

The four of them stood at the far end of the lobby, showering the mutants with a leadstorm as they swarmed out of the pit. Despite the amount of metal flying through the air, the mutants continued to make progress. Mitch knew they'd have to fall back soon, but to where?

"I'm out!" El Jesus said. With the mutants this close, he had no time to reload his shotgun. Instead he dropped back and drew his sword.

Steiner was next. "*Leer!*" the man said. He dropped both of his machine pistols to the floor and pulled his blade.

That left only Mitch and Duval with loaded guns. Mitch began to choose his targets more carefully, firing even shorter bursts. Despite his best efforts, the mutants continued to pour up into the elevator shaft. It would only be a matter of time before they joined the soldiers in the lobby.

Mitch's assault rifle finally ran dry. He tossed it aside in favor of his sword. He drew the sword quicky and took up a defensive stance between Steiner and El Jesus.

Duval's rifle came up empty then too. With nothing to deter them, the mutants began to crawl out of the shaft and into the lobby.

The men held their ground as Duval struggled to reload her weapon. Mitch glanced backward to see Severian step between Samuel and the coming horde. He stood there behind her, his sword in one hand and his book—now unattached—in the other.

"Any last words?" Steiner asked.

Mitch scowled at the man. "Shut the fuck up." He had nothing profound to say and didn't want to hear any feeble attempts from anyone else.

A horrible screeching sound came screaming out of the elevator shaft. For an instant, Mitch wondered if some new and different kind of mutant had come out to play now that the others nearly had them cornered.

Then the elevator car slammed into the bottom of the shaft like a meteor smashing into a moon. Dust and debris showered out of the shaft and into the lobby. If that kind of impact had happened outside, Mitch would have expected to see a mushroom cloud. Instead, the mess was forced in the only two directions available to it: up the shaft and into the lobby.

For a long moment, Mitch couldn't see a thing past the tip of his sword. The dust obscured everything. Whatever had happened, it had bought the soldiers some time. Now they had to take advantage of that.

"Reload!" Mitch said while the dust still hung in the air. He had no idea if anything could have survived that crash, but fate had given them a chance to go back to their guns. He meant to take it.

As Duval slapped a new clip into her weapon, Mitch and Steiner scooped up their guns and began changing the clips. El Jesus did the same with his shotgun, thumbing fresh shells into the weapon's magazine.

When the dust started to settle, the entire team stood locked and loaded, ready to go. Mitch took the point and nosed forward, his gun before him, and he peered down into the lift shaft. The wreck of the elevator car lay crumpled there, blocking off the pit. Rubble had fallen over everything, covering the remnants of the car.

Mitch looked up, wondering if Juba had managed to get out. Had the man sent the car plummeting down as a way to save the rest of them? If he was still alive, was he trapped up top or working his way down the shaft? Had he managed to stop the mutants that had been following them above? If not, why didn't Mitch hear any more shots?

Before Mitch could spend more time pondering Juba's fate, the rubble at the bottom of the shaft began to shift and move. A leg pushed free from the broken concrete, then an arm, then one boneblade and another.

Mitch swore and readied his gun to start blasting away at the creatures as soon as they were clear. Duval, Steiner, and El Jesus stood shoulder to shoulder with him, worn and dirty but ready to try it all over again.

Maybe the crash had killed some of them, Mitch thought, or at least sealed the top of the pit. Maybe some good had come of it. Maybe they still had a chance.

None of those possibilities sounded convincing in Mitch's head, especially as more and more of the mutants shoved the rubble off themselves and started toward him, snarling with inhuman rage as they rasped their boneblades across each other.

As the mutants moved forward, one of them pushed aside a massive piece of rubble, exposing a human arm still attached to a buried body. Blood trickled from the arm, red and fresh, and Mitch recognized the sleeve as Juba's.

The Mishiman's hand fell open then, and the grenade in it flopped out and rolled through the legs of one of the mutants. The creature looked down at it, but Mitch didn't see what happened next. He and the other soldiers had already turned to dive away.

44

"Down!" Mitch shouted.

Juba, as Mitch remembered, had been carrying a lot of ordnance. Besides the three belts of ammo, he'd had an entire box of grenades with him, plus who knew what else. When the grenade that tumbled from his dead hand went off, it must have blown everything else the man had with him, too.

The shock wave from the explosion knocked the entire squad off its feet. It carried Mitch clear across the elevator lobby to tumble against the far wall. As he fell back to the ground, he saw the others roll up against the back wall too.

The blast itself had deafened Mitch, so he didn't hear the shaft fall in on itself as much as he felt it. The ground shook and rumbled for only a few seconds, filling the room with thick dust once more, blinding Mitch as well. He curled himself into a ball against the back wall, covering his head as well as he could, and waited to learn his fate.

For a while it was so quiet that Mitch didn't know if it was all over or if he'd gone entirely deaf. Then he heard Samuel coughing out a lungful of dust.

Mitch struggled to his feet and peered back toward the shaft. As the clouds of dust settled once more, he saw that the doorway to the shaft was entirely blocked. Stones had filled the bottom of the shaft higher than the doorway. A pile of them had slipped into the room as well, going from the floor halfway into the place, all the way up to the top of the doorway.

"Anybody hurt?"

The six of them were safe from the mutants for now. Even if some of the creatures still lived or were streaming up from the pit, there was no way they were getting past that landslide of rubble.

Juba, of course, was gone.

Duval walked up to the rubble and stared at it as if she might be able to make it move with her eyes. When nothing happened, she lowered her gaze and bit her bottom lip.

"Hey, shit," El Jesus said.

Mitch nodded a final salute toward the man's resting place and then began to look around. Steiner and Severian had already started to hunt for some way out of the room. Samuel, meanwhile, faced where the elevator doors had been and muttered a benediction for Juba in Gaelic.

"Let's go," El Jesus said. "Let's go." As eager as he was, he still looked for others to lead the way, and they had no better options to offer than he.

There had only been two other ways out of the elevator lobby, and they had been sealed off too. Whether that had happened years or seconds ago, Mitch wasn't sure, but it hardly mattered. The fact was there was no way out of the room. They were trapped.

"Dead end," Duval said. Her voice had lost its usual sense of wonder.

"Who's got a deck of cards?" El Jesus said. The big man put down his shotgun and cracked his knuckles.

"MacGuire," said Duval.

El Jesus shook his head at the bitter joke. "Figures."

Steiner took up his sword again and went over to one of the blocked exits. The rocks flowing out of the collapsed stairwell had wrenched the door off its hinges. The ober-leutnant prodded at the broken bits of concrete with his blade, looking for a sign of weakness.

Looking grim, Samuel staggered over to the rocks in front of the elevator doors and sat down on the pile. He opened the Book of Law on his lap and began to flip through the Chronicles, searching for some kind of guidance.

Severian followed Samuel and stood over him as he pored through the book. When it became clear he didn't need her direct attention, she reached into her uniform and pulled out a chocolate bar. She spotted Mitch watching her and the monk, and she fished out another bar and handed it to him.

"Thanks," Mitch said, accepting her kindness.

In one corner, Samuel sat reading from his book. "They use tunnels to drag bodies to the Machine. It takes days, even weeks."

Finishing the chocolate, Mitch sat down next to Samuel and peered at the book. Whatever language it was in, he couldn't read a word of it.

"You got a lot of faith in that book."

Samuel allowed himself a wan smile, then shut the book's cover. "It's a very good book, Hunter. But in the end, even this book is just a book."

"You're a priest."

"Yes." He patted the leather-bound cover. "And I place my faith in something greater."

Mitch lowered his voice, speaking confidentially. He didn't like to talk about religion—or his lack of it—much. He didn't aspire to have any for himself, but he didn't see the point in tearing down what others had.

"Haven't seen much to have faith in," he said, no trace of bitterness in his voice. He'd gone beyond anger over the state of the worlds and accepted them for the horrors they held.

Samuel nodded. "You have seen the worst that Man can do." He looked Mitch right in the eyes. "But you have not seen the worst the Enemy can do."

Across the room, Steiner and Duval kept digging away at

the wall of rock. All they seemed to be doing was taking up more of the space in the room they were in, but they didn't question that and didn't stop working.

"So who got the tickets?" Duval said as she took a rock that Steiner handed to her.

"What?" The oberleutnant stopped, a large stone in his hands. The man hadn't been involved in the discussion on the skyship, and Duval's directness surprised him.

Unfazed, Duval persisted. "Your tickets."

Mitch shook his head. He could see the woman just would not let this go. He wondered then about Adelaide and Grace and if they'd made it offworld by now. He glanced up at the ceiling and realized he was so stuck on Earth it had buried him.

Steiner reached into his jacket and pulled out an envelope. He tossed it aside, and it fluttered to the ground. Mitch recognized the envelope, as did Duval. Their tickets had come in ones just like it. "Who cares?"

Duval looked up at Steiner. "I'm sorry," she said.

Mitch then realized what she had figured out. It wasn't that Steiner had held the tickets back. He didn't have anyone to give them to.

Steiner ignored her, though, and stayed focused on digging out the stairwell. El Jesus joined them, and she went back to work too, each of them now silent.

Samuel spoke to Mitch. "Do you understand what the Enemy is, Hunter? This Dark Star cast from heaven?"

It sounded like a bunch of bullshit, but Mitch shook his head.

The monk put his hands in front of him as he explained. "Everything that is comes from God. Everything you can see and feel, taste, touch—everything—is from God and of God."

Samuel paused for a moment to let that sink in. If he expected Mitch to counter his statement, he was disappointed.

"The Enemy is not of God. It came from outside. And as God is life, the Enemy is unlife. It is the end of every living thing, everywhere. For all time."

Mitch grimaced at the monk and left it at that.

"So I have faith that we will triumph," Samuel said. "Because the alternative is too terrible to contemplate."

"What if you don't believe in God?"

A hint of a smile curled Samuel's lips. "If you did not believe in God, you would not be here."

Mitch grunted to himself. He wasn't so sure he bought the monk's argument. He'd believed in helping his best friend's wife and kid. That was what had brought him here.

When he thought about it, though, Mitch realized he would have come along either way if he'd known what was really at stake. Back in that bar near Addy's cottage, he hadn't been sure he trusted what Samuel had told him. It had all sounded like the desperate ravings of a lunatic who took his literature too seriously. The tickets had convinced him that he didn't need to believe in what Samuel told him. They'd been reason enough for him to buy in.

Now that he was here, though, and had been through all this—now that it seemed they would all die here together—he knew that he'd have come either way. Fighting for the survival of humanity, even if there was only a small chance of it, beat the hell out of fighting for his corporation any day.

El Jesus stood up and groaned, wiping his face with his hands. "Hey, you guys gonna help?" he said to the monk. "Maybe you haven't noticed, but your mission is kind of fucked."

Samuel nodded, then removed a bottle of holy water from his robes.

Mitch bit his tongue. No blessing would get them out of here, no matter how heartfelt it might be.

"You should have a little faith." Samuel looked at El Jesus as he spoke, but he might as well have been talking to Mitch.

The monk poured the entire bottle of water onto the ground. Mitch thought about grabbing his wrist and stopping him but discarded the notion. After all, if they were trapped, the water would only mean a few more hours of life in this hole, tops, and what difference would that make?

Mitch and the others watched as the water trickled away from the center of the floor. It rolled slowly through the dust and around the stones in its way as it ran toward the corner across from the collapsed stairwell at which Steiner, El Jesus, and Duval had been working.

There it flowed down through a pair of small circular holes set in the floor.

45

Mitch made it to the grate first. "Give me a hand," he said.

He and Steiner cleared the rubble from it, and El Jesus reached down and pried it up with his bare hands. Beneath it stood a hole more than large enough for even the big man to fit through, fully loaded.

He stared down into it and allowed himself half a smile. "Something's down there."

Mitch got down on his knees and shone his light into the opening. Water trickled across the floor below, soft and shallow but steady. He leaned his head into the hole, half expecting a mutant to leap forward and slice it off.

Nothing happened.

He found himself staring down a tunnel—a wide pipe, actually—that led off into the darkness in both directions. He looked back and motioned for the others to be silent. Then he lowered himself down through the hole.

Mitch winced at the soft splash he made as he landed in the water, but it couldn't be helped. He shone his flashlight in either direction but saw nothing. The pipe ran off in both directions as far as the beam could reach. He backed up from the opening and signaled for the others to join him.

He thumbed the safety off his M50 and tried to cover both ends of the tunnel as the rest of the crew splashed down into the pipe one by one. Once they were all there, they looked at each other, wondering which direction they should take. Samuel pointed at the way the water flowed, and Mitch nodded in agreement.

Duval took point. Although Mitch guessed he could fight better than she would, she moved more quietly than anyone but Severian. The lady monk, though, could not speak and did not have the small-group training of the soldiers, so Duval got the job.

They made their way down the tunnel, moving as fast and quietly as they could. They followed its twists and turns until a soft light showed as a small disk in the distance.

Duval stole ahead to check it out while the others crept up behind her. When she became a silhouette framed in the circle at the end of the pipe, Mitch realized how much the tunnel seemed like the barrel of a gun. He wondered from which direction the bullets it fired might come.

Duval froze and stared out at the scene before her for a moment. Then she leaned back to signal the others to join her quietly. As they reached her, she moved off to the left.

When Mitch got to the opening of the pipe, he could barely believe his eyes. The water from the pipe flowed into a large tunnel and trickled fifteen feet down into a wide, open sewer that carried it away.

The line of mutants marching below didn't seem to notice the intruders. They kept their heads down, staring only at their feet or the back of the mutant before them. Overhead, stalactites formed from crud that had leaked through cracks in the ceiling hung like teeth on the inside of a monstrous mouth.

These mutants didn't have boneblades like the ones the squad had fought earlier, but hooks made of the same material, as gray and dead as the rest of their flesh. They walked at a steady pace in an unceasing line that ran in either direction as far as Mitch could see. Each of them carried a human body on its back.

Most of the people atop the mutants were dead, but a few

still breathed. They struggled feebly, barely alive, moaning and crying, even praying.

More than anything else, Mitch wanted to leap down into the tunnel and start hosing the mutants down. To do so would be suicide, he knew. Even if these worker mutants couldn't slice at him like the others, there were enough of them to bring him down with their bare hands. His ammo couldn't hold out forever, and sooner or later his arms would tire of swinging his sword.

That way lay doom.

Gritting his teeth, Mitch followed the others as they moved in single file down a narrow ledge that ran along the top of the tunnel. They crept forward as quietly as they could, each knowing that a single misstep could alert the mutants to their presence and kill them all.

Just yards from where they'd entered the tunnel, they came to a fissure in the rock. It formed a passageway that led away from the tunnel.

Duval signaled a stop. They all looked to Samuel to see which way to go.

"Poor bastards," El Jesus said, peering down at the mutants and their prisoners moving through the passage below. "Looks like they've been down there for weeks."

"We mustn't linger here," Samuel said.

"Where the hell are they taking them?" Mitch stared down at the line of people being borne off to some horrific fate by those who had been there before them. As he did, his eyes fell on a familiar face hanging over one mutant's back, and his blood ran cold.

"Is that—? Jesus, it's Nathan."

Mitch leaned over the ledge and stared. He didn't question how his friend had gotten there or how they'd managed to cross paths at just this point. He just locked his eyes on the man, searching for some sign of life.

"Sergeant?" Samuel whispered, curious about what could have made the soldier stop.

Mitch ignored him. At the moment, he didn't give a damn about the mission. Saving the world could wait until he was sure that he couldn't go back and fix his latest failure. Just when he was about to give up, to salute his dead friend and carry on in his memory, Nathan coughed.

"Hunter," the monk said, his curiosity turning to urgency. The longer they stayed on that ledge, the more they endangered their mission. They had to move along.

"I know him," Mitch said softly, jerking his chin at Nathan.

"Top?" El Jesus said.

Mitch didn't take his eyes off his friend as the mutant carrying him slowly marched past.

"It's Nathan."

El Jesus sucked at his teeth. "Fuck."

Mitch moved to follow the line of mutants. He didn't have to dive in and save Nathan now. He could bide his time, see where they took him, and make his move when the time was right—if that ever happened.

Samuel grabbed Mitch's arm. Mitch glared at the monk and pulled his elbow free.

"He's just one man," Samuel said. He didn't have to say that Mitch's concerns didn't measure up against saving the whole damned world. Mitch knew that. He didn't care.

"I know that man."

Steiner stepped up and shoved a gun in Mitch's face. He could smell the oil in the barrel.

"We have a mission," the oberleutnant said.

Mitch saw El Jesus's hands tighten on his shotgun, but he didn't know whose play the big man would back. Normally, he would have counted on the corporal's loyalty, but the welfare of a planet might have outweighed that in his mind.

Mitch stared deep into Steiner's eyes and waited. If the man was going to shoot him, he might as well make it easy for him. No matter what, though, Mitch refused to consider giving up on Nathan. Saving the world could wait.

If Steiner had a brain in his head, though, he'd have pulled his knife instead. A gunshot in the tunnel would ruin everything right there. Better to let Mitch wander off on his fool's errand. At least that way, if he got killed, it wouldn't bring the mutants down on everyone else. His death might even provide a distraction, pulling the mutants' attention away from the others.

Of course, the last time they'd gotten in a knife fight, it hadn't gone so well.

Mitch waited a moment longer for Steiner to pull the trigger. Seeing he was still alive, Mitch turned and walked away, following the line of mutants.

He moved slowly, hoping someone might join him. El Jesus's voice was the only thing that came after him.

"*Vaya con Dios,*" the big man said. His footsteps didn't follow. El Jesus had made his choice, and thinking about it, Mitch couldn't blame him. It comforted him to know the man would still be there trying to help the others.

Samuel didn't say a thing, and that disappointed Mitch most of all. The monk had been full of wisdom when Mitch had been on his side. Now the sergeant didn't even rate a blessing.

Mitch picked up his pace so he could catch up with the mutant carrying Nathan. As he closed on his quarry, he risked a glance back. He saw Severian standing there, staring after him. Then she followed the others into the fissure, and Mitch was on his own.

46

As Mitch moved along the ledge, he had to take care not to slip in the occasional bit of slime or get drenched by streams of water falling out of pipes similar to the one that had brought him there. If he fell down among the mutants, he had no idea what would happen to him, but he guessed it wouldn't be good.

As he moved, he hunted for a good place to stage a rescue. He thought about sweeping down and snatching Nathan from the creature carrying him, but where would he go? It wasn't like this was a cheap film and he was some hero swinging about on a rope.

Nathan groaned, and Mitch saw that the mutant dragging him along the ground had hooked his cargo through the shoulder. The flesh there had begun to separate and tear, and the agonizing pain seemed to be waking Nathan.

Mitch had to do something, though. He couldn't just follow Nathan forever and watch his friend squirm in pain like a worm on that hook. The farther into the tunnels they got, the longer the trip back out, and there was no guarantee that wherever the mutants were headed would be better than this.

Mitch spotted a steep slope of rock that led down to the sewer and decided to chance it. His rifle slung over his back, he slid down the slick rock, keeping his feet the whole way down.

With each foot he got closer to the tunnel floor, he expected a mutant to spot him and raise the alarm. He imagined they'd rip him to shreds with their hooks before Nathan ever knew he was there.

The cry never came.

Mitch's boot touched the damp, dank floor, but the mutants nearest to him didn't do a thing but keep marching in unison to a beat only they seemed to hear.

Nathan and his bearer had gotten far ahead of Mitch, as he'd taken his time climbing down. Nathan had been giving his mutant bearer trouble, and the creature had hauled him a bit off the beaten path, away from its fellows, so it could deal with him. Nathan had groaned louder and louder with every step, and just as Mitch had reached the sewer, he had managed to push himself off the mutant's hook.

As Nathan fell off the bonehook, the mutant dragging him stopped and turned around to recover him. Nathan put up his hands to fend the creature off with the little strength he had left.

Mitch started forward, being careful not to confront the other mutants. They might ignore him as long as he kept away from them, but he guessed that if he annoyed them directly they might have something to say about it.

The hook-handed mutant grabbed Nathan and started to draw back its terrible arm to finish him off. Mitch knew he would never be able to reach his friend in time to save him. He was going to have to risk a shot.

He drew his pistol and aimed it at the mutant. From this distance, though, he couldn't be sure he wouldn't hit Nathan instead. Before the mutant could bring its arm down, Mitch switched his aim and fired a single bullet.

It smashed into a massive stalactite hanging over Nathan. The bulk of the huge thing fell free and plummeted straight down.

The stalactite's point stabbed straight into the mutant leaning over Nathan, just as it brought down its hook.

Mitch raced forward, hoping his gamble had paid off. The mutant's blow might have still landed, or the stalactite might have gone straight through the creature and killed Nathan too. It had been a hell of a shot, but the only thing that mattered to Mitch was its result.

He rushed to Nathan's side, thankful that none of the other mutants seemed to care about the one he'd just killed. He knelt down next to his friend and propped him up. The wound in his shoulder oozed black fluid, and the skin around it showed the angry red of infection.

"Nathan," Mitch said. The man's eyes were open but unfocused. His skin felt slick with sweat and flushed with fever. It took a second for his eyes to snap together and then for him to realize his vision of his friend was real and not just a fantasy of his fevered mind.

"Mitch," he said, surprised and disappointed. His voice rasped with congestion. "Huh. They got you too."

"Don't talk. I'm getting you out of here."

Nathan grabbed at Mitch's jacket. "My girls? Where's my girls?"

Mitch nodded, a small smile on his lips. "They're safe. Halfway to Mars by now."

"Good. That's good." Although he was grateful for the news, this seemed to be the only thing he needed to hear. He fell limp in Mitch's arms and closed his eyes.

"No you don't," Mitch said as he wrenched his friend to his feet. He slung Nathan's good arm over his shoulder and gave the man's wound a painful nudge to wake him up.

"Come on."

Half dragging and half carrying his friend, Mitch began to make his way back down the tunnel.

47

When Mitch got to the steep slope that led back up toward the smaller tunnel and to the elevator foyer from there, he stared up at it and wondered how the hell he could get his wounded friend up it. He fell to his knees and let Nathan slide off his back.

"Mitch, what the fuck are you doing?" Nathan asked from where Mitch had propped him against the wall. His face was covered with blood, and he could barely breathe.

Mitch struggled to his feet and staggered over to the slope. "Make you a sling," he said, coughing out the words. "Get you out of this hole."

"I'm dying."

Mitch ignored that. He knew Nathan was dying and that if he didn't get him out of here fast his time would run out. "Goddammit, shut the fuck up will you? Just shut the fuck up, and let me do this thing."

He looked up at the slope and knew there was no way he could manage it. He'd saved Nathan from the Machine, but there was no way he could save his life. As he'd asked, Nathan remained quiet, at least for a while.

"Mars, huh?"

Mitch wiped the sweat out of his eyes. It had begun to sting. "Mars."

"How'd you swing that?"

Was Nathan impressed, or did he think Mitch had lied to him to keep up his spirits? "I did a job for a man."

"Yeah?"

Mitch felt his guts tighten at the thought of what he should be doing right now instead of this. He pushed that aside. "Save the world kind of thing."

"And how's that working out?"

Mitch gave a bitter laugh. *Not fucking well at all.*

Nathan started to gag. Mitch knelt next to him and shook him. "Hey, hey, hey," he said. "Jesus."

Nathan finally managed to clear his throat and start breathing again. As he did, he pulled back his shirt to expose his shoulder, the one through which he'd been hooked. Black streaks of the mutant infection had spread into his chest and up his neck like a web of cancer growing inside him.

More frustrated than he could bear, Mitch slumped down next to his friend, their backs both to the same wall.

"I thought, if I could save you," he started, the bitterness so harsh he could taste it on his tongue. "If I could do one good thing . . ."

"Do the mission," Nathan said.

Mitch bowed his head in misery. He couldn't bring himself to speak.

"You know, she missed you," Nathan said. "You know how I know? Because she never talked about you. Didn't even say your name."

Mitch shook his head. He didn't need to hear this. He just wanted his friend to live and be happy with the girl he'd stolen from him, along with their little daughter. That's what he wanted more than anything else.

"You could have come by."

"No, I couldn't." He had done it once, around Grace's fifth birthday. It had nearly killed him. He'd gone off on a weeklong drunk after that and had almost been charged as AWOL.

"I guess not."

Mitch finally looked at his friend. "I can't leave you here."

"I'm not asking you to," said Nathan. He gave Mitch a knowing look.

Mitch drew his sidearm—his Bolter—from its holster. It felt like he'd pulled his heart from his chest instead.

Nathan looked out at the opposite wall, his eyes unfocused as if they were gazing across some unknown vista from their past. "Tell Adelaide and Gracie. Tell them . . . Tell them . . . Tell them . . ." He turned away. Mitch thought he heard Nathan say, "I love them."

"Right." Mitch's throat felt so thick he thought he might choke on the word.

Nathan perked up for a moment and looked straight ahead again. "Oh. Remember that—"

Mitch snapped up his gun and squeezed the trigger. The bullet caught Nathan right in the temple and blew his brains along the wall on his other side.

Mitch holstered the smoking gun, then reached down to remove Nathan's dog tags. He added them to his ring of tags, then slipped them back into his belt pouch.

48

Hunter had disappointed Samuel, but the monk didn't see what he could do about it. He wasn't about to kill the man for abandoning their mission, although he hadn't stepped in when Steiner had threatened to. With so much at stake, he'd been willing to gamble with Hunter's life that Steiner had been bluffing, although it seemed that Hunter had been ready to roll those dice too.

He felt conflicted about that. He was a man of God, but where did you draw the line between good and evil when you were talking about defending humanity from the Enemy? Where were the limits? Should there be any?

The team—what was left of it—emerged into a gigantic cavern crisscrossed by several levels of beams that spanned from one distant side to the other and often met in various spots in the middle. Each of the beams stood narrow, high, and precarious, without a single railing in sight, perhaps a good metaphor for the path to paradise.

On some of the beams, the worker mutants marched along with their suffering cargo, taking them to only the Enemy knew where. They were close now, Samuel knew. They just had to make it past the last few parts.

Duval led the team into the cavern, and Samuel followed straight after her. Although she made a good scout, she was not willing to follow her instincts about which direction to go and so constantly looked to Samuel for guidance. This he willingly gave, although it tended to slow them down compared with the way they had moved when Hunter or Juba had been up front.

El Jesus came after the monk, then Steiner, and faithful Severian brought up the rear. Although Samuel had never had a conversation with the woman, he treasured her above all the others. Her faithfulness and her belief in the sanctity of her vows set her above every other member of the Brotherhood he'd ever met. She never compromised and always accomplished what she set out to do.

As they moved out onto the first beam, Duval stopped and waited for Samuel to direct her. He consulted the Chronicles quickly and found a part of the prophecy that showed him the way, or at least what he thought was the way. Prophecies were rarely as clear as a road map.

He gestured for Duval to go straight ahead. When they reached the center of the bridge, it met another that crossed it, and Samuel stopped again to get his bearings.

El Jesus had been peering below when Samuel stopped, and he almost ran into the monk. He lost his balance and barely avoided smacking into Samuel and sending them both over. As he windmilled his arms, trying to recover, Duval snaked back past Samuel and grabbed El Jesus by his shirt. She braced herself against his weight, stabilizing them both.

When El Jesus had started to go over, though, he'd nearly hit Steiner with his shotgun. The Bauhauser had reeled back to avoid the weapon, and that had caused him to tip right over the edge.

Steiner reached out as he dropped past the bridge and managed to grab it. His weight, plus that of the bomb he still carried on his back, pulled him downward and left him hanging there by his fingers.

Before anyone else could react, Severian was in motion. She dropped down and wrapped her legs around the thin bridge, then let herself flip over so that she hung upside down by her bent knees. With not a moment's hesitation, she reached for Steiner.

"The bag!" Samuel said, his heart in his throat. "We can't lose the bomb!"

El Jesus knelt down and held Severian's legs, ensuring she would not fall. Steiner let go with one hand and carefully worked the bomb-filled bag off his shoulder. He held it up to Severian, stretching as far as he could.

"Take it," Steiner said. "Take it!"

"Give me your hand!" El Jesus reached out from above, down on his knees on the beam.

Severian snagged one of the bag's straps in her fist. As soon as she did, Steiner's grip gave way, and he let go.

As Severian and El Jesus brought the bomb back up, Samuel and Duval peered over the edge of the bridge to bear witness to Steiner's fate. The oberleutnant fell about fifteen feet to a broad stone platform suspended in the middle of the room, on which several beams converged.

Worker mutants milled about the platform, ignoring the intruder. They didn't care about his presence at all, it seemed. As Steiner stood up and drew both of his pistols, Samuel breathed a deep sigh of relief, thinking the man would not have to use them.

Steiner, though, had seen something Samuel had not. He brought his guns up just as the workers in front of him parted to reveal a warrior mutant approaching the ober- leutnant, its boneblades at the ready.

Steiner let loose with both of his pistols at point-blank range. The mutant coming at him danced to the tune, the bullets blasting it back a burst at a time, shredding its flesh and knocking it straight off the platform.

By the time the first mutant fell, though, another had stepped up to take its place. Worse yet, Samuel could see others converging on Steiner's position from all around the chamber.

Steiner kept hosing down all comers. He blasted away

another mutant, then another and another, but soon his guns ran empty. Dropping his pistols, he drew his sword, but he paid for the time to switch weapons with a long gash down one arm.

"We must go on," Samuel said to the others. "We have to go on!"

Duval and El Jesus looked at him as if he were insane. The monk had to admit to himself that his words had sounded hollow even in his own ears.

"We're still human, Samuel," Duval said softly and sincerely. With that, she stepped off the bridge. She hit the platform below perfectly and rolled with her momentum, somersaulting down the arc until she came to her feet next to Steiner.

"Thank you," Steiner said to her.

Duval nodded at him. "It's an honor."

El Jesus leaped down straight after Duval. He pumped his gun as he went, then blasted a shell straight through the first mutant he saw, just before the creature tried to run Steiner through.

Then El Jesus pumped his shotgun again and blew another monster away with a white phosphorus shell. It exploded in a flash of white-hot light.

Severian begged Samuel with her eyes. The monk looked at her, then back down at the others, who were about to be massacred. He sighed and shook his head.

They'd given saving the world a good try, but it was over. There was only one thing to do.

"*In ainm Dé,*" he said.

Then he and Severian jumped down to the platform below and joined the battle in earnest.

As he hit the platform, Samuel already had his sword out and ready. Although he had not used his weapon in battle in years, Samuel trained with it regularly and knew which end to stab into his foes. Severian rolled to her feet beside him, her twin blades at the ready.

The two of them joined the fray, weaving a shield of razor-sharp steel around them. Any mutant unlucky enough to be caught in it lost its arms, legs, or head—and sometimes all of them at once.

El Jesus kept pumping shell after white phosphorus shell into the tide of mutants that came at them from every direction. Samuel noticed that the barrel of the man's gun had started to glow red.

Duval ran through clip after clip. Each time she had to reload, Steiner stepped up with his sword and protected her until she was ready again. Samuel glanced over at the man and saw a determined smile on his face, a wild light in his eyes.

He's actually enjoying this, Samuel thought. Try as he might, he couldn't find that emotion in himself. He was tired and terrified, not necessarily in that order.

Mutant after mutant fell before the team, but the tide never slowed. The workers had cleared out, leaving the hard work of killing active soldiers to their warrior kin, and there were plenty of them to take on the job.

The barrel of El Jesus's gun began to glow white hot, but the man didn't seem to notice. Samuel was about to shout a warning when Duval beat him to it.

"No!" she said, but her cry came too late.

El Jesus pulled the trigger of his gun one last time, and the weapon exploded in his hands. He vanished from Samuel's view in a burning white cloud.

The blast knocked Steiner back off his feet. He landed hard next to one of the arches that swept into the platform. His head snapped back and smacked into the stone, knocking him cold.

Her guns empty, Duval switched to her sword and charged into the horde of mutants. She swung her blade about left and right, but she could only last so long against such superior numbers. Soon she vanished beneath the countless mutants slashing at her.

That left only Samuel and Severian to stand against every mutant in the city, perhaps the world. He wondered now if he and Severian should have left the others to die. It would have been the wise thing, but would it have been right? It was too late now to know.

The monk began to pray in Gaelic, loud and strong, as he and Severian faced the horde encroaching on them from all sides. Every time a mutant lunged at them, Severian put herself between the creature and Samuel, but she could only attack so many at a time, even as fast as she was.

Samuel did the best he could against the others who swept in when her attention was elsewhere. His sword ran black with mutant gore, and he bled from a dozen tiny cuts on his arms and legs.

The worst part, Samuel thought, was that the mutants never tired. Here he was—his breath growing short and ragged, his arms beginning to feel like lead—and each one of them that came forward was as fresh as the first.

A boneblade pierced him through the back, and he fell to his knees. The pain was worse than anything he'd ever experienced, and try as he might he could not force himself back to his feet.

Samuel thrust at a mutant that came at him, but the creature's parry knocked his sword from his numb fingers. Defenseless now, he barely had time to bring the Book of Law up before him as a shield before the mutant went for the killing blow.

The creature's boneblade stabbed straight through the thick book. It pierced parchment and leather like they were little more than a thin veil, then shoved through his skin.

The blow pinned the book to Samuel's chest. His prayer faltered as he stared down at the wound and started to cough up blood.

Severian opened her mouth and screamed.

49

Mitch climbed back up the slope until he reached the ledge from which he'd left the others. From there, he worked his way back to the fissure at which he'd last seen them. Ducking in, he ran ahead, his sword drawn and ready, hoping to catch up with them soon. Instead, he came to a massive chamber full of crisscrossing beams, so many of them that it became impossible to see across them.

As he stood on the edge of the first beam, he realized he had no idea where to go. There were just too many choices—and too many mutants wandering around them.

"Come on," he said. "Come on, give me a sign."

As if in answer, he heard a horrible explosion straight ahead and down a bit. He dashed forward, hunting for the sound. A moment later he heard a woman scream.

The noises stopped then, and Mitch spent a few frantic moments trying to triangulate where he thought they'd come from. With nothing more to go on, he resorted to charging down one beam after another, hoping to do more than shove a worker mutant off the intricate gridwork.

Eventually, Mitch found the scene of the fight he'd heard, but when he got there, it was over. He shone his light around the platform, but it was empty: no soldiers, no mutants, nothing but bullet casings and lots of blood, both black and red. A few pages from a book—it could only have been Samuel's massive tome—lay scattered about the place, ripped loose from their binding, which he could not find.

To one side, Mitch spotted a large, charred corpse—the top part of which was missing—lying next to the remnants of a double-barreled shotgun. He crept over and looked down at the remains. A pair of dog tags lay next to the body, but they had melted from the intense heat that had blackened the man from head to toe.

"El Jesus," Mitch said. It sounded like goodbye.

Thinking of his fallen friend, Mitch didn't hear the mutant sneaking up behind him until it was almost too late. A woman's voice broke him from his reverie as it called out, "Hunter!"

Mitch spun about and used his sword to impale the attacker clean through the mouth, the tip of his blade jutting from the back of the monster's neck. Then, with a mighty twist, he took the thing's head off.

As Mitch glanced around to find his benefactor, Severian tumbled down from an arch above. She stared at him with eyes wild with grief, her lips contorting between sadness and rage.

"When's the last time you spoke?" Mitch asked.

Her voice came out in a husky whisper, as if she'd need the better part of a week to clear it properly.

"I can't remember."

Mitch closed his mouth. She'd broken a sacred vow to save his life. He couldn't imagine what that meant to her. He said the only thing he could think of.

"Thanks."

"I couldn't save them. They dragged them all the way to the Machine."

Mitch didn't know if she meant Samuel or Duval or even Steiner, but he supposed it didn't matter. He bent down and started collecting the loose pages from Samuel's book.

"What are you doing?"

"We need this damned book," Mitch said. They might

not be able to find much of it, but they'd make the most of what they could assemble, he hoped.

After gathering all the pages he could find, Mitch laid the parchment out on the platform and tried to read them.

"It is not permitted," Severian said.

Mitch ignored her and kept at it. Every page he could find had words in either Latin or Gaelic, neither of which he could understand. Still, he scanned both sides of each page, hoping to find something that could help. Samuel had put so much faith in the book that there had to be some use for it.

"They took everything," Severian said, her every word sounding as if it caused her pain.

Mitch found the final pages of the book. They featured illuminated illustrations of the massive Machine of which Samuel had spoken, the thing that turned humans into mutants—if it actually existed.

The last page of the book showed a drawing of a large sphere covered by a faint pattern of charcoal circles and glyphs. A hole had been burned through one of the circles.

"He kept looking at this damned stuff," Mitch said. He offered it to Severian. "What is this? Read it."

Severian shook her head. "I can't."

He shoved the pages at Severian. "Read it!"

She pushed him away, not with a snarl but with a flush of embarrassment. "I can't read."

Mitch's jaw dropped. "How can you believe in a book if you can't read it?"

"I don't need to read it to know it's true. That's the nature of faith."

"Fantastic."

Disgusted both with Severian and with a religion that would teach her such bullshit, he hurled the pages to the ground and walked away. Behind him, the woman scooped the pages up reverently and tucked them into her robes.

What the hell could he do now? They were down to two

of them and not a goddamn bomb between them. One of them must have had the thing when they were killed, captured, or whatever. A thing like that didn't just disappear.

If so, that meant there was a chance. Any chance was better than none, and as long as he was still breathing, Mitch meant to keep taking whatever opportunities he had.

He took a quick inventory of what he had: grenades, tripwires, two clips for his rifle, one for his pistol, and his sword. He arranged them around himself for easy access to everything.

"I don't believe any of that shit," he said as he chambered a round in his rifle.

"What do you believe in?"

It was just the kind of question he would expect from a monk.

"I'm not paid to believe," he said. "I'm paid to fuck shit up. You coming?"

50

Mitch and Severian wandered around the chamber of bridges, looking for a way out. Eventually Mitch figured out that they should look for worker mutants toting bodies and follow them wherever they went.

That worked well, although Mitch's impatience meant that they not only followed the workers but shoved straight past them when possible.

The path of the worker mutants wound farther and farther down, deep into the earth. Mitch and Severian kept along it until they reached the bottom. There the workers shuffled out of the chamber into a large tunnel bored through solid rock.

This tunnel let out into what appeared at first to be a massive natural cavern the size of a sports stadium. The only light in the place came from a flickering red glow that beamed up out of two holes in the cave floor.

As Mitch stepped into the chamber, though, he realized that the floor was made not of stone but of metal. In fact, the entire chamber was floored with the stuff, which rose in a smooth arc until it covered the walls as well.

Mitch realized then that they weren't inside a cave but in the middle of a massive machine. The Machine. This had to be it, the one Samuel kept going on about as he read the book, the thing they'd come to destroy.

The Machine's housing stood at least ten stories tall.

Mitch couldn't be sure, as darkness shrouded the distant ceiling. Strange designs encrusted the walls and floors, reminding him of the graffiti he'd seen on the outside of the buried building they'd passed through on the way here. Most of the place was colored black, but red had been splashed all over it. Whether it was paint or blood, Mitch couldn't tell, but the coppery smell in the air had to be coming from somewhere.

There was one entrance into the chamber. Through it, worker mutants carried their human cargo and dumped the bodies into one of the holes, never to be seen again. Most of the area was either rust-red or pitch-black, but the paths they walked along were a bright, slick crimson.

Besides the scent of copper, Mitch could detect the stench of the slaughterhouse: shit, piss, and rot. The heat that rose from the floor made the air feel close and dry like an oven, but for the fluids that dripped steadily from the bodies the mutants carried in.

As best Mitch could tell, the workers dropped the bigger bodies into one hole and the smaller or broken bodies into the other. He suspected this had to do with the raw materials necessary for making the two main types of mutants they'd seen in this place: warriors and workers.

The mutants never said a word, not even grunting with the unending effort of hauling their burdens along. The victims had all fallen silent too, none of them giving so much as an involuntary twitch.

Mitch handed a stack of grenades to Severian and explained his plan. If they couldn't destroy the Machine, they could at least cut off access to it. To manage that, they only had to blow the entrance into the place away.

Mitch chose one side of the entrance and sent Severian off to tackle the other. As they went their separate ways, Mitch noticed how their boots clanked on the floor, making a hollow sound. He realized then that they weren't inside the Machine, just walking across its outer hull. He wondered how large the thing must be, then shoved the thought away.

Mitch climbed the rocks around the left side of the tunnel's entrance as best he could. When he found a place near the top where he had a good foothold, he started fishing out his grenades and hammering them into a crack in the rock, using the butt of his pistol as a hammer.

Although he wasn't sure it mattered, he timed the fall of his blows with the churning rhythm coming up from below. None of the mutants glanced up at him even once. After jamming four grenades into the crack, he replaced the fuse of the last grenade with a tripwire that he ran through all four of the grenades' triggers.

As he finished up, Mitch looked across the top of the entrance to Severian. She had been doing the same thing, except that she was using the hilt of her sword instead of a pistol to pound the grenades in. When she finished, she looked up and nodded at Mitch.

Looking down, Mitch could see that the red-painted path the mutants followed to the twin holes resembled a long dagger pointing toward the center of the Machine. At the far end, a crosspiece formed a hilt capped by a semicircle. A word, or perhaps a name, had been emblazoned across the hilt: Algeroth.

The two of them clambered down and met up near a pile of broken rock they'd spotted along one wall, right where it met the alien hull of the Machine. They took cover behind it and then waited.

As Mitch and Severian watched, a worker mutant limped in with another man Mitch recognized on its back.

"Shit, they're hauling Steiner," he said. As he spoke, Steiner opened his eyes, and Mitch saw the man was still alive.

Mitch pulled the tripwire, and their daisy chain of grenades exploded all at once. Two tons of rock came sliding down in the distance, burying the end of the tunnel entirely.

As soon as the grenades blew, Mitch charged toward the center of the chamber. Getting nearer, he saw that the worker in front of the one dragging Steiner had Duval with him.

When Mitch reached the nearest of the glowing holes, the mutant carrying Duval had just pulled her off its back and was preparing to toss her into the Machine. It was then that Mitch saw she still had the black bag strapped to her, the one with the bomb in it. With a single face-smashing blow, he sent the creature reeling back into the hole instead.

The mutant holding Steiner dropped the man to face the new attacker. Severian kicked the worker in the chest, and it fell into the hole after its compatriot.

Mitch and Severian moved to help Steiner and Duval to their feet. They had gotten to their hands and knees and were gazing down into the hole into which they'd almost been thrown.

Inside, Mitch saw the outer face of a gigantic wheel spinning slowly by, grinding along on unseen gears. Every so many feet, a corpse appeared on the edge of the wheel, impaled on one of its countless spikes.

Duval had been beaten black and blue. Dozens of tiny cuts and a couple nasty ones covered her skin. She'd stopped bleeding and could stand on her own after Mitch helped her up. She nodded her gratitude to him.

Steiner, on the other hand, was a mess. Much of his flesh had been charred like El Jesus's, and the pink flesh that showed under the crisp, blackened skin oozed blood. His eyes, though, shone with both pain and determination.

Mitch pulled out the pack of cigarettes he had taken from the body of that dead soldier in the trenches what seemed like a lifetime ago. He shook out the last stick and lit it. He took one good pull off it and put it in Steiner's mouth.

The Bauhauser took a long drag from the cigarette and

coughed, then took another. Mitch helped him sit up, and Steiner stayed there under his own power.

"You still hold a gun?" Mitch asked.

"Only with my right." Steiner held up his left hand. The fingers had been fused into a club of melted flesh.

Mitch grimaced. The smell from the man's burned skin turned his stomach, but he had no time to get sick over it now.

"Can you hold a rope?"

51

Mitch pulled a rope from Duval's pack and started to un-coil it. The tunnel was blocked solid. No mutants could come through that way, and that gave them free access to the holes.

He handed Severian one end of the rope and gestured for her to stand next to Duval at the side of the hole. He took the other end and walked it and Steiner over to a stalagmite stabbing out of the Machine's metal floor. He set the ober-leutnant down a few feet from it, then tied the rope around the base and tested it to make sure it was secure. He left the coiled part of the rope behind Steiner and put the part past that in his good hand.

"I can't hold all three of you."

"They're going in." Mitch jerked his head at Severian and Duval. "I need you to help me make sure we can get them back out."

Mitch moved a bit farther down the line and got a two-handed grip on it.

By that time, Duval had secured the rope around both Severian and herself. She pulled Severian close and held her as she lowered them down the hole.

Mitch put his back into letting the rope play out a bit at a time. Even with Steiner's help, it was harder than he'd thought it would be. Severian and Duval didn't weigh much individually, but put them together and load them up with all their gear and they were bigger than even El Jesus had been.

Behind him, Mitch heard something tumble over. He looked back over his shoulder and saw the rubble in front of the tunnel starting to move.

"They're coming through," he said to Steiner, jerking his head toward the entrance. "That tunnel's not going to hold."

Mitch's grip on the rope began to give, and it slipped through his hands. He tried to slow it down, and the friction caused his hands to smoke with the heat.

"These rocks are not going to hold their weight much longer," Steiner said. Looking at the metallic floor, Mitch wondered how well the stalagmite could be attached to it, and he knew Steiner was right.

He wondered how the women were doing in the Machine and how much farther they had to go before they reached someplace they could stand. He hoped it wouldn't take much longer.

"Can't go any faster," he said.

The rope lurched forward, whistling through Mitch's hands. He knew that if he grabbed it and held on tight the sudden jerk would pull him off balance, and then he would be finished. The weight of the women would haul him straight into the hole after them, and they would all end up as fodder for that awful Machine.

Mitch tightened his grip on the rope as fast as he could. He could smell the rising scent of his burning flesh.

Although he managed to keep his balance, the weight of the women dragged him forward, closer and closer to the hole. He dug in his heels as hard as he could, but he could find no purchase on the smooth metallic floor. He knew he would only have one chance to catch himself on the very lip of the hole, and if he failed, the women and he would die.

"Oh!" With one final effort and the hole coming up fast, Mitch shoved his heels into the floor and pushed back as hard as he could. The strain nearly stood him up in his tracks, but he fought back down to keep his angle flat.

"Oh, shit!" At the hole's edge, his boots finally caught, but the force nearly blew out his knees. He hauled up against it with all his might and stopped there dead on the lip.

Blood welled up between his fingers. He wondered if the fluid would make the rope slippery, but he held his hands so tight on it that nothing could come between the fibers and his flesh.

"Ah!"

He glanced behind him to see what had happened to Steiner.

The Bauhauser was gone.

Mitch growled and wrapped the rope around his waist. Using himself as a large pin, he slowly played out the rope, letting the women descend at a more reasonable clip.

"Steiner." Mitch called for the man. He turned back and finally spotted the oberleutnant limping toward the open tunnel, which now was choked with the shadows of mutants digging their way through the rubble.

"Steiner!"

The Bauhauser started to say something. In the vast metallic chamber, his voice echoed off the walls, and his words came to Mitch's ears. They were in the man's native tongue.

"Ich bin Maximillian von Steiner, und ich schicke Sie alles zur Hölle."

Steiner turned back to Mitch. When he saw the sergeant watching him, he snapped a salute with his left hand.

Something shiny dangled from the man's fingers, and Mitch realized it was the pin to one of the grenades he wore on a bandolier around his chest.

Mitch's eyes widened. Before he could say a word, Steiner exploded.

The blast filled the tunnel with fire and then brought it

down. The force of the explosion knocked Mitch back toward the hole, and he went tumbling in. The rope slipped from his hands as he fell.

Mitch saw the spike sticking up from the great wheel as he tumbled toward it, but he had no way to avoid it. He twisted around the best he could, but when he smashed down on the unforgiving metal, he felt the sharp tip stab up through his flesh, slashing open his neck.

Another spike popped out of the Machine and drove straight through his arm, pinning him to the Machine. For a moment, Mitch exulted in the fact he was still breathing. Then he wondered if, trapped as he was, that was such a good thing after all. It meant he would be alive for whatever happened next.

52

As the wheel ground slowly around, Mitch struggled against the spike in his arm, but it held him fast. He gritted his teeth to make one last attempt with every bit of his strength, but at that moment clamps snaked out from the wheel, binding him to it by his arms and legs.

Mitch snarled in frustration but could do nothing to free himself. The wheel kept turning. When it reached the next station, a diagnostic array emerged from inside the wheel and scanned his body with white-hot energy. The heat evaporated the blood and dirt caked on his body, turning it all to dust, and it singed his hair and left his clothes and skin scorched and smoking.

"Jesus, no!" Mitch shouted, but the Machine ignored his complaint.

Next, a mechanical arm unfolded from the side of the wheel and spat staples into him like bullets from a machine gun. The small silver bands sutured together his many cuts, including the fresh one on his neck. The bleeding from it stopped.

Relieved of worrying about his wounds, Mitch renewed his struggles against his bonds, but they held fast. As he thrashed about, a robotic, spike-tipped cannula snaked down and moved over his body, scanning him with a strange light emanating from its electric eye. Where the light touched his flesh, his skin became translucent, revealing his muscles and veins. Soon enough, the cannula found what it was looking for, the big vein in the crook of his arm, and stabbed into him, burying its sharpened end in that vessel.

Black slime flowed through the cannula tube and into Mitch's blood. He screamed both in pain and at the burning violation.

The cannula yanked back. The veins of Mitch's arm started to turn black, radiating out from the site of the injection. He wanted to grab his arm and squeeze it until the poison ran back out, but he couldn't even touch it.

As Mitch watched, his hand on that side began to mutate. The third and fourth fingers started to grow together and become longer. He recognized the pattern. They were starting to form a boneblade.

Another cannula dropped down and moved over Mitch's head, looking for the right spot in his skull. He jerked his head away, but the damn thing followed him like it was alive. He moved his head again, and still it came after him, coiled like a cobra ready to strike.

This gave Mitch an idea. Most of the people tossed down onto this wheel were either dead or near it. He felt like hell, but he had to have been one of the Machine's healthiest subjects.

He craned his head as far as he could toward his left arm. He watched, forcing himself to be patient, as the tip of the cannula homed in on his exposed temple. Then, just as it struck, he whipped his head out of the way.

The sharp end of the cannula slammed into the binding on his arm and tore it. The rip wasn't much, but it was enough. Mitch wrenched his arm free, pulling himself off the awful spike that ran through it too, and the cannula went haywire, flinging itself all about.

Mitch drew his sidearm and used the butt of it to smash the strap on his right arm. He sat up and reached down to free his legs. As he did, the wheel brought him within range of another cannula. He tore his leg free and kicked the damned thing to pieces.

53

Duval hated everything about this, but she clearly didn't have a choice. They only had a single rope left among them, and they'd lost all their winches and clips in the battles before. It was either trust the men to hold them both or let them lower her into the Machine by herself.

She clung to Severian as if the woman were her daughter. Something about Severian reminded her of her little girl, a clean innocence that few adults had. Even though she'd seen Severian dismember mutant after mutant with her blades, Duval felt a need to protect her from the evils to come.

As they began their descent into the hole, Duval stared down and realized that she'd be lucky to save herself, much less anyone else.

Two massive wheels spun beneath them. One carried the larger, healthier victims, while the other ferried the weaker corpses to their ultimate doom.

Each wheel stood vertically, mounted on an axle like a gigantic Ferris wheel. As a body was tossed through the hole on the top, it caught on one of the hundreds of vicious spikes that stabbed out of the wheel's outer ring. Then the movement of the wheels brought the bodies around to various stations at which unspeakable things were done to them.

Duval got a good view of the first of these horrors as she

and Severian slowly descended to the gore-caked floor below. As they got closer, the horrible smells of spilled bodily fluids and worse got to her, and she struggled to keep down the contents of her stomach. She didn't want to puke on Severian if she could help it.

Duval had angled the rope so that they would come down just to the inside of the wheel nearest them. As they came level with the top of the wheels, they started to fall. Something had happened to Mitch or Max or the rope or all damned three, and now she was going to die in this mute woman's arms. Despite herself, she let out a little scream.

As the floor rushed up at them, the rope started to catch. Someone above was trying to save them. She only hoped he would manage it in time.

The world jerked to a stop, and Duval let out a short howl of pain. Between the rope biting into her waist and Severian clutching her so tightly, she thought she might be cut in two.

"Thank God," Severian said in a voice raspy and low.

Duval nearly jumped out of the rope. "You can talk?"

Severian nodded.

Duval looked down at bits of the Machine spinning beneath them. A control station sat atop the axis that connected the two wheels. Over the axis stood a piecework bridge that seemed to transport fuel throughout the system. Most of the time the pieces formed a line, but at regular intervals they would spin about to the perpendicular instead. Gouts of flame burst from holes in the pieces, too, burning off waste gasses.

Below that, razor-sharp steel blades spun on a central driveshaft beneath the control station. Their tips fitted into the wheels' spokes and kept them moving along. If they fell onto those, it would all be over.

It looked insane, and Duval somehow couldn't think of a good enough reason for her to be here. Then Constance and

Jack's faces sprang to her mind, and the memory of their laughter calmed her down.

Just then, a horrible explosion sounded overhead, and the rope gave way again. Duval screamed, but they didn't have far to fall. They ended up on their knees on one of the bridge sections that ran over the wheels' axis. She almost cheered to find herself alive.

Duval and Severian scrambled to their feet and unwound the slack rope from around them. Neither of them seemed to have been hurt in the fall, but their surroundings were too astonishing for them to celebrate that at the moment.

The two women avoided the gouts of fire and waited for the piece they were on to align with the others next to it. Then they moved toward the center platform. As they did, jets of flame spurted out of exhausts situated on the pieces. Severian saw them coming and hauled Duval back just before she would have been cooked.

When they reached the central platform, Duval was at a loss as to what to do. She reached into the black bag and withdrew the velvet sack in which the parts of the bomb were stored.

She pulled out the main part of the bomb. It looked like a metallic circle engraved with alien designs. The triggering mechanism was a steely ball with similar markings.

She had no idea what to do with them.

She looked to Severian, but the woman was staring at something coming toward them on the bridge pieces over the axis.

It was Mitch, or at least it had once been.

His skin had been cut and seared, then stitched up with staples. His hair had been scorched off the side of his head so that he looked like a walking burn victim. The veins on his arm and chest had turned black, and the gunk slowly spread up toward his neck as she watched.

Mitch had his knife in his hand, poised, ready to strike. She saw then that he had become the latest victim of the

Machine, and she grabbed Severian and prepared to race away from him. She knew she might have to, but she couldn't bear the thought of trying to kill him unless it was absolutely necessary.

Gouts of flame spouted from the axle again, blocking Duval and Severian's retreat. They turned to face Mitch, their swords raised before them. Duval didn't want to hurt him, but it seemed they had no choice.

Mitch staggered over toward them, struggling with balancing on the rotating axle, and drove the knife straight into his arm. He jabbed the tip into the spot where the cannula had injected him with its poison, and he dug deep. Then he pulled the blade out and squeezed the wound. Thick black gel oozed out like pus from an old cut.

"Hunter?" Duval asked, her voice uncertain. She still wasn't sure it was really Mitch in there.

Mitch raised the new cut to his mouth and sucked at it as hard as he could. He nearly choked on the black gunk but managed to spit it out on the floor. He looked up at them still holding their swords at the ready and said, "Get those pigstickers out of my face."

"Are you . . . ?" Duval started. She couldn't finish the thought.

Mitch gave her a look that curled her toes. "What do you think? Give me that bomb. Give me that fucking bomb!"

Duval paused, unsure that she could trust him with the device while that junk ran through his veins. He pointed over her shoulder then, and she spun around to a horde of warrior mutants standing on the other side of the axle, waiting for the bridge on that side of the platform to come around again. She looked down and saw more warriors coming up to intercept them from the other side as well.

"Give me the fucking bomb!" Mitch said.

Hoping she wouldn't regret it, Duval handed him the bomb in its battered duffel bag. Severian tossed him the detonator. He caught it in his free hand and grinned.

54

Mitch strode forward with the bomb and detonator, ready to get the job done at last. As he reached the central platform, though, warrior mutants appeared on either side of them, walking toward them through the hollow spot over the wheels' axis.

Duval rushed to greet one group of mutants with her sword, and Severian charged across the platform to cut off the other. Duval was a soldier, no expert in the sword. She held the blade before her and swung it like a club. It didn't look pretty, but it killed any mutant that came within her range.

Severian, on the other side, swung her blade in an intricate pattern—a kata—weaving an impassable wall of steel. The warriors that came at her fell to the distant floor in large, wet pieces.

Sweat beaded on Mitch's face as he lurched toward the control panel situated on the central platform. He reached up to wipe the sweat from his face, and his fingers came away black.

He didn't understand how to work the Machine at all, but he didn't have to. He just had to figure out how to blow it up.

He looked at the great circle in the center of the platform. A broad band of metal stretched across it, with a smaller circle of metal at each end. Mitch gave the circle nearest him a test push, and it gave.

He leaned down and put his back into it. Slowly but surely, the band of metal spun on an axis in the center of the larger circle. This exposed a large empty circle under one of the metal strip's ends. It was the perfect size for the bomb.

Mitch pulled the bomb from the bag and held it over the hole. He hesitated for a moment. Would this work, or had the old monk been crazy? At this point, Mitch barely saw the difference.

"Anytime!" Duval said as she knocked another warrior to its doom.

Mitch gritted his teeth. This had to work. He didn't see any other way. The bomb might go off as soon as he inserted it, but he figured that his life was a small price to pay for bringing the damned Machine down.

In one swift move, he slammed the bomb home.

Nothing happened.

Mitch waited for a moment. Had they gotten this all wrong? Should he grab the bomb and try something else? Maybe there was a place for it in the Machine's base.

A small hole opened up in the area directly across from the bomb, on the other side of the console. Mitch held up the detonator and saw that the hole was the right shape. He moved around and made to slam the detonator home when another hole popped open next to the first on the console, then another and another and another.

The platform was covered with several holes, each of them looking the exact right size for the detonator. "You've got to be shitting me," Mitch said.

"Just put it in the hole!" Duval said, shouting at Mitch over her shoulder.

"Which hole?"

"Any hole!"

Mitch shoved the detonator into a hole right in front of him. It seemed that the device was just a hair too big. He twisted it, pounded on it, smashed it, but it made no difference. The hole was the wrong size.

"Piece of shit!" Mitch said. "It doesn't fit!"

Mitch glanced over at Duval. She was getting tired. A boneblade worked past her defenses and laid open her shoulder.

In retaliation, she shoved her blade into the warrior's chest, stabbing it straight through. The mutant fell to the side, but her sword got jammed, and she couldn't pull it out in time. As the mutant fell from the bridge piece, it took the blade with it.

Another warrior stepped onto the bridge to confront her. As it did, the bridge section finally spun perpendicular again, tossing the warrior to the ground and cutting off the central platform from the giant wheels.

Severian fell back too. She turned to join the others for their brief respite. Behind her, a warrior leaped across the gap formed by the missing bridge section.

Mitch started to shout a warning to her but knew that it would be too late. Flame spouted from the axle at that point, though, and incinerated the mutant as it landed. It plummeted into the abyss below like a falling star.

Mitch glanced around. They had no guns and just one sword left. The bomb didn't work. Even if he could fit the detonator in, he didn't have any idea where to find the key to turn it. And they had about thirty seconds before the bridges locked back into place and let the mutants swarm over them in final battle.

"It's not working," he said to the women.

They stared at him, exhausted and just as scared as he. Mitch pounded his head and stared at the holes in the panels. There had to be a way to make this damned thing work. He looked at the panel again and realized that there was something familiar about it—or at least the pattern of the holes in it.

"Give me the pages," he said.

"What?" Severian said.

"From the book!" He shoved his hand out at her, demanding the sheets of paper.

Severian reached into her robes and pulled out the tattered pages of the Chronicles, which she'd stuffed next to her heart for safekeeping. Mitch snatched the pages from her and shuffled through them until he found what he was looking for: the final page of the book, the one that looked like a charcoal rubbing. He found it and shoved the other papers at Severian. Then he held it up to the panel in front of him.

"What are you doing?" Duval asked.

Mitch pointed at the pattern of circles. "It's a rubbing of this thing, and it shows where—"

"The detonator," Duval said, finally catching on.

Mitch nodded. He wondered where the Brotherhood had found this device they'd lugged here. Had they gone into the Machine and stolen it, or had the mutants somehow left it someplace?

Was it really a bomb? Some sort of self-destruct mechanism? And if so, why hadn't they used it before now?

He stared up at the wheels on either side of him. He couldn't see their outer faces from here, but he knew they were coated with mutants being manufactured from the dead. Why someone had installed such a mechanism wasn't vital now. Destroying the Machine was the only thing important, no matter how it might be done.

The bridge pieces on either side of the platform spat fire again. Soon they would line up with the platform, and the mutants would come streaming at them.

"I lost my sword," Duval said.

Without looking at her, Mitch tossed her his knife. She caught it, looked at how small it was compared to her sword, and rolled her eyes.

Severian spun her blades, flinging off the accumulated blood and gore. The women took up their positions at either side of the control platform. The bridges clanked into place, and the warriors advanced.

Duval leaped forward, using her speed and experience to her advantage. She was a virtuoso with a knife, but its short blade put her in reach of the mutants' boneblades in a way the sword hadn't.

On the other side, Severian tirelessly took out one mutant after another. She seemed like she'd been born for this role.

The trouble, Mitch knew, wasn't that the women weren't good. It was that they would eventually tire, while the mutants could keep coming until they killed them all.

Mitch moved the paper all about the panels, hunting for the pattern shown there. After a few long moments, he found it. The rubbings on the page and the surface of the bomb lined up perfectly. The hole in the page revealed just where the detonator ought to go.

Mitch took a deep breath, then slid the detonator into the hole. He heard a satisfying click.

He tried to turn it but couldn't. The thing was too smooth, and he couldn't get any leverage. However, it was split by a central groove.

Mitch stared for a while at the slit. The monk back at the monastery had mentioned a key. He'd claimed it would be somewhere in the Machine.

Mitch looked all around. The Machine was huge. It could be anywhere in the chamber housing it. They were doomed. They'd never find it.

Mitch turned to Severian just as she sliced a mutant in two with a single powerful stroke. The corpse fell apart, and from behind it walked up the next mutant in line. This one, though, was horribly familiar, and Severian stood there stunned by the sight of it.

"Samuel," she said.

The monk had lost his hair, and his skin looked warped and slick from the strange black fluids snaking underneath it. His eyes were filled with shiny black from rim to rim, and his teeth looked like those of a starving animal. Steel staples held together what must have once been a gaping wound in his chest, visible through the torn tunic, which hung unrepaired.

The creature who had once been Brother Samuel stepped forward and raised his single boneblade at Severian. To Mitch, it seemed that he saluted his former charge right before he prepared to kill her.

The mutant monk opened his mouth and shouted a single word. *"Legion!"*

55

Mitch raced to the edge of the platform. He couldn't get around Severian, and without a weapon he wasn't sure he wanted to.

"Severian, no!" he shouted. "That's not Samuel!"

Severian raised her blade at the ready. Mitch had seen such combat positions before in a duel between samurai.

He drew his Bolter and fired his last few shots into the mutant. They did little more than slow the creature down. He'd lost his sword and rifle when he'd been strapped to the wheel, and he missed them sorely now.

"Kill him!" Mitch said. "Kill him!"

Mitch glanced back to where Duval stood, hoping they might find some help from that quarter. She had somehow lost his knife, but she fought on barehanded against the line of mutants.

The bridge pieces spun perpendicular once more. That cut off the line of mutants and left her with only one more mutant to face. Exhausted, she raised her hands to take the creature on. With a single kick, she knocked it off the small bit of bridge.

As the mutant went, though, it knocked into Duval. She lost her balance and fell off the bridge too.

Mitch peered down over the side of the control platform. Duval tumbled into the path of one of the spinning blades on the driveshaft, and it sliced her neatly in half at the waist.

The two parts of her corpse tumbled into the murky, steam-shrouded distance below.

Mitch spun back to see Severian and Samuel rush toward each other. They slammed into a tight embrace that shook the platform with its force. Their faces were inches apart.

Samuel's boneblade emerged from the middle of Severian's back. He'd run her through.

For a moment, Samuel seemed to be a man again, not a mutant, and he looked at Severian with eyes filled with grief.

"Shhh," she whispered to him. "You are Samuel. It's all right."

As she slid off the boneblade and into the abyss below, Severian flung her sword behind her. It clattered along the platform before coming to a rest near the control panel.

Mitch dived for the sword, but Samuel lunged at him, keeping him from it. Unarmed, Mitch spun away and rolled to his feet.

Samuel came after him hard and fast. Mitch dodged as best he could, but the platform was small: He had nowhere to hide, much less run.

He tried hammering at the mutant with his fists, but try as he might he could not find a hole in the monk's defenses. His arms felt like rags hanging from his shoulders, whereas the mutant never tired. He knew it would only be a matter of seconds before he made a mistake.

A glancing blow from the boneblade knocked Mitch off balance, and he fell back onto a set of pipes at the platform's edge. Grunting, Samuel raised his boneblade for a killing blow with every ounce of his weight behind it.

Mitch flung himself out of the way just in time. Samuel's momentum carried him right past his target so that he buried the tip of his blade in the cluster of pipes. The mutant monk tried to pull the blade free but found that it was stuck.

Mitch removed the ring of dog tags from his belt pouch

and wrapped them around his hand to protect his fist. As Samuel started to pull the boneblade free, Mitch stomped on his elbow, snapping the blade in two. Then he kicked Samuel in the chest, and the blade broke off entirely. Black goo fountained out of the wound.

Still Samuel showed no sensation of pain. Instead, he stared at the stump of his arm in utter fascination. Then he looked up to see Mitch standing over him, his metal-bound fist ready.

Mitch grabbed the monk by his robes and hammered him with everything he had left, a punch-drunk prizefighter giving it his all in the final round.

Smack!

"That's for Nathan."

Smack!

"That's for El Jesus."

Smack!

"That's for Severian."

Mitch growled at the pain in his fist as he hauled Samuel closer for one last blow.

"And this is for Samuel."

The punch knocked Samuel backward, teeth flying and black blood spurting. The mutant staggered to his feet, but Mitch wouldn't let up. He charged into him and smashed him back against the panels—against the detonator.

Samuel shoved Mitch back with his remaining arm, knocking him off his feet. As he fell, Mitch's gaze landed on the tip of Severian's glittering sword.

It was then that Mitch saw that the sword was the key he'd been hunting for, the last piece he needed to activate the bomb. He just needed to shove it in the detonator, which Samuel was lying on top of right now.

Mitch scooped up the sword, brought it into an overhand grip, and stabbed it straight down through Samuel. His aim was true. It passed right through the mutant monk and slipped into the slit in the detonator behind him.

Samuel hung there, impaled, though the life did not go out of him yet. Mitch grabbed the blade with both hands and twisted it to the right. Through Samuel's body, he felt the detonator turn and then sink into the sphere of the bomb.

The mutant went limp, and the panel behind him lit up.

56

Mitch lifted his head and waited for some sign of the end. The entire Machine began to shake. The mutants lined up on the bridge sections fell off, and Mitch grabbed hold of the control panel to avoid sharing their fate.

He pushed himself to his feet. The entire chamber shuddered. He could feel energy pulsing beneath his feet, building up within the Machine, which now had no place for it to go.

Mitch blew out a long, tired breath. He knew this was it. Everyone else was dead, and he was about to die too. At least they'd saved the world. He looked down over the edge of the platform and saw that the blades that had sliced through Duval still spun below him. If anything, they now moved faster.

A bloody hand reached out and grabbed Mitch by the arm. He recoiled, then turned to see Samuel gazing at him, his eyes only half-filled with blackness now. His mouth moved as he tried to speak.

Putting his hand on the hilt of Severian's sword, Mitch decided to risk leaning in to hear what the monk had to say.

In a cracked whisper from his broken mouth, Samuel spoke. "Have faith."

Mitch stared at the monk. Hanging there, dying once more, he almost seemed human again.

The monk gave Mitch a weak but knowing smile. "Have faith," he said.

Mitch spun toward the other side of the platform and walked to the edge. He looked down and saw the blades spinning still. Even if he made it past them, he had no idea what might lie beyond. There was no way to know.

And there was no other choice.

He closed his eyes and let himself fall over the edge. He felt the spinning blades scrape past him as he plummeted between a pair of them.

Mitch braced himself for the impact, wondering if it would break his spine or just his legs. Then he zipped through a wide hole—an open drain—in the bottom of the Machine and kept falling, now into nearly total blackness.

Hitting the surface of the lake of water, oil, and other horrible fluids shocked Mitch. He hadn't known it was coming and so hadn't taken a breath before he found himself deep under it.

He wanted to fight to the surface to grab a lungful of air, but just as the water finally slowed him to a halt, something flared hot and white above. At first the light blinded him, but then he saw everything. He recognized the building energy and the horrible roar it made that shook every ounce of the lake.

A spaceship. He was under a spaceship.

The Machine had been part of a spaceship.

The water above him began to get hot. Realizing that the surface of the lake he was in must have been burning and boiling away in the Machine's exhaust, he swam for the bottom as hard as he could. His lungs aching for air, he kicked down, down, down, struggling through the water toward the coolest, darkest part he could find.

By the time he reached the bottom of the lake, the light had beaten him there. The place was littered with skulls and bones many layers deep, pieces of people that had fallen from the Machine's giant wheels.

Hugging the bottom, Mitch looked up at the bright blue inferno above, the spaceship's exhaust jet sinking toward him as the lake continued to boil away.

The light around him shifted from blue to red to black as the Machine and the blazing pillar of flame behind it finally lifted away toward the sky. The roar of the exhaust faded to silence.

Mitch's lungs demanded air. Fortunately, he didn't have far to swim, as the spaceship had boiled much of the lake away.

He broke the surface gasping for air and took in a huge gulp of the steam still rising from the lake's lowered surface. It seared his lungs, but next to trying to breathe the water it felt like a cool breeze.

Mitch swam toward the shore. Soon the water became shallow enough for him to scrape his legs, and he crawled along on his hands and knees instead. He had been beaten and battered to within inches of death, but he couldn't remember the last time he'd felt so happy just to be alive. The pain and exhaustion and the loss of his friends blunted the edge of that, but there would be time for remembering them later.

As Mitch came to the bone-covered shore, he fell down upon it and rolled onto his back. He lay there for a long time, looking up and breathing.

As the steam faded, the stars appeared in the night sky—first one, then another, and another, until a sea of tiny lights shone down at him. High above, the spaceship's glowing exhaust crossed the sky like a shooting star heading for the darkest parts of the heavens.

Mitch reached into his shirt for the pack of cigarettes he'd carried with him since the day he'd seen his first mutant. He had one left. It was bent and nearly broken, but it was all he had.

He crumpled the pack and tossed it in the lake, where it

sank to rest among the bones. Then he fished his lighter out of his pocket and flicked it open.

Bent as it was, the cigarette still lit.

"Christ."

He gazed up at the sky and watched a circle of sparkling stars framed by the edges of the great pit that had for so long been the Machine's home. He wondered where the spaceship might be headed. Back to wherever it had come from, he hoped.

That wasn't his problem, though. He'd done his job. He'd fucked shit up. And after he finished this last cigarette, he'd get right back to doing that again.